The Last Call

C. L. Peck

ISBN: 0996373012
ISBN-13: 978-0996373012

DEDICATION

I would like to dedicate this book to my amazing friend, Susan Aston. She has always been my pillar of spiritual strength, the one I can turn to when I am lost and struggling. Her unconditional love and lack of judgment has been a shelter for me during my personal storms.

ACKNOWLEDGMENTS

This book would not be what it is without the dedication, patience, and support provided by my husband and best friend, Tony Peck. He urged me to keep going and spent countless hours editing my work.

Thank you to my exceptionally talented illustrator, Marty Petersen. I have loved working with him as we collaborated to make the words I put on paper come to life in my children's books. But this project was extra special. The magnificent cover of "The Last Call" provided a wealth of inspiration during the writing process.

Thank you to my parents, Harry and Delores Keiffer. Their love and support is unending and forever appreciated.

I also would like to add some words of thanks to Kevin Miller. Your candor and insight are much appreciated, for you had the task of editing the first draft – lucky you. I hope this final version proves that I took your valuable advice to heart.

This list would not be complete without me offering up a huge thank you to my Heavenly Father. Thank you for gifting me with this story. Even if it doesn't touch another living soul, it touched mine. It brought me closer to you and filled me with a renewed faith and hope, and for that I am most grateful!

And do this, knowing the time, that now it is high time to awake out of sleep; for now our salvation is nearer than when we first believed.

Romans 13:11

PROLOGUE

Anya loved spending Sundays with her grandmother. Sometimes she wished she could stay at home and play with her friends, like she did on Saturdays, but her mother had to work on Sundays, so that meant staying with Grandma Dee until Mom got home around dinner time. That was fine with Anya, though, because what 8-year-old girl doesn't like to be spoiled?

A typical Sunday started with breakfast with Mom, usually a "healthy" meal featuring egg whites and wheat toast, but Anya knew that something tastier was in store once Grandma Dee was done with church and picked her up around noon.

Today, as she slid into the front seat of the huge, comfy Cadillac, Grandma announced that they would catch a matinee at the movie theater after they had lunch. Where they would eat was always up to Anya, and today she had her heart set on McDonald's. Her mother never let her eat fast food, but Anya and her Grandma had "an understanding."

"Every kid should have some fun every now and then, and it's a grandmother's job to make sure that happens," Grandma Dee said. "So if my little angel wants to have a Big Mac today, then that's what she'll have. Just remember: No telling your mother!"

"I promise, Grandma," Anya said with a giggle.

As they pulled up to a stoplight, Anya's eyes fell on the big Baskin-Robbins sign across the street. Ice cream was her favorite dessert, and she wondered if she could talk her grandma into stopping there on the way home from the movies.

"Can we, Grandma? After the movie?" she asked, pointing to the ice cream parlor and putting on her cutest face. Her grandmother smiled wide and gave her a firm nod. "Sure, honey. Do you want a cone or a cup?"

Anya turned back to look at the store, secretly wishing she could bring home an entire ice cream cake, even though her birthday was still months away. "Oh well," she thought, as the Cadillac slowly started to move through the intersection, "a waffle cone is better than nothing."

"Pralines and cream in a cone, please."

At that moment, Anya turned back to her grandmother to flash a grateful grin, but she was instantly consumed by confusion and then horror when her eyes fell on an empty driver's seat. She screamed as the big car, with no foot on the brake pedal, rolled through the intersection and crashed into a mailbox on the far corner.

"Grandma!" Anya screamed as she frantically unbuckled her seat belt and looked behind her at the intersection, hoping that her grandmother had simply gotten out of the car for some strange reason. Again, she looked at the empty driver's seat, but panic took full hold of her when all she found was Grandma Dee's seat belt, still buckled.

"Grandma! Where are you?!"

The Antichrist is the beast who derives his power from Satan, the Dragon. Together they will use the False prophet, the second beast, to help them accomplish their evil works on earth.

Revelation 13:1-8

2020

Noah Parks was taking his good fortune for granted. He had risen to great heights in his field at an unexplainable pace. He was the lead general assignment reporter for the nation's largest newspaper in New York City. This was something that, until now, just didn't happen to a man of 28 years of age. And Noah was not wasting a minute of the prestige. There were perks, and he gladly accepted them.

His mother and his older sister Anna, both deeply religious, had lectured him about his so-called immoral behavior. They had warned him that if he became a reporter, he might be put into positions where he would be tempted to use unethical tactics. But what had their morals and ethics ever done for them?

In Noah's opinion, they were living in denial and losing out on the finer things life had to offer. They had pleaded with him to return to his faith, but honestly, what was there to return to? Why should he serve and worship some "being" that had let him down? Their God hadn't been there for Noah when he needed him.

So he would scoff and leave the room whenever his mother and his sister would start in on how "all powerful" and "all knowing" God was. In his mind, if God really has these abilities, then he knows the horrific things that are going to transpire in people's lives, and yet he withholds his power to stop it? Yeah, that's a god worth serving.

As Noah began to slowly unbutton the silk shirt of the voluptuous young lady whose company he was thoroughly enjoying, he heard their voices in his head.

"Noah, it is critical that you repent from your sins. You have been losing your integrity and morals since, well, since you know when."

Noah sighed as he combed his hands through his thick, brown locks and rolled his hazel eyes. "Get out of my head," he thought to himself. To help drown out their influence, Noah took a large gulp of the red wine he and his companion were drinking.

Noah ran his skillful fingers through her long, amber hair and gently kissed her neck. The woman let out a soft moan when Noah's cell phone began to ring. More than a little annoyed, he went to hit the "ignore" button when he noticed it was his boss calling. What the heck? It was Sunday night. Noah looked at the young woman with an irresistible pout. Noah shook his head. Why couldn't he remember her name? No matter. It wasn't like he was planning on taking this anywhere.

"Excuse me, I have to take this call, but don't go anywhere. I promise I will be right back to finish where I left off." He playfully nibbled on her ear.

His mystery date giggled. "Don't be gone too long," she purred.

Noah professionally masked his irritation as he answered the phone. "Hey Abigail, what can I do for you?"

Abigail's voice resonated a sense of panic. "Something unbelievable has just happened. You need to get your butt in here! Oh, and don't bother trying to drive. You are going to have to come in by foot."

Noah was confused. "What? Why can't I take my car?"

"Just do what I say and do it now." He heard a click and she was gone.

Noah was both intrigued and offended. Abigail had never spoken to him in such a disrespectful manner before, and for her sake she better have a darn good reason for doing so now.

For a moment Noah had forgotten about the young woman who was most likely curled up naked in his bed. Why was it that big stories always had the worst timing?

Noah laid his seductive charms on thick, apologizing to the woman and vowing to call her tomorrow. Like that would ever happen. He hadn't even asked for her phone number. Noah felt no shame pushing the young woman out of his posh, high-rise apartment in the middle of the night. After all, he had given her more than enough money for a cab ride.

As Noah stepped out of the elevator, he went to offer Kurt the bellman a cordial wave and noticed that Kurt wasn't there. He didn't give it much thought until he walked out of the lobby and onto the street. Noah stood in shock. "What in the world is going on?"

Mayhem and chaos surrounded him. Traffic was bumper to bumper, and throngs of pedestrians jammed the sidewalks. Noah pushed through the crowds, fighting his way toward the office, only a few blocks away. His phone rang. It was Abigail. "Hello?"

Her voice was frantic. "Where are you? We need to get on this story ASAP."

"Yeah, well you could've warned me that I was going to be fighting my way through a mob."

Before Noah could finish, someone had bumped his arm. His phone went crashing to the ground and the impact shattered the screen. "Great, just wonderful." He was picking up his phone when another stranger

4

accidentally stepped on his hand.

It felt like an eternity before Noah finally reached the top floor of the newspaper building. Abigail, typically a calm and collected city editor, was a total wreck.

"What in God's name is going on out there?" Noah said, bursting into her office. "People are acting like the bloody world is coming to an end."

Abigail's face turned ghost white at his final words. "In a sense, it is."

Noah chuckled. "Yeah, right. Are you going to tell me what's going on, or are you just going to send me out there blind?"

"Noah, I'm not playing around!" It was then that Noah realized Abigail was sincerely frightened. She was pacing uncontrollably, and he saw the panic in her eyes as she looked up at him before continuing her thought.

"It's happened. The Rapture has happened, Noah!"

Noah was beginning to think she had lost it. "Jesus, Abigail. The Rapture? You seriously believe in all that malarkey?"

"Yeah, yeah I do. Maybe not until now, but now I most certainly believe. And you would too if you would have been watching the news instead of seducing the intern."

Noah rolled his eyes at her as she continued. "Millions of people have gone missing, and we need to find out why – especially since it sure as heck can't be because of some hokey religious nonsense, according to you."

Noah could not hide his shock.

"What do you mean millions of people have gone missing? What do you call all the people I had to fight my way through to get here?"

"According to the reports we have been receiving, this phenomenon isn't limited to the United States," she said. "People have disappeared all around the globe. People sitting next to their families watching TV, people driving cars, riding on buses and trains. A couple of planes have crashed. They've just... they're just gone, leaving the rest of us to figure it out."

Her voice was somber.

"My mom is one of them, Noah. She's gone... she just disappeared while driving with Anya in the car!"

He also forced everyone, small and great, rich and poor, free and slave, to receive a mark on his right hand or on his forehead, so that no one could buy or sell unless he had the mark, which is the name of the beast or the number of his name.

Revelation 13:16-17

2022

Joshua Hansen had been a respected rookie agent of the Secret Service for U.S. President Martin Knox. That had been a couple years ago, before the current world leader, President Angra Mainyu, had decided to occupy the White House for use as his personal headquarters.

Somehow through the change of regime, Joshua had been hand-picked to stay on staff. Not long after he had taken up his new post for Mainyu, Joshua overheard a rumor among his fellow agents about the president's chief adviser, Persephone Miller – that she had chosen to retain a few of the former U.S. president's agents because they were well trained, but had not held their positions long enough to hold a deep alliance with their regarded and popular former leader.

Joshua distrusted Miller. There was something unsettling about her. There was no denying that she was extremely intelligent and apparently the best woman for the position, but she reminded Joshua of a snake – cunning and coiled, ready to strike, without a care about the consequences. Many bowed down to her as if she were a god. Others swore she was the Antichrist.

All Joshua knew was that he wanted nothing to do with her. Her subtle sexual advances toward him, which had proven quite successful with some of his fellow agents, made him sick to his stomach. She made no attempt to hide the fact that she was merely using them for her own sexual satisfaction – and that if she were ever accused of having relations with them, she would openly deny stooping to such a level. Since all of the other agents were married, this suited them just fine.

Joshua had kept his opinions to himself, with one exception. He told Noah everything.

The two of them had been best friends since either of them could remember. Their mothers had pictures of them playing together in a playpen. They had been inseparable for most of their lives, but a tragic incident had severed their friendship for a few years.

It wasn't until the Rapture that they started talking again. Joshua believed it was the loss of their loved ones during the Rapture that had brought them back together. He had lost his entire family, and Noah had lost everyone except his young nieces. Noah had insisted that the twins come live with him in New York, but Martha and Mary had refused. They wanted nothing to do with the city.

They had been 16 at the time the Rapture took place, almost adults. The girls convinced Noah that they would be perfectly safe out in the country. They had been raised on the family farm, which had been passed down from generation to generation. They knew everything there was to know about running a homestead. They insisted that the land and the animals would sustain them, just like their ancestors before them. Noah eventually relented to their wishes, albeit reluctantly. Now, recent events had both Noah and Joshua wondering if it was time to pack up and join the girls back in their hometown.

The majority of the people throughout the world viewed President Mainyu as if he were a miraculous savior, but Joshua and Noah were exposed to a different side of the president and Ms. Miller.

As a reporter, Noah was no longer free to report events as they actually happened. The press was now being censored. The remaining civilians of the world were told only what their leader wanted them to hear, and the truth was not always part of that equation.

As their world changed around them, Joshua and Noah agreed that they would remain in their respective positions just long enough to gather any intelligence on what was really happening. Information was everything.

Noah was quietly interviewing people who made up the small minority that did not support their new leader. This group was made up of those who either had returned to their Christian faith or who had converted to Christianity after the Rapture. These people claimed that their food and water had been rationed, their Bibles burned, and their means of transportation confiscated. According to this group, the authorities claimed that their possessions were being taken for the good of the world, that the "world's army" was in need of such supplies.

Almost all of the factories worldwide had to be shut down after the Rapture. There were not enough people to keep them all running. Joshua had witnessed one very telling interaction that still haunted him. A bold man who had been assigned the position of keeping order in one of the territories in the Middle East had asked President Mainyu a sensible question: "Since we are now one nation, unified, why do we need an army? Who is there for us to fight? Wouldn't it be more prudent to use those resources to improve the living conditions of your citizens?"

The president replied by stating that there were rebels out there who would like nothing more than to destroy the current peace. He claimed that these men and women were sinfully addicted to violence and denounced any authority over themselves. Miller had added that their pride would be their downfall.

The next day, as the territorial leader flew back home, his plane's engines "malfunctioned" and the people mourned their loss.

Not long after that, people started appearing with a small mark on their hands or their foreheads. Miller had announced in a press conference that the government had started an experimental phase of a system to organize the world's civilians to make sure every citizen received their due supply of food and water. "We want to make sure that everyone receives fair rations," she explained.

After these unsettling events, Joshua and Noah devised a plan to tap the president's personal quarters. Joshua had the bug hidden in the sole of his shoe. Being part of the security detail allowed him access to all areas of the White House.

Joshua lacked any physical proof, but his gut told him that Persephone Miller was acting as more than just the president's chief adviser. The fact that President Mainyu's wife had been taken during the Rapture meant that there would be no one to notice should Miller take it upon herself to fill the void.

Joshua knew that what he was about to attempt was insane. The consequences of his actions, should he be caught, would be permanent.

The president and Miller were in the Oval Office meeting with his army's commanding general. Joshua stepped into the main security control room. He made idle chitchat with a coworker, Joe Phillips, as he discreetly scanned the monitor screens. The president's personal quarters were empty and no one was patrolling its corridors.

Left alone for a moment as Joe stepped out to use the restroom, he decided to act. Joshua tapped into the system and jammed the feed from the surveillance cameras, freezing the picture on all the monitors. He took a deep breath, trying to calm his nerves. It was imperative that he stay cool. Soon Joe returned. "Well, I better get back to my rounds. See ya, Joe."

Joe nodded. "Have a good one, Josh."

He hurried to the corridor that led to the president's room. Joshua gave a sigh of relief. It was empty. He casually strolled down the hallway until he reached his destination. He gave a solid knock on the door. When no one answered, he quickly slipped inside. The key was placing the bug where it would pick up conversations from every corner of the room. The other obstacle he had to work around was the fact that the room was swept for bugs each day. Fortunately, he knew precisely where not to plant the bug.

Before he could finish the job, he heard footsteps approaching. Joshua's heart pounded. He closed the closet door behind him just as the president and Persephone entered the room. He heard a click as one of them locked the door behind them. Next he heard the curtains being drawn shut.

The next 15 minutes were more than just a little awkward for Joshua.

Here he was, trapped inside a closet behind a few trench coats, as the world's leader and his chief of staff engaged in intimate relations. Joshua felt like an unwilling voyeur.

Joshua froze as he heard footsteps, and then the knob on the closet door started to turn. He held his breath as the door began to open. He was sure his days on this planet were over.

Miller's voice traveled across the room in Joshua's direction. "What are you doing, my love?"

The door stopped, remaining slightly ajar.

"I'm grabbing a new suit. What do you think I'm doing?"

Persephone sighed. "You can't just change suits. Angra, have I not taught you a thing about

discretion? You do realize that you owe your rise to power and the ability to hold your presidency to me. Without my skills, you would have failed miserably."

Her playful laugh had undertones of hidden derisive disgust.

"Yes, my sweet angel, I have never forgotten your worth. However, I sometimes feel as though you have forgotten mine." There was an uneasy sense of tension in their banter.

Her voice was as smooth as butter. "And tell me, what attributes do you bring to the table?"

The president's voice had a nasty bite to it. "Need I remind you that our master chose me for this task? You possess the skills of deception needed for your position, but you are severely lacking in the charm department. Without me, people would see you for the shrewd and conniving witch that you are. Oh, and by the way, don't think that I am not privy to the little trysts you have with my security agents. But, in order for our master's plan to come to fruition, it is vital that we remember to work as a team."

Persephone's voice sounded ruffled. "There's no need to be nasty. I was merely attempting to point out that if you suddenly change your suit at this hour of the day, it may raise unwanted suspicion. We cannot risk being caught. We have so much left to accomplish."

Joshua breathed a sigh of relief as the closet door closed with a click.

"By the way, Persephone, have we arrived at a solution for how we are going to dispose of those who refuse to take the mark?"

Joshua could hear the pleasure in her voice as she informed the president. "Yes, we have a viable plan in place as we speak."

"Good. Now, what about Operation Julienne? Have we heard from the operative?"

Her voice wore an edge of irritation. "No, we have not yet received any word."

"And why the hell not?"

Joshua jumped as President Mainyu's voice burst out in an angry rage.

This was a side of the president Joshua was unfamiliar with.

Her voice became sweet and seductive. "Now Angra, please calm down. There is no need to worry. These things take time. A thorough plan requires patience. You cannot rush these things."

He was still clearly frustrated. "So, what you are telling me is that we are supposed to just sit here, in the dark, like ignorant fools? I need to know if this Army of Angels is legitimate or some story conjured up by the rebels to inspire hope among their ranks. And I need to know now!"

She tried to stifle an irritated sigh. "Angra, please understand that if per chance this story is actually genuine and not some fabrication, we need to give him some time. If this renegade army is real, do you honestly think that they are going to allow just anybody to join their forces? He will need time to gain their trust if he is to obtain any real information. If he moves too quickly, his motives are bound to be questioned. It will look suspicious, and any hope of success will be lost."

Mainyu was still cynical. "Just remember that the Great Tribulation is quickly approaching. If he waits too long, there will be no need for his services." The president was annoyed. "Get dressed and meet me in my office. Saul wants to speak with us regarding one of my agents. He claims there is a mole in the Secret Service."

Persephone scoffed. "Do you honestly think that if there was a mole I wouldn't know about it? My actions do have a purpose."

Angra let out a wry laugh. "Do you really think men are that weak? What makes you think that they aren't playing you? You don't really think all of them have fallen prey to the seductive wiles of Persephone Miller, do you?"

"Go to hell. Oh, but then you would probably like that, wouldn't you?" she hissed. "For your information, I have photographs. The naked truth, if you will. Any false move on their part, and their wives and children will receive a hand-delivered copy."

"Impressive. You do have your uses. But from what I have heard, there is one who eludes you. How are you going to control him?"

"Don't worry about him."

NOAH

Noah parked his Porsche in the visitors section as the guard at the gate had instructed. He was to be escorted by military personnel from this point forward.

Noah felt a little unsure about the arrangement Abigail had set up. They were both shocked that they had even been granted permission to step onto Andrews Air Force Base. Since President Mainyu had taken over the base, access to his military headquarters had been impossible to obtain.

Noah couldn't help but wonder what had changed. Rumors had been spreading across the country that Mainyu and his top leaders from around the world were building an elite military force. The big question was why? Against whom did Mainyu intend to use such formidable force? He already held the world in his hands.

Noah's thoughts were interrupted as a Humvee pulled up next to him. A young soldier stepped out of the vehicle. "Noah Parks?"

Noah nodded, a little taken aback by the formality.

The soldier opened the passenger door for Noah then climbed into the back seat behind the driver. Noah could feel the soldier's eyes watching his every move. Trust was obviously something this group did not believe in. The soldier's right hand instinctively rested on his sidearm and Noah's trained eyes immediately detected a small mark on the man's hand.

The driver's demeanor was a little more cordial, but still aloof. "Welcome to Andrews Air Force Base, Mr. Parks. I am Staff Sergeant Nichols, and this is Staff Sergeant Manuel. We are honored that your paper is doing a story on the military."

Noah was curious. The driver also had a small mark on his right hand, but his was different from Manuel's.

Noah nodded toward Nichols' hand. "I noticed that the marks on your hands are different, yet you both hold the same rank and appear to be from the same unit. Can you tell me what the marks stand for?"

Noah was certain that the mark had nothing to do with the military. He had seen civilians wearing the mark as well, but he was hoping that this approach might spur the soldiers to offer an explanation as to the reason behind these marks.

Manuel curtly replied. "Sir, the marks are not military-issued."

"This one is going to be a hard nut to crack," Noah thought to himself.

Nichols politely offered up a vague explanation. "Sir, the marks are not issued by the World's

Army, but it is mandatory that every soldier possess the mark."

Noah nodded. "What do the numbers stand for?"

Nichols started to reply, but Manuel cut him off. "Sir, the number represents what part of the world you are originally from." Manuel shot Nichols a cold look in the rear-view mirror.

With that, Noah decided to drop the issue. He took mental notes as they drove through the base. More than one area housed row upon row of military vehicles that had been modified with upgraded armor and large .50-caliber guns. The Humvee stopped at a flashing red light, allowing Noah to watch a squad of soldiers training in the distance. His stomach churned, but his face remained composed.

Noah turned to Nichols. "Excuse me, sergeant, but I have noticed that we haven't stopped at any of the training sites, and I would like to check out the new weapons."

Manuel spoke up. "Sir, we have been assigned to take you straight to the golf course, where you can interview some of the top brass."

Noah hid his disappointment. "Wow, what an honor. I was hardly expecting such royal treatment," he said with a smile as the Humvee pulled up to the golf course and stopped alongside a putting green, where a group of officers had gathered in the distance.

Before Noah could step out of the vehicle, the radio crackled and there was a great commotion among the uniformed men all around him. Nichols picked up the receiver as Noah shut the door behind him. He stood outside the vehicle, unable to hear conversation inside.

After a moment, Nichols curtly informed Noah that his meeting had been canceled. Something had the entire base on high alert. Manuel ordered Noah to return to the Humvee and Nichols sped off in the direction of the front gate.

Manuel addressed Noah. "Sir, I regret to inform you that due to a medical emergency, your meeting will have to be postponed."

Noah's voice kept its cool charm. "Of course. These things tend to happen in my line of work. May I inquire as to what happened?"

Manuel stared straight forward. "Sir, at this moment the incident is deemed classified."

The soldier looked down at Noah's hand and then into his eyes. "By the way, Mr. Parks, where was it you said you were from?"

Noah was skilled at reading people's faces. The slightest movement could reveal a wealth of information, and at this moment, he was certain the tables had turned. Noah turned away. He gazed out at the mass of soldiers running in formation with their weapons and packs, as if they were being deployed on a mission.

"I didn't."

JOSHUA

Joshua waited to hear the door close from inside the closet. His heart was still pounding. He had never intended to be in the president's quarters this long. It was only a matter of time before Joe noticed that the system had been tampered with.

He looked back at the curtain rod where he had planned on planting the listening device, but his gut told him to get out of there. Joshua exited the president's room, hurried down the long corridor, and turned the corner when he heard Joe's voice in his earpiece.

"All security personnel, be advised. We have a breach. I repeat, we have a breach. Our monitoring system has been compromised. Report to your stations immediately."

Joshua entered the nearest bathroom, flushing the device down the toilet as fast as he could. He attempted to poise himself when his boss called him on his radio. "Agent Hansen, this is Captain O'Malley. I need you to report to the Aviary immediately."

Joshua's heart skipped a beat. The Aviary was code for the Oval Office. It didn't take a genius to know that he was their prime suspect. He was also the only agent who had not taken the president's mark. Joshua quickly responded. "Affirmative. On my way."

He headed in the direction of the Oval Office, noting that each of the hall cameras had a red blinking light. In his earpiece, he heard constant chatter among his Secret Service colleagues as they reacted to the security threat.

Joshua took a sharp turn into the kitchen. He stood underneath the security camera, avoiding its field of view, before he slipped into a closet and quickly changed into a sous chef's uniform. Fortunately for him, more than half the agents on staff had dark hair and brown eyes, making it easier for him to blend in.

Joshua entered the deep freezer as one of his coworkers inspected a seafood delivery truck. Joshua kept the freezer door cracked open just enough to allow him to keep an eye on the fish truck. He watched Agent Randall sign off on the inspection sheet before moving to the bakery truck behind it.

It was now or never. Joshua slid out of the kitchen and quietly climbed into the back of the refrigerated fish truck. The cold was beginning to wear on him when the truck finally began to move.

"Thank goodness," he thought to himself. He wasn't sure how much longer he could tolerate the bone-chilling conditions.

The truck came to a stop and Joshua heard the heavy doors creak open, allowing light to flood in. He held his breath. Due to the security breach, he had anticipated Agent Randall's signature would not be enough to allow the vehicle to pass through the gates without further inspection. Joshua was counting on the pungent odor and the freezing temperature to deter the agents from carrying out a thorough search.

He pinned himself behind a stack of boxes in the back against the wall, purposefully avoiding the corners, which were likely places to be searched. Joshua steadied his breath as Agent Gomez pointed his flashlight at the driver's side corner. Joshua then heard Gomez's footsteps pass right in front of his shield of boxes to investigate the passenger side corner when Captain O'Malley's voice came over Gomez's radio. "All agents be on the lookout for Agent Hansen. Repeat, all agents be on the lookout for Agent Hansen."

Gomez turned and slowly began to head toward the door, but his instincts were too good. He raised his flashlight toward Joshua's hiding spot, then shrugged as the light shone on an empty space. Joshua had slipped out from behind the boxes and was leaning up against the opposite side. Once he heard Gomez's footsteps trailing off, Joshua slipped back into his original position seconds before Gomez's flashlight scanned the empty spaces of the vehicle one last time. The doors slowly creaked shut and Gomez pounded his fist on the back of the truck, giving the driver the go-ahead.

Joshua moved his way to the rear of the truck and waited.

NOAH

Noah leaned against his car, feeling relieved to be off the base but frustrated at the lack of information he was able to obtain. He purposely put a few miles between himself and the base before stopping to top off his gas tank.

Noah was staring off into space when his cell phone began playing AC/DC's "Hell's Bells." Noah answered. "Hey, my interview was cut short. Do you think you can play hooky? Maybe we can get in nine holes before grabbing a bite to eat later?"

Joshua was out of breath. "Where are you?"

Noah was alarmed. "A couple miles from Andrews. Why? What's going on?"

Joshua looked around. He had left the delivery truck and its unconscious driver in the back alleyway of the vehicle's next scheduled stop. Joshua was trying to put as much distance between himself and the truck as possible. He had decided to walk through an affluent residential area. There were too many security cameras scattered around the city and he knew he looked conspicuous wandering around in a cook's uniform.

"I had to abort the mission. It's a long story. I'm on the run. I barely made it out of the White House. I need you to get to D.C. and pick me up. I need to get out of here! It's bad, Noah. It's worse than we suspected."

Noah's head was spinning. He plugged Joshua's location into his GPS and drove as fast as he possibly could without drawing any unwanted attention, which was not an easy task in a Porsche 911.

Noah tried to stifle his laughter as Joshua climbed into the car wearing his disguise.

Joshua shot him a dirty look. "I don't want to hear it. In fact, you need to pull over and switch places with me."

Noah gave him a sideways glance. "Are you crazy? Do you really think I'm going to let you drive my car?"

"Yeah, I do." Joshua was insistent. "Right now, they're using satellites and traffic cameras to track me. I know my way around this city, not to mention I've had actual driver's training at the academy. You drive this thing like an old lady. So pull over and get out."

Noah sighed. "Fine." He pulled over and relinquished the driver's seat to Joshua. "Happy?"

Joshua smirked. "Under any other circumstances, yes, but the fact that I am now a fugitive kind of takes the fun out of it."

Noah sneered. "Good."

Joshua rolled his eyes before apprising Noah of the day's events. Once he had finished, Noah shared what information he was able to gather from his time on Andrews Air Force Base.

"I'm telling you, I have been around long enough to know the signs. They are gearing up for war."

Joshua looked at Noah. "I agree with you, but I don't get it. Who do they plan on invading?"

Noah's voice was grim. "Us."

Joshua's eyes widened with comprehension. "You are saying that Miller's plan for dealing with the people who refuse to take the mark is annihilation?"

Noah nodded. "Look, I don't believe in all this religious stuff, but at the same time, if the people don't want to be branded like cattle, they shouldn't be forced to do so."

He looked off in the distance before continuing. "You should have seen these soldiers. There was something not right about them. To be honest, I couldn't get off of that base fast enough."

Joshua stopped the Porsche abruptly. Noah was annoyed. "Hey man, what's wrong with you? Look, I only agreed to let you drive my car because of your 'special training'."

Joshua was focused on the road. "Exactly."

He nodded to the long line of stopped vehicles off in the distance. "That's a military roadblock ahead of us," Joshua said as he nonchalantly turned the car around.

Noah panicked. "Oh-kay. Mind telling me what your plan is? Because from where I am sitting, it looks like you are heading right back toward the lunatics who are hunting you like a dog."

Joshua ignored Noah as he casually turned into a parking lot. He parked the Porsche in a sea of vehicles.

Noah looked at him as if he had lost his mind. "Now what are you doing?"

Joshua nodded toward the door. "Come on. We are ditching the

Porsche. Stay low, but act casual."

"Why are we ditching my $90,000 car? You know darn well that she can outrun any of their vehicles." Noah was befuddled.

Joshua gave Noah a sly look. "Dude, speed is not what we need right now. We can't outrun roadblocks. And besides, every single cop in the city is searching for your car."

Joshua started jimmying the door lock on a Jeep Rubicon. "Now this, this is what we need."

Noah looked back longingly at his car. "Screw it. You're right. Let's hurry up and get the heck out of here."

Hopping in behind the wheel, Joshua looked over at Noah. "Where to, James?"

Noah thought for a moment. "The way I see it, we have two missions. First, we need to high-tail it to my family's farm and check in on Mary and Martha. Then we need to find out about this Army of Angels."

JOSHUA

Joshua drove the Rubicon over dirt roads and mountainous terrain as far as the gas tank would take them. They made sure to park the Jeep pointed north, opposite of the way they were heading, underneath a grove of pines. The two men broke branches off nearby trees until they had completely covered the vehicle from view.

They were tempted to steal another vehicle, but that would just leave a trail for the authorities, and using their bank cards was not an option. So they walked.

Noah had been in an irritable mood for hours. "We are screwed! What the heck are we supposed to do?"

They had been walking for half the day and still had not found anywhere suitable for putting up camp. Joshua, ignoring Noah, stopped to survey the land when he heard a familiar click.

"Freeze." The voice belonged to a male, probably in his mid-twenties. "Turn around slowly with your hands in the air."

Joshua did as the man instructed. His heart sank when he turned to find the man holding a .45 to Noah's head. Joshua quickly scanned the man's hands and forehead. To his relief, they were clean of any marks. The man waved his gun at Joshua. "You, take out your gun and put it on the ground."

Joshua removed his sidearm from his waistband and dropped it to the ground.

"Now walk in front of us."

Joshua slowly walked around Noah and the stranger. Once he was in front of them, the man barked out further orders. "Walk straight until I tell you otherwise." Joshua did as he was told.

Noah attempted to reason with the man. "Look, we don't want any trouble. All we want is to be on our way."

The stranger hit Noah in the head with the butt of his gun, staggering Noah and allowing him to quickly scoop up Joshua's pistol.

"Listen to me, pretty boy. All you need to do is shut up and do as you're told. I don't recall asking you to speak."

They walked in silence until the man told Joshua to veer toward the left, up the side of the mountain. The three continued to trudge up the steep slope for about 15 minutes when out of nowhere a cabin appeared. It was well hidden behind tall pine trees and shrubs. The man's voice broke the silence. "Hey Parker, come on out here."

Joshua noticed that the man kept his voice down. Another man around the same age came out from around the corner. Parker sounded annoyed. "Great, Kyle, what the heck have you done? Why on earth would you bring these two here?"

Kyle looked shocked. "What should I have done with them? Let them wander around like a couple of hens, clucking and making all sorts of noise and drawing attention to us?"

Parker sighed. "You have a point. These city boys look pretty clueless." Joshua noticed that Parker did not bear the mark. He also didn't miss Parker's subtle glances at his and Noah's hands and foreheads.

Joshua ventured to speak. "If it is alright with the two of you, I do have some questions."

Parker looked around nervously. "Not out here. Let's go inside. You don't want to be caught outside after dark." Parker noticed the knot on the side of Noah's face. "What happened to pretty boy?"

Kyle offered up a sheepish grin. "I might have knocked him on the head a little."

Parker shook his head. "Haven't I warned you about your rash behavior? It's like you don't have a lick of sense about you. What would you have done if you had knocked him unconscious?"

Noah and Joshua walked inside the cabin, shocked to see a group of about 10 people staring at them. Parker turned to a woman who was standing in a nearby doorway.

"Trisha, would you please grab this man a package of frozen vegetables?. It seems that someone decided to knock him upside the head." Parker shot Kyle a scolding look.

Noah held his tongue as long as he could. He was a reporter, and true to his nature, he needed answers. "Look, I tried telling Kyle that all we want is to be left alone. We don't mean anyone any harm. But I can't help but wonder what all of you are doing way out here in the middle of nowhere. Why aren't you living in your homes?"

Parker ignored the question and looked at Noah, then Joshua. "Where are you two from?" The three men looked at each other for a long, silent moment.

Joshua turned to Noah, who nodded his consent. Joshua spoke up. "I'm from D.C. and my friend is from New York."

"Well, you two are a long way away from home," Parker said, handing each of them a piece of paper.

Noah was horrified. "Are you kidding me?" He looked at Joshua in disbelief. "What are we going to do?"

There, staring back at them, was a flier with their faces on it. Modern-day wanted posters.

Noah looked at Parker. "Where did you get these?"

Parker sat in a leather chair across from Noah and Joshua. "We sneak into the town library every few days and use the computer. My nephew, Tristan, knows how to hack into their system. He downloaded these today."

Noah attempted to size up the young man. He guessed he was probably a year or two older than his nieces, but his sandy blond hair, blue eyes, and tanned skin told Noah that Tristan wasn't from around these parts.

Noah nodded to him. "So, what part of California are you from?"

Tristan looked shocked. "How'd you know I was from California?"

Noah chuckled. "Your surfer look kind of gives it away."

Noah took a deep breath as he reflected on the ramifications of the flier. "This means everybody and their brother knows that we are wanted by the government. We can't show our faces anywhere."

Parker nodded when a tall, slender man named Adam stood up. His tone was aggressive. "That is why the two of you need to leave. I don't know what you did to piss them off, but I sure as heck know what will happen to us if we're caught aiding and abetting fugitives."

Parker stood up and faced Adam. "We have already discussed this, and it's my decision," he said as he walked over to Joshua and handed him the gun Kyle had taken from him. "They can stay until morning. I won't send them out there in the middle of the night. It's too dangerous. You know once the sun sets no one stands a chance out there."

Adam let out an exasperated sigh. "Think about it, Parker. You are sentencing us to death. Your wife, her grandfather, your son."

Parker stared at Adam intently. "No one is forcing you to stay. You and your family are free to go."

Adam sat down, seething with anger. Parker looked over at him. "Besides, they would not be the first fugitives we have aided and abetted."

Adam snorted. "That was different."

Noah was about to ask Parker what he meant when Parker's Great Pyrenees, Jack, began to growl. The hairs on the giant dog's back were standing straight up. Parker's other Pyrenees, Jill, had been napping by the front door.

They heard a gunshot ring out in the distance just seconds before Jill jumped to her feet. She bared her teeth, snarling and growling at the door. Joshua stood up, drawing his weapon as he saw the door knob slowly turn. Noah silently pointed to the three deadbolts on the door that appeared to be keeping the intruder out. At least for now.

MARY

Mary hopped behind the oversized steering wheel of the vintage Ford. The 1950 F1 pickup had been in the family since her grandpa had driven it home straight from the dealership. Decades later, her grandpa and her father had collaborated to restore "Ole Jean" back to her original glory. They left the interior the factory cream color, but spruced up the exterior with a root beer brown paint job that sparkled in the sunlight. They had presented the new version of Jean to Mary and her twin sister, Martha, on their 16th birthday.

They had been on top of the world. It wasn't the first time they had driven Jean. Their father had taught them how to drive when they were 12 years old. It's just the way things are done when you live on a farm. But now, Jean and the farm were all they had left of their family, with the exception of their Uncle Noah.

Their mother had died of breast cancer when they were 14. Their father had been their rock. He had remained strong and frequently comforted his daughters with his quirky sense of humor. Mary believed in her heart that her father's steadfast belief in God is what provided him such remarkable peace within life's storms. She also believed that his faith was the reason for his disappearance during the Rapture. Their Grandma and Grandpa Parks had vanished as well. Their mother's death was not the first time their devoted grandparents' faith had been severely tested, but like their father, they had refused to let the enemy turn them.

Martha put the last case of produce in the bed of the truck before joining Mary. As Martha opened the passenger door, the brisk fall air chilled the truck's cab, causing Mary to shiver. Martha also shuddered from the cold. She looked out past the farm, admiring the brilliant autumn canvas of the Smoky Mountains. "This will be our last trip until the winter harvest is ready."

Mary nodded. Fall had always been her favorite time of year. There was something magical and invigorating about it. It never ceased to lift her spirits. Neither did the song that was blaring out of the truck's speakers. Mary and Martha were rocking out to Danny Gokey's song, "More Than You Think I Am." Their off-tune voices clashed with his as the truck rolled down the dirt path toward town.

As they entered the sleepy mountain community of Gatlinburg – once a bustling resort destination prior to what the girls had coined D-Day, which stood for Disappearance Day – an ominous scene left them with a sense of dread. Several cars were backed up behind a roadblock and military personnel patrolled the narrow streets.

Martha reached over and turned off the music. Radio stations had been prohibited from playing "religious" music, leaving listeners stuck with having to scrounge for old CDs and anything they might have on their iPods.

Mary's heart was racing as they approached the checkpoint. Martha looked at Mary and whispered, "What the heck is going on? It feels like we are being invaded."

Mary shook her head as a soldier approached the truck. "I need to see your license and vehicle registration, ma'am." Mary nodded. She handed the documents to the soldier, who studied them at length. Mary shot Martha a nervous glance. The soldier looked up. His eyes had an emptiness to them that caused Mary's stomach to turn.

"Ma'am, I am going to have to ask you to pull your vehicle off to the side."

Mary swallowed hard. Her mouth was dry. "Is there a problem?"

The soldier looked past her. "Ma'am, I repeat, please move your vehicle off to the side." He pointed to Mary's left, where a group of soldiers were forming.

Mary did as he ordered. She attempted to steady her hands, which were shaking uncontrollably. Another soldier who appeared to be in charge approached the truck. He wore the bars of a lieutenant. "Ma'am, I need the two of you to step away from the vehicle."

Mary took a deep breath. She nodded to Martha, signaling for them to do as they were told. The soldiers began to search the vehicle. Martha spoke up. "Excuse me, but can you please tell us what is going on? Why are you searching our truck?"

The soldier approached Martha. "Ma'am, I am going to need to see your ID as well."

Martha hesitated. Feeling violated, she fought the urge to tell them where they could go, and slowly handed over her driver's license.

The soldier studied both of their identifications as if he were trying to commit the information to memory. He finally addressed them. "Where are you headed with this produce?"

Mary picked up on the soldier's subtle glance at their hands and foreheads. She had heard some of the people in town saying that the government had issued a law that prohibited any person who did not wear the presidential mark from buying or selling any goods.

Martha had started to speak when Mary abruptly cut her off. "We are taking the produce to a few families that we are friends with."

The lieutenant shot her a stern look. "Not anymore. From now on, you are prohibited from taking any produce off of your property." His voice was as cold as his eyes. He looked at their driver's licenses one last time before handing them back.

He curtly addressed Mary. "I see that your last name is Rivers, yet your company sign on your truck reads Parks Produce."

Mary was leery. She wondered where he was going with this. "Yes, that is correct."

The soldier scrutinized her closely. "Any relation to Noah Parks?"

Mary steeled herself. She willed her voice to remain calm as she smiled up at the soldier.

"Yes. That would be my uncle." She feigned concern. "Is he all right? Has something happened to him?"

Mary felt as if she were going to be sick. She wanted to vomit all over the lieutenant's polished boots, but she held herself together.

The soldier ignored her question. "When was the last time you had contact with your uncle?"

Mary shrugged her shoulders and sighed. "Geez, let me think. It has been quite some time. He hasn't been around here since before the Ra-..." She caught herself. She had been told that President Mainyu had forbidden the use of the term "Rapture."

"Since before the disappearance," she finished.

Martha chimed in. "He has never been a fan of the country. It is impossible to pull him away from the big city." She sighed. "Sort of easier for him to blend in, ya know?" She laughed. "Here he always sort of stuck out like a sore thumb."

The lieutenant's eyes narrowed. "I suggest you two ladies consider making it a priority to receive the president's mark. Until then, it would be prudent to obey the law, which prohibits anyone without it from buying or selling any merchandise. You may return to your home."

The twins nodded their consent. Mary turned the truck around and headed back toward the farm. She controlled her anger to a whisper.

"Can you believe the injustice? Where do they come off telling us that we can't even give our produce away? How are we going to survive if we can't sell our fruits and vegetables? If Dad hadn't installed the solar panels and the farm didn't have its own well, we would be doomed."

As Mary approached their turnoff, Martha interrupted her. "Go straight."

Mary looked at her sister. "What? Martha we can't be wasting gas. You heard that guy. If we don't take that bloody mark, we won't be able to buy gas ever again."

"Just do it!" Martha insisted.

Martha had been watching her side-view mirror during their drive home. She suspected they were being followed.

Mary continued down the highway for about a mile when Martha told her to pull over on the side of the road. Mary had had about enough of everyone barking orders at her. She pulled the truck onto the shoulder, but before it came to a complete stop, Martha jumped out.

Martha raised her finger to her lips, signaling for Mary to keep quiet. She ran around to the back of the truck, bent down, and then Mary saw her sister throw an object deep into the forest. Martha jumped back in the truck.

"Oh-kay...," Mary exclaimed. "Mind sharing with the class?"

Martha spoke in a hushed tone. "Yes, but first drive straight for a block or so before turning around and heading back home."

Mary did as her sister instructed while Martha explained her erratic behavior.

"I was keeping my eye on the other soldiers while you were talking with Prince Charming. I don't know what's happened, but they are after Uncle Noah. That roadblock wasn't about the mark."

Mary looked confused. "You think the roadblock was for Uncle Noah?"

Martha nodded her head. "Yep. And while we were being questioned, another soldier was busy putting a tracking device on the truck. They must think that Uncle Noah is coming here."

Mary became alarmed as the pieces fell into place. "That has to be the reason we can't reach him."

JOSHUA

The intrusion of the property around the cabin had been uneventful but nonetheless disturbing, so the men rotated shifts, standing guard throughout the long night.

Joshua had the last shift after a restless night's sleep. Jack had taken a liking to Joshua. The big dog never left his side and Joshua found his company comforting. This dog had been bred to protect; it was his nature, but he was affectionate as well.

Joshua kept checking his watch. He couldn't wait for the sun to rise. He had had about all he could stand of being penned up inside.

Parker and his men boarded up the barn and the cabin every night. It was like living inside a box. Noah had always been the claustrophobic one, but Joshua had to admit that he was feeling his friend's pain.

He took one last look at the time. "Thank God." It was 6:30, about 15 minutes until sunrise. Joshua made a mental list of everything he needed to do before he and Noah hit the road. They had decided to stick to the Appalachian Trail. Of course, they would have to stay off the beaten path, making their route more perilous.

It was then that both Jack and Jill went berserk. They ran to every point of entrance, barking ferociously and baring their teeth. The group was jolted awake, and there was a hard knock at the front door. Jill was standing on her hind legs, feverishly clawing at the door. Joshua didn't know why, but it always freaked him out when the hair on an animal's back stood straight up. It was a primal response to danger.

Parker whispered something to Adam, then headed to the door.

"Who is it?"

Joshua hadn't expected Parker's voice to sound so calm.

A gruff voice responded. "This is Major Henry of the World Army. We need you to open up so we can speak with you, sir."

Parker looked back to check on the others. "Sure, no problem. Just give me a minute to put my dogs in the other room."

Adam was leading everyone down into a small cellar when Parker entered the master bedroom. As the last person entered the dark hole in the ground, Parker closed the cellar door and quickly replaced the heavy wool rug and antique chest. He intentionally left an irate set of Great Pyrenees behind the heavy pine door.

Parker rushed back to the front door. He had unlocked one of the deadbolts when he remembered the cross above the entryway. He grabbed the cross and stashed it underneath one of the cushions on the couch before he returned to unlock the remaining two deadbolts. The wrought iron hinges creaked in protest as he pulled open the massive wood door.

Major Henry stood tall and expressionless as the sun rose behind him. His voice sent chills up and down Parker's spine. "Sir, I need you to step aside. My men need to do a thorough search of your residence."

Across the yard, Major Henry's men had already torn down the boarding and ransacked his barn. Parker offered the major a polite smile, skillfully hiding the rage that burned inside him. Several soldiers filed past him and began searching every nook and cranny of his home.

Major Henry looked Parker up and down with suspicion. "We are searching for two men who are wanted by the government. They are considered armed and dangerous."

He handed Parker the fliers of Noah and Joshua. "We have reason to believe they might be in this area." The major glared at him before continuing. "It is imperative, for your safety, that we locate these two men. Have you seen them?"

Parker shook his head. "Nope, but I can't imagine two city slickers lasting too long out here." Parker gestured toward the boarded windows. "As you can see, this area is home to some pretty aggressive bears."

Henry was still eyeballing Parker when a soldier returned from the back part of the cabin. He addressed the major. "Sir, we have searched the premises, with the exception of one room, and have found no trace of them."

Major Henry was annoyed. "Your orders were to search the entire property."

The soldier squirmed. "Sir, yes sir, but the dogs..."

Jack and Jill had been aggressively vocalizing their dislike of the intruders. The major looked at Parker. "Restrain your animals so my men can enter," he snapped.

Parker nodded. "It will take me just a minute."

Parker leashed the dogs and stood in the corner of the room. The two canines tugged hard on their leashes and snarled viciously at the strangers.

The soldiers briskly searched under the bed, in the shower, the closet, and behind the curtains before exiting the room. Parker quickly locked the dogs in the room before following the major's men back to the front of the house.

He felt a sense of relief as he watched the men leave his home and climb into their Humvees. Parker was shutting the door when Major Henry stopped and turned around. "By the way, I noticed items in your home that indicate a woman and a child live here."

Parker swallowed before answering. "Yes. My wife and my son." This was information he was not happy to share.

The officer tilted his head. "But they're not here?"

Parker shook his head. "No. We had a disagreement. She went to her sister's house to cool off."

Major Henry nodded. "I see... Good day, sir."

Parker shut the door. His hands were shaking as he locked the deadbolts behind him. He waited until Jack and Jill had settled down before he opened the cellar door.

As he pulled back the trap door, Joshua's gun was staring him right in the face. "Hey, easy there, Trigger."

Seeing it was Parker, Joshua slid his weapon back into its holster. "Sorry man, but we couldn't hear much down here. Just a lot of footsteps over our heads."

Jack came lumbering up to Joshua, slobbering on him with big kisses. Joshua chuckled as he ruffled the dog's fur. "And some pretty upset puppy dogs. Isn't that right, Mr. Tough Guy?" Jill let out a playful bark. "And you, yes, you are one ferocious girl, aren't you?" Jill wagged her tail before returning to Parker's side.

The group gathered in the living room. Some members left to prepare breakfast while Parker shared the details of Major Henry's visit with Noah and Joshua.

Adam could hardly sit still. "I knew it. I knew these two were nothing but trouble." He was becoming frantic. "We've been made. They know we are here. They know you haven't taken the mark. It is just a matter of time before they return. Parker, we've got to get out of here."

Parker sighed. "I'm not going to lie. This isn't good." He looked at his uninvited house guests. "I need the two of you to lead our group far away from here."

Noah looked up. "Wait. What?" Noah had no clue how the two of them were going to hike through the treacherous mountains without getting caught, but now Parker wanted them to take along all of these people. There was just no way. There were too many of them.

Joshua spoke up. "It's the least we can do after everything you have done for us."

Noah rolled his eyes. "Great. Just great."

Joshua shot Noah a sharp look before turning his attention back to Parker. "But what I don't understand is why you're asking us to lead them."

Parker looked over at Adam, bracing himself for his friend's reaction. "Because I intend to stay here."

Adam blew up in anger. He stared at Noah and Joshua as if it was their fault. "Are you happy now?"

That was too much for Joshua, who lost his cool. Both men stood toe to toe. Adam had a few inches on him, but that had never intimidated Joshua.

"I have had enough of you and your attitude," he said. "Has anyone ever told you you need to learn when to shut up?"

Noah looked away to hide his smirk. He loved this side of Joshua.

Joshua was still railing on Adam. "If you want to blame someone, why don't you blame your buddy Kyle over there. We were minding our own business when he decided to pull a gun on us. And to answer your question, no, no I am not happy. My life has been turned upside down ever since this bloody Rapture, and it just keeps getting worse. So if you intend to join us, I highly suggest that you can the attitude."

Trisha had entered the room during the heated confrontation carrying a tray of food. She calmly stood there, watching the scene unfold. Once Joshua's temper subsided and he sat back down, she asked, "Anyone hungry?"

MARTHA

Martha sat up against her pillows, twirling her long, chestnut brown hair, something she did when she was apprehensive. She and Mary had stayed up late into the night discussing their options, which were extremely limited.

The rooster sound on her alarm clock began to crow, signaling it was time to start the day. Martha laughed to herself as she heard Rupert, their rooster, begin to crow in response out in the yard. "Yeah, yeah, yeah. I get it. Everyone's hungry."

She was slipping into her work clothes when Rascal, their Australian shepherd, started to bark aggressively at something near the barn. Martha put on her boots, grabbed her jacket, and ran outside. Since the farm was nestled in a valley, it was common for a layer of fog to settle in over the land. Between the fog and the early, predawn sky, her visibility was minimal.

Martha called out to Rascal, but he ignored her. He was locked on to something.

"Darn it!" Martha prayed it wasn't a bear or a mountain lion. She nearly jumped out of her skin when she felt Mary nudge her. She tried to scream, but nothing came out.

Mary was quite adept at sneaking around like a lioness on the hunt. She handed Martha a shotgun and proceeded toward the barn seconds before all hell broke loose.

Every animal inside was suddenly emitting a distress call. Rascal was at the barn door, pacing back and forth, frantic to get inside. As the girls reached the entrance to the barn, Martha froze. The heavy beam that locked the double doors was missing. She whispered to Mary, "This is not a wild animal we are dealing with."

Mary nodded. Martha raised the shotgun as Mary pulled open the heavy door. Rascal squeezed through the small opening and lunged toward a dark figure in the distance.

A young man screamed out in pain. "Get him off of me!"

Martha took aim at the stranger's chest, calling Rascal off. The dog let go of his bite, but stood snarling over the trespasser. Mary searched the stalls, randomly stabbing a pitchfork into the animals' straw beds.

"Martha, for Pete's sake don't shoot! It's me!" The young man pulled off a black ski mask, revealing his identity.

"Luke?" The twins exclaimed simultaneously. Mary ran over and threw her arms around their friend, who was the preacher's son. Martha sat down on the milking stool. Her muscles were too weak to support her after the excitement. She was suddenly overcome with a nervous laugh that soon had Mary and Luke joining in. Soon the three lifelong friends were close to tears from laughing so hard. Rascal turned his head to the side, confused by their behavior.

Once Martha had gained control of herself, she questioned Luke. "What in the world are you doing poking around out here in the dark?"

Mary nodded as she gently slapped Luke upside his head. "Yeah, what were you thinking?"

As Mary and Martha stared at him with their striking sets of hazel eyes, Luke was quickly brought back to reality. He ran his hands through his sandy blond hair as he cleared his throat. Tears welled up in his eyes. Without saying a word he unzipped his coat, reached into an inside pocket and pulled out two pieces of paper. He handed them to the girls.

Martha looked down at the paper. There, smiling back at her with a sophisticated grin, was her Uncle Noah.

She looked up at Luke. "I knew it. I knew that roadblock had something to do with my uncle."

Mary looked confused. "What? This is Joshua."

Martha's eyes opened wide. "They are both fugitives?"

Luke nodded his head. "They have been searching all the homes in Gatlinburg and the outskirts since yesterday. They arrived at my house a few hours ago."

Martha watched her friend wipe tears from his bright blue eyes. It dawned on her that there was more to the story. "Wait, you wouldn't be this upset over my uncle and Joshua. What else happened?"

Luke closed his eyes and shook his head, trying to compose himself. "They showed up in the middle of the night. They began to search our house and demanded to know if my father knew where our two hometown heroes might be. My dad insisted that we hadn't seen them, that as far as he knew, no one had."

Luke paused and his voice turned angry. "But they continued to search our property, insisting that my father unlock the church. My father refused and then a soldier hit him in the head with his gun." Tears were flowing down Luke's cheeks. "I started to go after them when my mom stopped me. A couple of soldiers threw my dad into one of their vehicles, and the rest of them broke into the church. While they were busy ransacking the church, my mother gave me the fliers and told me to head here. She promised that she and my sisters would come as soon as it was safe to get away."

Luke wiped his nose with the back of his hand. "I managed to sneak out of the house without them noticing. I made it into the forest just before the sky lit up with fire. They torched the church!"

Martha looked at Luke's guilt-ridden face. "Knock it off," she ordered. She knew what her friend was feeling. Blaming yourself for not doing more. Feeling guilty that it was them instead of you. Angry at God for allowing it to happen in the first place. Feeling guilty for being angry. Ever since her mother's death, she was all too familiar with the misery Luke was experiencing.

Luke looked deep into Martha's eyes. "I'm so sorry."

Martha slowly shook her head. "Don't sweat it." She stood up, stretching her legs. "Why don't I hurry up and take care of the chores out here and you can join Mary in the kitchen. I'm starving, and I always think better with a full stomach." She offered Luke a warm smile.

Luke gave her a quizzical look. "You sure? I'm better out here than I am in the kitchen."

Martha nodded. "Yeah, Rascal and I got this. I need you in there making sure Miss Mary doesn't eat up all the bacon. I bet you didn't know that she was a bacon hog," she said, laughing at her own play on words.

Mary playfully stuck her tongue out at Martha. "Oh, bite me," she said, grabbing Luke's arm. "Come on, it's warmer inside anyway, and you and I can split the bacon fifty-fifty," she laughed.

Mary waited until they were inside the house before she started to interrogate Luke. "Pray tell, what was that all about?"

Luke looked confused. "What was what all about?"

Mary busied herself with preparing breakfast. "What are you sorry for?" She asked, narrowing her eyes.

Luke shrugged his shoulders. "It's a long story."

Mary smiled. "Good, because I have plenty of time. So talk to me."

Mary usually respected her sister's privacy, but this time curiosity got the better of her. Martha and Luke had been an item during most of high school, but about a year after their mother's death, out of nowhere, they just split up. Martha had never talked to Mary about it, which wasn't like her. In fact, it was at that time Martha began to pull away from a lot of things. Mary had overheard Martha arguing with their father about attending church. She told him that she didn't believe in his heartless God, and didn't feel like she should have to be a hypocrite just to make the family look good in the eyes of their peers. The thing was, Mary had been dying to share her feelings with Martha because she too was livid with God.

Luke looked uncomfortable. "I don't know ... I really don't think it's my place to tell you. And besides, I only know my side of the story."

Mary nodded her head. "Yeah, I get it. I'm sorry for prying. Not that it is an excuse, but I have just felt so distant from Martha since the two of you broke up."

Mary's eyes were moist. "We used to have this special bond, that weird twins thing everyone talks about. But something happened, and she just kind of pulled away. It's not like she is mean to me, but she just sort of keeps everything to herself." Mary took a deep breath. "It makes me feel so lonely, especially now that my dad is gone."

Luke gazed off in the distance, his voice solemn. "I know what you mean." He suddenly slapped his hands on the marble countertop, startling Mary. "So, we need to put our heads together and figure out what we're going to do. Should we stay here, or should we hide out in the wilderness? And what the heck is going on with your Uncle Noah and Joshua?"

The screen door slammed shut as Rascal ran in to check his bowl for any scraps. Martha took off the old denim jacket that had belonged to her father and hung it on one of the hooks by the back door. Her voice floated across the kitchen toward Mary and Luke.

"I say we stay here. This way we have food, shelter, and weapons should we need them. And to answer your question, I believe my uncle and Joshua discovered something that the government would kill over to keep it from getting out to the public."

Mary felt sick to her stomach. "I can't bear to lose another family member. So how do we find them?"

Martha wore a confident expression. "By staying right here. Uncle Noah knows that the farm is the best place to hole up. He's coming home. We just need to stay alive until they get here."

NOAH

Noah lay awake, staring up at the dark sky. He knew it was an optical illusion, but being this high up in the mountains felt like he could reach up and pluck the stars right out of the sky. He tossed and turned, partly because his mind refused to shut down, but Adam's obnoxious snoring didn't help.

The group had been out on the trail for a couple of days. Parker and Tristan had made a covert trip into town and raided the old outdoor supply store. It had been boarded up since the Rapture, but it still had enough supplies for the entire group.

Normally Noah wouldn't consider a group of eight very large, but as they were sneaking around in the woods trying to evade trained soldiers, it felt like an overwhelming number. The fact that three women and two young boys comprised over half their group made the odds of success slim.

Noah's eyelids were finally beginning to feel heavy. He welcomed the warm, pleasant sensation of sleep when his heart suddenly kicked into overdrive. He held his breath, straining to listen. He was almost positive he heard a branch snap a few yards away. Then he heard the faint rustle of footsteps landing on top of pine needles slowly moving toward him.

He wrestled to free himself from his sleeping bag and crawled over to wake Joshua. Jack was already awake. A hushed growl came from deep in his throat as he lay curled up next to Joshua. The dog never left his side. Parker was sad to see him go, but admitted that the group could benefit from his presence.

Joshua had become a light sleeper. There was something about being hunted that will do that to a man. He was awake and sliding out of his sleeping bag before Noah reached him. Both men pulled their pistols and squinted into the darkness. Noah secretly prayed it was a wild animal. Right

35

now, he would take the nastiest grizzly bear over soldiers of the World Army.

They quietly woke the other adults, but before the rest of their group had a chance to arm themselves, they heard several guns click in succession.

Noah felt his body's reaction to fear travel through his core. He also felt a surge of anger rush over him. They had come so far, only to be captured? Part of him wondered if he ever truly believed that they had a real chance of escaping the enemy's grasp.

A low voice traveled through the distance. "Who are you? What are you doing out here?"

The intruders drew closer and into view, their weapons aimed at Noah's group. To his surprise and relief, Noah saw that they wore civilian clothes. But he caught himself. The strangers could very well be loyal to the World Army. And then there was the fact that both Noah and Joshua had bounties on their heads. Joshua was worth $200,000 while Noah was only worth $100,000, but that was still a hefty chunk of change.

Noah was about to offer up a false name when the man who appeared to be their leader moved in. "Wait a minute. I know who you two are. I've seen portraits of your lovely mugs."

The man laughed, and the group of men hiding behind him in the shadows emerged and lowered their weapons.

Noah and Joshua's mouths fell to the floor. They resisted the urge to holler for joy as they stared into the face of America's famous four-star Admiral Peter Marcus, former commander of the Navy SEALs.

Marcus chuckled under his breath at their reaction. He pulled a piece of paper out of one of his pockets and handed it to Noah. "That, boys, is why I am worth $500,000." Noah stared at Marcus' wanted poster and then handed it to Joshua.

Marcus pointed at Joshua. "I remember meeting you on several occasions at the White House under President Knox. He was the best president I ever worked for. He was a remarkable man, and he sure took notice of you."

Joshua looked surprised. "Me?"

Marcus nodded. "Yep. He once told me to keep my eye on you. That you were going places."

Joshua felt melancholy. Before the Rapture, he was being groomed to be the president's personal guard. "He knew how to build you up. Made you believe in yourself... then he disappeared."

Marcus sighed. "I often wonder where we would be right now if the Rapture hadn't robbed us of people like him. I don't know about you boys, but I lost a lot of good people that day."

Marcus looked off into the distance. The sun was slowly pushing back the night. He turned to Noah. "And you, Mr. Hot Shot Reporter. I remember knocking some balls around with you. Best interview I ever had. You were a cocky son of a gun, but I like the way your mind works."

Noah blushed like a little boy. "Thank you, sir. That means a lot coming from you."

The three men reminisced for a few minutes before getting down to details. Marcus looked at Noah and Joshua. "So what are your plans? You can't just wander around out here, but something tells me you already know that."

Noah responded. "We picked up these guys back in Shenandoah." Noah nodded toward the group. "And if our bearings are correct, we just passed through the Roanoke area yesterday. From here we plan on heading south. My family has a farm in the Smoky Mountains. The way we see it, it is the best place we know to dig in."

Marcus nodded. "Sounds like a pretty decent plan." He looked Noah and Joshua up and down. "Neither one of you would happen to be Christian would you?"

A sneer flashed across Noah's face. "No. Why do you ask?"

Marcus took a long pause before answering. "I'm going to be honest with you boys. You don't stand a chance against Mainyu's army. There's something unnatural about them." Marcus looked around. The women in Noah's group had already started breakfast for everyone.

Marcus lowered his voice and leaned in toward Noah and Joshua. "I'm not a religious man, but I do know this. Something eerie happens to those who take the mark. My company and I ran into a group of fighters about a month ago. They called themselves the Army of Angels. We trained with them for a while. According to them, the mark is the sign of the devil. Once you take the mark, your soul is damned for all eternity. No going back, ever."

This sent chills down Noah's back. "So what are you suggesting?"

Marcus sighed. "Find them. Find the Army of Angels. They are the only group to face the World's Army and live to tell about it."

Joshua piped in. "But what about you? Why aren't you guys still with them?"

Marcus shrugged. "Sometimes in my gut I feel like we made a huge mistake by leaving. They are a little too, um, spiritual for me and my boys, but I'll tell you this much – I haven't had a moment's worth of peace since we left them."

Noah looked at Marcus. "I met a few of Mainyu's guys. There is something really creepy about them, but I can't put my finger on what it is."

Marcus whispered. "According to the Army of Angels, these soldiers' souls have been possessed by demons."

Noah looked at Joshua. He knew it sounded absurd, but after his experience at Andrews he almost believed it. Noah had recalled something from all his years of attending church with his family about a satanic mark and something they called the Great Tribulation.

Noah cleared his throat. "If all this is true, then that would mean that we are at the end of times."

MARY

Mary was busy making a hearty chicken stew with homemade cheese biscuits. It had always been her grandpa's favorite. The sun was setting, which meant Martha should be coming in from the barn at any minute. Mary was trying to stay calm. Since he arrived, Luke had been helping the girls with their chores around the farm. Martha had been finishing up sooner than usual with his help, but tonight they were still out there.

Rascal sat in front of the kitchen door whining, which added to Mary's concern. The thought of something happening to them terrified her. Martha had always been the brave one. Mary had been the wimp.

Even when her mother was dying, laying there wracked with pain and asking for Mary, Mary chickened out. She never got to say goodbye to her mother. Her fear of death paralyzed her. She had prayed and begged God to save her mother, which he did not do, so then she prayed and pleaded with him to take away her fear of death so she could say goodbye. But again she was let down. After that, she became bitter. She hated God for abandoning her during her time of need.

Unlike Martha, who outwardly displayed her resentment toward God, Mary tucked it away deep in her heart, sheltering the truth. She went to great lengths to harbor it from those she knew and loved, happy to play the hypocrite her sister loathed and refused to be. Her Uncle Noah and Martha were a lot alike when it came to that.

But Mary learned what she had always known: No one can hide the condition of their heart from God. He knew the truth she hid inside her soul. Hence, she was left behind, left behind to live in the hell she had secretly chosen. She would never forget the shocked expression that washed over Martha on the day of the Rapture when Mary remained on earth, right by her side. Even Martha hadn't a clue to the true condition of

Mary's tarnished soul.

Mary was lost in her regrets when the door flew open, startling her. She jumped, burning her arm on the oven and nearly dropping the biscuits.

"Well it's about time. I was wor-..." She turned to find Luke's younger sister, Margo, standing in her kitchen. Margo was shaking uncontrollably and she was covered in blood.

Mary put the biscuits on the stove and rushed to Margo's side. "Oh my God, Margo, what happened? Are you okay?"

Margo nodded her head, unable to speak, as Martha and Luke burst through the door carrying Luke's mother. Angela Parish was nearly unconscious. She was soaked in blood. Her arms were ripped to shreds. It appeared she had been attacked by a wild animal.

Mary froze for a moment. Her mind struggled to make sense of the scene being played out in front of her. Martha shouted to her. "Mary, run upstairs and throw an old blanket on mom and dad's bed."

Rascal was growling at the darkness outside. Luke spoke to his little sister. "Margo, can you please do me a favor and shut the door? Make sure you lock it, okay?" Without saying a word, Margo did as she was asked. As soon as the door was locked, she ran to her brother's side.

Mary was soaking hand towels in hot water as the four of them entered what had been her parents' bedroom. She hadn't been in here since D-Day. She noticed Luke's sister Ella was not with them, but she was too afraid to ask why. From the looks of things, she didn't want to know.

Mary dressed Angela's wounds while Luke started a fire in the wood-burning stove. Martha helped clean the blood off Margo and dressed her in one of their old flannel nightgowns. They were eating their dinner around the bed when Angela began thrashing and screaming for Ella. She threw her arms around Luke and began to bawl into his shoulder. Margo squeezed in with them.

They forced Angela to eat, and once Margo fell asleep at her mother's side, Angela shared the night's horrific details. Not wanting to wake Margo, she spoke in hushed tones.

"It was unbelievable. We weren't far from your farm. We had decided to travel through the forest, trying to keep out of the soldiers' sight. They're desecrating the town. They started going door to door, demanding that people take the mark. Those who refused were taken against their will. We don't know where they're taking them. They started on the opposite end of town and are coming this way. It won't be long before they're here."

Mary's stomach turned. She resisted the urge to vomit. She grabbed Martha's hand and noticed her sister's face become defiant.

Luke's voice cracked as he questioned his mom. "Then what happened? What did this to you? Where is Ella?"

Angela shook her head as tears poured down her face. "I don't know. It all happened so fast. It was a blur." She took a deep breath. "We were making good time when out of nowhere this beast-like thing jumped down from a tree and started attacking Ella. I tried to save her..." Angela's voice failed her and she sobbed. It took a few minutes before she could continue. "I couldn't... the monster cut me up during the struggle, but Ella... it mauled her to death. That was when I picked up Margo and ran here as hard as I could."

Luke didn't know what to make of what his mother said. She had to be in shock. He decided it would be best to leave it alone for now. He encouraged his mother to try to get some rest.

It wasn't until the next morning when Margo woke up and told the three of them the same story that a foreboding feeling filled the room.

Martha and Luke headed out to retrieve Ella's body so they could give her a proper burial, but when they returned to the farm empty-handed, their uneasiness grew. There had been no sign of Ella. No tracks, no blood trail. It was as if she had just disappeared.

JOSHUA

The last week had been a grueling one. The terrain was increasingly difficult and wearing them down. Ever since Marcus' men were able to sneak up on them so easily, the members of the group had agreed it would be in their best interest to rotate keeping watch. They split the night watch into two shifts. It was a necessity, but the lack of sleep was taking its toll.

Joshua led the group and Noah covered the rear. Sometimes the slopes were so steep the travelers had to grab onto anything they could to pull themselves up without falling backwards.

Joshua found it exhausting always being on full alert. It was one thing to do it for a living. You got to go home and let your guard down. But now it was 24 hours a day, 7 days a week.

It didn't help that Noah and Adam were constantly at each other's throats. Before the group had left the cabin, Parker had appointed Noah as first in charge with Joshua as his second in command. This was something that didn't sit well with Adam. Parker had tried to explain to Adam that he had a family that needed his protection. He also pointed out the fact that Noah and Joshua had spent time amongst their enemy. They had a slight advantage of knowing how they think, what their next move may be.

Night was closing in on the group. Joshua scanned the landscape, searching for adequate cover. Not finding anything sufficient, he led his comrades further south. Finally, they stumbled across a small cave. The group rejoiced. They were tired, their muscles ached, and their stomachs protested the absence of food.

The journey had been more than physically taxing. Joshua struggled with the irony of his situation. Here he was, risking life and limb to survive. He fought death with every ounce of his being, but for what? He had lost his entire family in the Rapture. He didn't have a wife or kids to live for. In fact, he had been alone for a very long time.

He had been in love once. Deeply in love. But God had seen fit to take her away from him. He still had nightmares about that night. He was driving her home from their anniversary party. She was sitting next to him on the bench seat of his truck, resting her head on his shoulder like she always did, when the lights of the oncoming car veered right toward them.

There was nowhere to go. It was a two-lane road that dropped off on their right. There was a car coming up from their rear. Joshua slammed on the brakes as hard as he could, but it wasn't enough. The impact sent them sailing over the side of the road. Their bodies were thrown around the cab like a pair of rag dolls. The truck finally came to a stop, the roof of the cab smashed in by a giant boulder.

Joshua shuddered. He had never been able to wash the image of Emma's broken body from his mind. It haunted him even after all this time. The worst part was that Joshua had lost more than Emma that night. He also lost his best friend, and his Savior. Noah blamed him for his sister's death, vowing never to forgive Joshua, and Joshua blamed God, vowing never to forgive him.

MARTHA

Martha threw on her father's old jacket. She loved to run her hands over the worn denim. For some strange reason, it always comforted her. She pulled the lambskin lining in close to protect her from the cold bite in the air and walked briskly toward the old treehouse she had spent so many hours in as a kid.

She climbed the wooden ladder and pushed open the trap door. She hadn't been up in the treehouse since the day her mother died. She didn't know what had drawn her all out here, but she yearned for some time alone.

The farm was becoming crowded as a few more of their neighborhood friends had managed to escape the soldiers, finding refuge at the farm. Martha was anxious for her uncle to come home. She secretly worried that something had happened to him. She had expected him to be here by now. She knew it was just a matter of time before the soldiers attacked the farm. Actually, the fact that they hadn't unnerved her. What were they waiting for?

Luke's presence had been a blessing, but it had also unearthed painful memories. She couldn't look at him without being wracked with guilt. She knew she had broken his heart, never even offering him an explanation. But how could she tell him? The truth would have hurt him more.

She was sitting on a giant pillow, soaking up the solitude, when she noticed the trap door slowly start to open. Her blood began to race through her veins. She searched the small space for anything she could use as a weapon and picked up one of her volleyball trophies.

It was an odd place to keep such memorabilia, but after her mother had become sick, she pushed away anything that reminded her of life before her mother's death. Her father had begged her to store her trophies out here

44

rather than throw them away. She had given in for his sake. She knew her anger and bitterness added to his sorrow, but it was like a disease she couldn't kick. It spread through her like cancer. And how ironic was that?

She raised the trophy above her head, ready to knock the head off of whatever came through the door. Man or beast, she would not be some helpless victim.

Martha let out a long exhale as she saw Luke's face pop up through the trap door. Damn! She would rather have faced a beast than Luke. It was as though God just wasn't going to let it go.

Luke's face lit up when he saw her. "I thought I saw you come out here. I'm not sure it was the wisest move considering all that has taken place, but..." Luke looked around. They had shared a lot of good memories in this place. "I can't say I blame you."

Martha fought back tears. It was easier to deny her feelings for him from a distance. Her voice was soft. "Yeah, I always felt safe up here." She let out a laugh. "Did you know that one time I was so furious with my mom that I decided to run away. This was as far as I got." They both laughed.

Luke sat with his back against the wall a few feet away. He stared at a poster of singer Avril Lavigne. "I remember when you sang Avril's song 'Complicated' at the talent show in fifth grade."

Martha snorted. "Oh my gosh, and all the boys sang, 'why do you have to be so constipated,'" she said, rolling her eyes at the memory.

"Hey, we were your biggest fans," Luke jokingly protested.

Martha chuckled. "Oh, is that what you call it? I'm sure all of Avril's fans used to pull her hair, too."

Luke shrugged his shoulders. "What can I say? We were young, dumb, and in puppy love."

He looked at Martha with that gentle expression that always made her melt. He clicked his tongue before he spoke again. "I was wondering, since the world seems to be crumbling around us and all hell is breaking loose... would you be willing to tell me what happened?"

"There's not much to tell. I just couldn't handle it anymore." She didn't want to do this. She had been avoiding this painful discussion for years.

Luke spoke to her in a gentle tone. "Marty, I am so sorry. If I could take it back, I would."

Tears threatened to spill from the corners of her eyes. "Damn it. No, don't cry. Suck it up, girl," she told herself.

Luke's eyes were pleading with her. Fine. She might as well just get it over with. She owed him that much.

Her voice was weak. "Luke, it's not your fault. I never blamed you." His face expressed a mixture of surprise and relief. "I loved you. As you know, after my mom died, I became angry with God. No secret there. You and I had been fighting our feelings and our hormones for a very long time. The

45

only thing holding us back was our faith." Luke nodded his agreement. "Once I turned my back on God, I didn't give a rat's behind about what God thought. I am the one who initiated taking things to the next level. I pushed you into having sex."

Luke blushed. "It's not like I put up much of a fight."

Martha laughed. "You had raging hormones, and I was clumsily doing everything I could to seduce you." She paused for a moment. "The thing is... I cherish the time we had together. I am thankful that I was able to experience that with you."

Luke fought the urge to rush to her side and hold her. He didn't want to scare her off. He had waited forever for her to open up to him. "Then what happened?"

She looked at him for a moment. Before responding, she closed her eyes, unable to face him. "I got pregnant."

She heard the air rush from his lungs. A silence filled the space between them. Finally she heard his voice. It was soft, nonjudgmental – not what she had anticipated. "Why didn't you tell me?"

Her voice cracked. "Because... because it was my fault. I talked you into it. I taunted you and teased you until you couldn't resist any longer. I knew how much you struggled with it. I knew it wracked you with guilt. I wasn't going to add an abortion to your burden."

He couldn't resist. He moved over to comfort her. "We had other options. I would have gladly married you." He wiped the tears from her cheeks. "I would still be honored to call you my wife. Don't you know how much I love you?"

Martha buried her head into his chest. She couldn't stop crying for quite some time. When she regained her composure, she answered him. "Yes, yes I knew how much you cared for me. But I wanted nothing to do with the institution of marriage. It reminded me of God, something I wanted to have no part of. Something I loathed."

She winced as she saw the pain on his face, the pain she had caused. "Luke, I am so sorry. It was wrong of me to make that decision by myself. It was your child, too."

Tears ran down his face as he mouthed, "It's okay."

"That's why I pulled away. I couldn't look at you without drowning in guilt. You reminded me of my worst sin."

Luke continued to hold her, silently praying for their forgiveness. After a long time had passed, he whispered in her ear. "You know what my dad would always say: 'We are not defined by our sin. We are defined by His blood.'"

NOAH

Noah rubbed his blurry eyes, fighting to stay awake. He hated the second shift. As a reporter, he was required to work late. Sleeping in had been his reward, but when he covered the second shift of the watch, there was no sleeping after 3 a.m. Noah was the first to admit that he wasn't the most pleasant person when he suffered from sleep deprivation. The only other member of the group who was worse than him was Adam, and that wasn't saying much.

Noah hated these long nights. They had parted ways with Admiral Marcus' band of rebels the same day they had been ambushed by them. Marcus had recruited about 80 former soldiers. Their plan was to cross the country and build an army to defeat President Mainyu. They were making their way to Texas when they left.

Noah missed the brief sense of security Marcus' men had provided, but he knew his little group could not tag along. It put his comrades in more danger than it offered them protection. If the Army of the Dead, as some called it, was working this hard to find Noah and Joshua, he could only imagine their efforts to find Marcus and his men.

Engulfed in solitude, Noah's mind wandered. He was anxious to reach the farm, worried sick about Mary and Martha. He knew the girls would have tried to call him a thousand times by now. Mary would be scared to death. She was the sensitive one, much like his older sister. Noah's heart ached for Anna. "Oh, how I wish you were here. I could use some of your sage advice right now. I wouldn't even roll my eyes once."

Then there was Martha. She was just as sensitive, but she showed it differently. She didn't let her fear stop her like her sister did, and she tended to disguise her pain with an in-your-face attitude. It was her line of defense. Everyone always said she acted more like Noah than either one of her parents. Martha was always her sister's protector. She was never one to back down from a fight. Her parents tended to lean toward compromise, but Martha called it like she saw it. Right or wrong, she owned it.

Noah chuckled to himself as he remembered the day Martha was sent home from kindergarten for punching a little boy on the playground. The boy had been bullying Mary, calling her names and teasing her, but when he pushed Mary out of line for the swings, Martha responded by punching him in the face. That was his little monkey. She didn't mess around.

Noah had been lost in his memories when he thought he heard a commotion in the distance. He looked around to see if anyone was awake. Jack's head was propped up, his ears raised, signaling that he heard something.

Tristan sat up and turned toward Noah. Noah whispered, "Do you hear that?"

Tristan nodded. Noah woke Joshua and the three of them decided that Tristan would stand guard over the camp while Noah and Joshua left to investigate.

Noah shadowed Joshua as he adeptly maneuvered his way through the pitch-black forest, causing Noah to question, yet again, why Parker had put him in charge with Joshua as his second. To Noah's way of thinking, Parker got it backwards.

As they headed south, they passed a sign off in the distance that read "Jefferson National Forest." Not long after they passed the sign, they came upon the source of the noise. They scaled an enormous boulder that formed part of the mountainside.

As they peered over the edge, Noah's first reaction was that of elation. But as his mind made sense of the carnage that lay scattered just a few yards in front of them, Noah turned numb. And then terror gripped him.

Noah heard Joshua mutter under his breath. "Holy..."

There, right in front of them, Marcus' men were engaged in battle with soldiers of the World's Army. Now Noah knew why some referred to them as the Army of Darkness, or the Army of the Dead. The soldiers moved with such precision, such speed that it seemed beyond humanly possible. They did not appear to fear death. It was as though they were already dead.

But the incomprehensible part was that Marcus' men, a group of elite American soldiers, were being mowed down, like they were children playing "war," by only a handful of the enemy's men.

Noah's jaw dropped as he watched the Americans unleash waves of automatic fire at the soldiers, to no avail. The bullets seemed to ricochet off the bodies of Mainyu's men, with some of the rounds appearing to reverse course and hit the Americans. Some of Marcus' men appeared to comprehend the futility of their situation. They tried to flee, but the enemy's soldiers swooped in like vapor and took them out, one by one.

Joshua swallowed hard. "Please tell me you are seeing what I'm seeing, because if someone tried telling me that this actually took place, I wouldn't believe them in a hundred years."

Noah nodded his head in disbelief and tried to keep his voice low. "This is either the real deal, or we both ate the same mushrooms. Why aren't those guys using guns? Is this an entirely different unit?"

The Dark Soldiers wielded heavy steel swords. The ends of the swords were alight with fire. As the steel cut through their victims' flesh, the flames appeared to leave some sort of poison behind. Each slain man would writhe in pain as a putrid stench filled the air. The wound would sizzle and bubble where the flames had made contact.

Noah panicked as Joshua drew his weapon and began to move toward the fight. Noah pulled him back. "What are you doing?"

Rage danced in Joshua's eyes. "I'm going to go help them. I can't just sit here while they are being slaughtered."

Noah held his best friend down. "No, no way. Have you lost your mind? What makes you think your fate would be any different? Do you really think you are going to jump in and save the day?"

Joshua shook his head. "No, but I can't just sit here like a coward."

Noah looked his friend dead in the eye. "I need you. My nieces need you. Tristan, Adam, Kyle, and the rest of the group… they need you. Sacrificing your life will not amount to anything. Staying alive, hashing out a game plan, finding the Army of Angels… all this leads to hope. That is not being cowardly, that is being smart."

Joshua slid back down behind the rock wall. "Okay, maybe you're right."

Noah let out a sigh of relief. He chuckled under his breath. "Hey, remember what Coach Madden always used to say?"

The two recited in unison. "Fight smarter, not harder."

When Noah looked back over the rock, he saw that Admiral Marcus was the last man standing. He fought bravely and with honor, but his human strength was no match for his opponent. Noah closed his eyes as Marcus fell lifeless to the ground.

Noah turned to retrace their steps when his foot dislodged a small piece of the rock. As it rolled down the mountainside, he heard one of the dark soldiers speak. "Did you hear that?"

Joshua and Noah plastered their bodies up against the rock. They did their best to steady their breathing. One of the soldiers came over to investigate, but when he reached the side of the mountain, small debris gave way under his weight and he quickly retreated.

Noah and Joshua waited for the soldiers to leave. Noah wondered what they were doing. His muscles were shaking from exhaustion as the minutes ticked by. From what he could tell, it sounded like they were doing something with the dead bodies.

MARY

Mary was worn out. She had been busy tending to Angela's wounds on top of overseeing the meals for all their guests. Mary had noticed a change in Martha since Luke had been around. Her sister was beginning to soften around the edges. She still had her feisty spirit; that would probably never change. But the anger seemed to be subsiding.

Mary smiled to herself as she remembered overhearing her mother saying to her father, "I know no one will ever be good enough for the girls in your eyes, but I'm telling you, Luke and Martha are meant to be together."

Her father had groaned, causing her mom to laugh at his antics. "Don't worry. You will always be the number one guy in her life, but seriously, who else besides you has the ability to calm her down the way he does? He knows how to deal with her."

Her mother had started to giggle as she heard her father protest. "Fine, maybe you're right, but do we really have to talk about it? They're only 15. I still have three more years before I have to deal with offering my approval to anyone." She could still hear her father's obstinate tone.

Luke, Angela, and Margo had taken up residence in their parents' bedroom. The Carsons and their children were staying in Mary's grandparents' old room, and the Millers and their newborn son were occupying Uncle Noah's room. The house was filling up fast.

Mary grabbed one of the old patchwork quilts that either her mother or grandmother had made. She pulled a couple of photo albums from the built-in shelves and curled up in her grandpa's oversized leather chair next to the fire.

Once she was settled in, her cat Pumpkin plopped down on the ottoman on top of her feet. Pumpkin was an old Maine Coon who preferred to lounge around somewhere close to Mary. But during his youth he had been quite the hunter, leaving plenty of little and sometimes not so little gifts on the front porch. Whenever Mary was the one to stumble across one of his presents, she would run away squealing. Even then, death of any kind freaked her out.

Mary rubbed Pumpkin's belly with her foot. The fire crackled and popped, throwing out a warm glow throughout the room. It was bright enough for Mary to look through the old family photos without having to turn on a light.

As she flipped through the pages, she quietly laughed to herself, remembering the fond moments she had spent with her family. They had not been rich, and with the exception of their Uncle Noah, they did not hold fancy college degrees. But they had been close and they had been happy.

Mary looked proudly at the photo her grandparents had taken of her uncle, standing in front of his loaded-down car the day he had left to pursue his college education at Columbia University. She could still hear her grandmother's voice saying, "Ever since I can remember, that boy dreamed of becoming a journalist. Look at him now." There was a twinkle of pride in her eyes, and a tone of concern in her voice.

Mary turned the page and paused. There was a second picture taken that day. This one included Uncle Noah's twin sister, Emma. The two of them had been inseparable. The next picture included Joshua: The three amigos.

A queasy feeling spread through Mary. For someone terrified of death, she had been given a healthy dose of it. First her Aunt Emma, then her mother. And if that weren't enough, her father and grandparents had disappeared in the Rapture.

Emma had been the baby girl of the family. Anna, Mary and Martha's mother, had been the eldest sibling. Then came Noah and Emma. She remembered how her uncle would always tease Emma about being the baby of the family because she had been slow out of the gate. Noah had been born first. Now that she stopped to think about it, it was a lot like she and Martha. Martha had been born first, and like their Uncle Noah, Martha had always been overly protective of her younger sibling.

Mary remembered how much she adored her Aunt Emma. Her aunt had brains and beauty. She had been Homecoming Queen and valedictorian of her class. After her first year away at college, she returned home engaged to marry her high school sweetheart and best friend, Joshua Hansen. She had excelled at Harvard University. She was aggressively working toward being accepted into Harvard Law School. She wanted to be a civil rights attorney. Her hero was Supreme Court Justice Thurgood Marshall. Everyone who knew her believed she had what it took to accomplish her goal.

Mary wiped away tears as Emma stared up at her, her long, rich, brown hair blowing in the wind as her bright green eyes sparkled. Mary could still hear her playful laugh. She remembered how excited she was whenever her aunt was around. Her energy was contagious, but then her exuberance and her breath had been snuffed out much too soon. She had been only 19 years old when she passed.

Losing Emma had been a blow below the belt. Yes, they learned how to deal with the unbearable pain, they learned how to suppress their emotions, and they went on living, but a great chunk of who they were had been chiseled out of their hearts. It healed, but the missing piece never grew back, especially for her Uncle Noah.

Mary turned and looked as she heard the stairs creaking behind her. It was Martha. Her sister grabbed a quilt out of the large basket and sat down on the couch. "What are you doing up so late?"

Mary lifted up the photo album. Martha nodded. Her eyes fell on their aunt. Martha gazed into the fire, watching it dance around the logs. "Do you think it hurts?"

Mary gave her a quizzical look. "Do I think what hurts?"

Martha's voice was low. "Death. Do you think death hurts?"

Mary shuddered. "I don't know."

Martha continued to stare into the fire. "I think that it must be peaceful. Sure, the moments leading up to your last breath might be painful, but think about it – all the anguish, all the pain, is gone."

Mary nodded. "I wonder if this is all there is? Do you believe in life after death? If so, do you think they miss us as much as we miss them?"

Martha shook her head. "Honestly, I don't know what I believe anymore."

NOAH

Noah's mind was still racing from the unimaginable scene he and Joshua had witnessed. For the first few days, they had decided to keep the news to themselves, maybe because they were still trying to come to grips with what had transpired. Maybe they were afraid the group would think they had lost it, or maybe it was a little of both.

Noah and Joshua finally agreed to tell the others about what had happened to Marcus and his men. It was unfair to keep the truth from them. Keeping someone in the dark as a means to protect them never really worked out for the best.

Adam went crazy when he found out. He pushed Noah up against the side of the mountain, holding him there as his fingers wrapped around Noah's throat. "What else have you been hiding from us? I knew you couldn't be trusted!"

Noah had had enough of Adam's hostile treatment. "Get your hands off of me," Noah hissed.

Adam tightened his grip. Joshua rose to his feet, but before he could reach them, Noah rammed his knee into Adam's groin. As Adam bent over in pain, Noah grabbed Adam's head, bringing it down on his knee. But before he could inflict further damage, Joshua and Tristan were pulling him off of Adam.

Noah spoke through clenched teeth. "Don't you ever lay a hand on me again, or so help me God you will not live to tell about it."

Joshua turned to look at Adam. "One more act of defiance and you will be banned from the group." There was a part of Joshua that wanted to let his friend finish the man off. Adam had been a thorn in their side since they first met him back at Parker's cabin.

Tristan looked at Adam in disbelief. He knew the tension between

Adam and Noah had been escalating, but he never suspected Adam would resort to violence. He had been keeping something from Noah and Joshua, not wanting things to spiral out of control, but now there was no point in holding his tongue.

He cleared his throat. "I didn't say anything because I didn't want to aggravate the situation, but now, well..." He looked at Adam with contempt. "Adam has been trying to convince the rest of us to turn both of you in to the authorities. I should have told you sooner, but I honestly thought he was all talk."

Joshua put a hand on Tristan's shoulder. "Don't blame yourself. You did nothing wrong. You hear me?" Joshua had been paying attention to Tristan when he heard Adam's wife cry out, "No! Please God, no!"

Noah had his gun aimed at Adam, a cold, furious expression on his face. For a moment, Joshua thought his friend was going to pull the trigger. Joshua hesitated for a moment. He knew he should rush in and stop Noah, but there was a small part of him that wanted Noah to do it. They would be justified in their eyes. Adam had threatened to sentence them to death, so why should he feel obligated to protect his life?

A collective sigh of relief echoed within the group as Noah lowered his weapon. He ran his hands through his hair, shook his head and muttered under his breath. "I've got to get out of here."

Joshua ran after his friend, but Noah turned him away. "You need to stay behind. I just have to clear my head, but I don't trust that son of a ... I need you to keep an eye on him while I'm gone." Joshua nodded and returned to the group.

Noah slowly picked his way through the trees. It was a new moon, and the sky was pitch black. It suddenly dawned on him that the only light visible for miles was the faint flickering of a small campfire crackling deep within the forest. The harsh scent of smoke clashed with the fresh, clean aroma emanating from the tall pines that stood like noble guardians over the dense terrain. An evil feeling lingered in the night air, sending chills up and down Noah's spine.

After hearing Tristan's revelation, Noah desperately wanted to abandon the group. They had dragged this band around through the forest for what seemed like weeks. And for what? For them to traitorously turn them in for a handsome reward? Noah sat down on the cold ground. His back was pressed up against the trunk of a tall pine as he continued to wrestle with his conscience.

Noah decided to look at the circumstances through Tristan's eyes. The young man had been loyal, obedient, and respectful to both Noah and Joshua the entire trip. It was then that Noah admitted to himself that these terrified souls had yet to engage in their first battle. Still, they knew that a bloody encounter with the demonic forces that had been set loose to

55

destroy the human population was inevitable.

The rumors that had spread throughout the countryside were more than alarming. The hideous creatures that formed the Army of Darkness were ghastly beings that possessed supernatural strength, and it was said they became stronger with each soul they struck down. After the massacre he and Joshua had witnessed, Noah knew the rumors were just the tip of the iceberg. Deep down, Noah knew he couldn't sentence all of them to death because of the behavior of one man. He resolved to do his best to protect them.

As Noah's emotions subsided, the smell of the campfire finally registered with him. Someone else was lurking deep in the woods, not far from where they were camped. With his senses on high alert, he quickly headed back to the group.

When Noah finally reached Joshua and the others, he wasted no time informing them that they were not alone. Members of the group voiced their concerns and ideas, with the exception of one. Adam was no longer allowed to speak during group meetings.

Everyone voiced their hesitancy to approach the camp. What if it was a trap? What if it wasn't the Army of Angels, but rather the dreadful demons lying in wait?

Adam stubbornly defied his order of silence. "Why would the Army of Angels be burning a fire out here in the wilderness? I would think they would have more common sense than to send up a smoke signal to the enemy."

Joshua slapped him upside the head. "Silence. You no longer have a say."

Noah contemplated everyone's concerns. "Joshua and I will go. Even if it's the Army of the Dead, at least we will know what we are dealing with." Noah nodded to Tristan. "I am leaving Tristan in charge."

He glared at Adam, begging him to defy his order. Adam rolled his eyes but remained quiet.

Noah pulled Tristan off to the side. "About a football field's length south of here, there is a cave. I want you to take the group there. Joshua and I will meet you there, but should we not return by sunrise, I want you to promise me that you will lead the others on to my family's farm."

Noah looked Tristan straight in the eyes as he watched determination slowly replace trepidation in the young man's face. Tristan nodded.

Noah grabbed Tristan by the back of his head and pulled him in for a quick hug. "Thank you. I have faith in you, and God willing, Joshua and I will be back in no time."

Noah and Joshua left to scout out whoever inhabited the dense forest less than a mile away.

Noah sent up a silent prayer. "Dear God, please let it be the Army of

Angels." It was the first conversation Noah had had with God since the death of his twin sister. Noah looked over at Joshua and wondered if he still thought of Emma.

Tristan and the others did their best to camouflage themselves as they waited for Noah and Joshua to return. Their suspense grew with every passing minute. Tristan found it nearly impossible to remain calm. He took in a slow, deep breath and whispered a prayer up to the heavens.

DEBORAH

Deborah was a young, petite woman whose eyes were notorious for changing color from a dazzling green to what they were now – a smoldering, smoky blue. Those who had accompanied her across the severe terrain and fought alongside her in the fierce, bloody battles knew all too well that the blue eyes foretold of imminent peril.

Deborah sat with a group of soldiers a few feet away from the fire, her long blonde hair tied up in a bun so it would not become a hindrance in the event of a battle. She looked up suddenly and then rose to her feet.

"Someone is near."

Her soldiers reached for their weapons, already rising to their feet, but she put up a hand to stop them.

"Do not be alarmed; it's not the enemy, but they are hiding over there, to the east. Stay here so we don't frighten them."

She stood up and, with an unassuming air, strode over to where Noah and Joshua were attempting to conceal themselves.

"Gentlemen, please show yourselves. We are no threat to you."

Noah nodded at Joshua, and the two stood up cautiously. Noah's deep voice broke the silence. "We are searching for the Army of Angels. Do you know where they might be?"

Noah could hardly disguise his shock and amazement. Why would the seasoned soldiers remain around the fire and send this delicate – not to mention young – woman over to face two good-sized men?

Deborah's eyes narrowed, as if she were reading his thoughts.

"Why are you searching for the Army of Angels?"

Noah didn't appreciate being questioned by this young woman. Who did she think she was? The Army of the Dead could strike at any time. They didn't have time for such nonsense. Why were the soldiers ignoring them?

"I don't see how that is any of your business! I'm sure you are well aware of the danger that lurks in these lands, and I do not have time to answer your tedious questions. I need to speak to your leader. This is urgent!"

Deborah nodded, taking a long, deep breath before she replied. "Well, I see that patience and diplomacy are not your strong suit. Gentlemen, I will ask you one last time what your business is with the Army of Angels. If you refuse to answer, then I am afraid I will have to ask you to leave this area."

Deborah's friendly demeanor disappeared, replaced with an imposing look that would cause even the most seasoned soldier to think twice about calling her bluff.

Joshua spoke into the dead silence that followed.

"We're sorry." Deborah ignored the exasperated look Noah shot his friend. "We did not mean to offend you. We are exhausted and our nerves have been worn thin. We have been traveling for what seems like forever, narrowly escaping what we have heard people refer to as the Army of Darkness, and we have heard rumors that an Army of Angels exists and that they're the only ones who have faced the demons and lived. We seek the Army of Angels because we need to know how to fight the dark army. We do not ask this just for ourselves. We have a small group of people, including women and children, who rely on us. Please, if you know where we can find them, we would be more than grateful."

Noah continued to glare at Joshua, failing to notice that his friend's words had managed to ease the steely gaze on Deborah's face. Her voice was pleasant.

"Please wait here a minute. I must confer with someone. Oh, and don't worry, you are perfectly safe for now. No harm is lingering in the shadows – yet."

As Deborah wandered off into the darkness, she could hear Noah venting at Joshua. "Why on earth would you reveal the existence of the rest of our group? What if she's a scout for the Army of the Dead? What if she's calling them right now? You just managed to put all of our lives in danger. And I thought we had to worry about Adam!"

Joshua stared at his shoes. Humiliated, he fumbled around, trying to explain his actions. "I don't know what came over me. For some reason I just felt compelled to be completely honest with her. I can't explain it."

Noah's voice relaxed. "She probably used some freaky spell or something." Noah shuddered before he continued to express his thoughts. "Did you notice the way her face changed? That wasn't natural." He tried to shake off the chills that rattled through him when he envisioned the steely expression that had overtaken Deborah's elegant face. "It freaked me out!"

Joshua's eyes lit up. "That's exactly when I felt compelled to tell her everything. I don't think it's an evil thing, though. I think she's part of the

Army of Angels. I felt safe when she was here. Something about her calms me."

Joshua looked around nervously. He felt vulnerable since her absence.

"Save it, man," Noah said. "There's something about her all right, but I wouldn't use the word 'calming' to describe it."

Before Joshua could respond, Deborah emerged from the forest and headed in their direction. Noah held his breath in anticipation, scouring the clearing, half expecting an army of freakish soldiers, like the ones they saw annihilate Marcus and his men, to come charging toward them at any moment.

Deborah shook her head. "I see that trust is not one of your strong points, either." A sly smile escaped her lips.

"Why should I trust you?" Noah said, his eyes burning with defiance. "You have ignored my questions and refused to tell us who you are. You might be able to bewitch my friend with your pretty face, but it takes more than a hot piece of tail to make me lose my head."

Joshua turned bright red. It was true, he did find this stranger more than attractive, but who wouldn't? She was gorgeous. Joshua wanted to slap Noah. His curt words were uncalled for. If she had been planning to shed any light on the location of the Army of Angels, he doubted she would divulge any information to them now.

Deborah turned her attention to Noah. "My name is Deborah. If it were up to me, I would let you meet the Army of the Dead and go on my way. But it's not up to me. I sure can't see it, but I guess there is more to you than meets the eye, and ear. Your friend has shown a true calling. You should be thankful for his ability to read a situation accurately."

She smiled at Joshua before turning her attention back to Noah. "Your people are not safe where they are. Go and bring them back here. However, there is one condition. If they want to live, they need to follow my orders. If they refuse to listen, I will not be able to save them, nor will you."

"Wait a minute." Noah looked her up and down suspiciously. "Why should we listen to you? We're looking for the Army of Angels, not some ragtag group of survivors."

"Fine, suit yourself." Deborah turned to leave.

"Wait, Deborah, look… my name is Joshua and my friend is Noah. We are grateful for any assistance you can provide us, but we really need to find the Army of Angels. Do you know where they are?"

Deborah paused and looked back. "Joshua, I suggest you hurry if you wish your friends to remain safe." She looked him straight in the eye. "I am the commander of the Army of Angels. I answer to God and God alone. You are welcome to join us if you would like. I do not extend this offer to everyone."

She shifted her gaze to Noah. "But God has chosen you." She did not miss Noah's snort of derision. Ignoring it, she continued. "It is up to you to answer his call. Now, as I stated earlier, danger is fast approaching. I must return to my troops. We don't have much time to prepare."

Even Joshua was stunned by this revelation. How on Earth could she be in charge of the Army of Angels? With no time to ponder such questions, they hurried off to their group. If Deborah was telling the truth, they didn't have time to waste if they hoped to see another day.

NOAH

Upon returning to Deborah's camp with his followers, Noah scanned the small group of warriors, searching for their leader. He finally spotted her perched on a large branch halfway up a towering pine, a few feet away from the blazing fire.

Adam had protested the idea, insisting that it was a deceptive ploy of the enemy. If Noah was honest with himself, he had to admit that he worried Adam's suspicions were correct. Heck, he had those very same fears, but what else were they going to do? They couldn't hide from the Army of Darkness forever.

For a moment, Noah found himself admiring Deborah. Her pale skin shone like a magnificent full moon against the dark of night. Her head was tilted up slightly, her eyes were closed, and her full lips were moving, as if she were talking to someone.

The other members of his group were oblivious to her presence. Their only focus was the food offered to them and the much welcomed warmth the fire provided as a respite from the frigid mountain air.

Noah overheard some of the group voicing their disbelief when they learned that the Army of Angels was led by a petite, young woman. It might have been a little easier to believe if she had been some kind of Amazon warrioress.

Noah's blood boiled. He could hear Adam insisting that they take shelter within the nearby cave, even though this went against Deborah's explicit orders. When Noah and his followers first arrived, she immediately notified the newcomers that the cave was off limits, period. And that was all she would say on the matter.

The worst part was that Noah agreed with Adam. He hated having to admit that, even if it was just to himself. Noah tried to drown out Adam's voice as he recited several practical reasons why it made sense for them to gather under the protection of the cave. They would be sheltered from the cold and their campfire would not be visible, not to mention the fact that they would be hidden from the enemy's line of sight.

Noah carefully watched Deborah. He desperately wanted to believe that they had found the army Marcus had told them about, but Noah could not wrap his head around the fact that Deborah was their leader. This revelation shook not only his faith, but the faith of the members in his group.

Adam's voice continued to bellow on and on behind him. "Noah has tricked us. If this woman truly is the commander of the Army of Angels, then how can we seriously believe the stories we have heard about them? Noah has fallen for some fairy tale created to give hope to survivors like us."

Joshua sat on a log by the fire. His resolve remained firm and he challenged Adam's theory. "I find it ironic that you claim to be a Christian, yet you are the first to doubt, you are the first to accuse, and you have the least amount of hope."

Tristan offered up an "Amen!"

Joshua continued to argue his perspective. "Doesn't the Bible tell of many stories where the underdog defeated a powerful enemy? What about David and Goliath?"

Joshua stood up and walked over to Adam. He stood toe to toe with him. "That woman was gracious enough to allow us to seek refuge here, within their camp. She could have refused and let us fend for ourselves, unprotected and vulnerable." Joshua noticed that the members of their group were nodding their heads in agreement. "Deborah and her people have provided us with hope, and we need to cling to this hope and follow her leadership."

Adam scoffed. "You mean follow them right into the enemy's hands."

A sly smile spread across Joshua's face. "Speaking of hands, if they are scheming with the Army of Darkness as you claim, why aren't they wearing the mark?"

Noah gasped. That was an insightful fact. Deborah and her soldiers did not possess the mark, something that would be mandatory for them to work with the dark army.

The bantering continued. Adam seemed to be in love with the sound of his own voice, which Noah was most definitely not. The group continued to squabble over the issue until it became nothing but white noise. Noah's attention drifted elsewhere.

He was a little ashamed to admit it, but Noah had grown accustomed to being in charge. His ego had been sorely bruised when he found himself facing off with a five-foot beauty. Noah marveled at how one so tiny and insignificant in stature could be so powerful in presence. Was it merely the Army of Angels' reputation that made others stand up and take notice? He couldn't deny how captivating she was, but it was more than just her appearance. There was something more, but Noah couldn't put his finger on it. It dawned on him that it was her elegance and beauty that prohibited them from comprehending her full potential.

In a way, it reminded him of his sister, Emma. Many people struggled to accept that she could be both beautiful and extremely intelligent. It was if a woman had to be one or the other, but she couldn't be both. Was he labeling Deborah the way others had labeled Emma?

Noah didn't know how long he had been lost in his thoughts, but he suddenly was painfully aware that Deborah was watching him intently. It had been many years since his cheeks had turned such a crimson color, but this woman seemed to possess some unexplainable power over him. He had not found himself drawn to another human being like this since, well, never.

In one graceful, effortless leap, Deborah alighted from her post in the tree and nearly floated over to him. Her face was peaceful and calm.

"May I please have a moment of your time, in private?"

Noah stood and followed her without a word. Instead of feeling superior and strong as he walked beside her, he felt more like a lumbering oaf.

Once they were several feet above the gathering, higher up the mountainside, Deborah climbed up another tall pine facing the people below them. Noah noticed that she always positioned herself where she was able to keep watch over her troops and their followers. Deborah lowered her hand to assist him up to the branch, but he waved her off and, after a few moments of intense labor, was sitting beside her, breathing heavily. To his relief, she did not laugh or comment on his awkwardness. She merely smiled.

"You will soon become quite adept at maneuvering yourself in and out of trees. It will become second nature to you, I promise."

"Why is that?"

She responded without taking her eyes off the gathering below. "Survival."

Silence fell over them. Noah could not help but wonder what empowered her. She led a small platoon of eight men and four women – five, if you included her. Although they were small in number, this group had fought the formidable Army of Darkness on several occasions and survived. It was a feat no one else had accomplished. It didn't make sense. None of it made any sense.

Her soft voice broke into his thoughts. "What is troubling you?"

Noah was startled. Was he that easy to read? He tried to mask his awe and curiosity.

"I was just wondering how you and your company have managed to survive when larger groups of trained soldiers have failed."

"You are referring to Marcus' men, are you not?"

"You heard about what happened to them?"

Deborah nodded. "Yes." Her voice carried a somber note.

"Why didn't you do something to stop it? Marcus was a good man."

"You would not understand even if I told you."

Now Noah's pride was wounded. Was she calling him an imbecile?

"Why wouldn't I understand? I'm an intelligent man. I graduated from Columbia, for Pete's sake. What could you possibly have to tell me that I could not understand?"

As he heard the words spill from his mouth, he knew she was right; he didn't understand.

"I apologize if I offended you. That was not my intention. But the truth is you are not a believer, and there is no way for an unbeliever to discern, let alone accept, the truths of my world. Your mind has been trained to understand and comprehend the scientific facts, but what we are dealing with, scientific minds discard as nonsense."

Noah looked confused. "Are you trying to tell me this has something to do with the Christian faith?"

She nodded. "Precisely. The battle we are facing is not of this world! God's ways are not our ways. He tends to do things that confound the wise, leaving us baffled, so that the only explanation we can turn to is him."

Noah was frustrated. "So you are telling me that he sat back and did nothing to save Marcus' men, on purpose?"

Deborah let out a deep sigh. "Let me put it to you this way. We had been patrolling the area around a small family farm in the Smoky Mountains. God had called on us to protect some people down there."

Noah's heart did a back flip. "Where in the Smoky Mountains?"

His interest and concern did not go unnoticed. She gave him a quizzical look. "It was in a small town named Gatlinburg. Have you heard of it?"

Noah's heart was pounding so hard he was sure she could hear it. "Yes, that is where Joshua and I are from, and my family has a small farm there." Noah knew this could not be mere coincidence. "Why did you leave?"

"We had been holding back the Army of the Dead for a couple of weeks, when out of nowhere they disappeared. We had heard rumors that Marcus and his guys were closing in on Jefferson National Park. We started moving in that direction, hoping to get to them in time, but we cannot move like the enemy moves."

Noah's voice was sharp. "Why didn't your God save them? He could have prevented their deaths if he had wanted to, according to what all the believers I know have to say about him."

Deborah knew this would be difficult for him to understand. "Yes, he could have, but then the victory would have gone to Marcus and not God."

"So you choose to serve a selfish God who would allow innocent men to die so he can relish in victory?"

"No. Marcus and his men trained with us. They were brave, noble men. We were very fond of them. God desired for them to serve him, but they chose another path. They walked away from him to fight the enemy on their own. What they could not understand was that no one can defeat these soldiers without God. This battle is between heaven and hell, and it is the last chance we have to save our souls."

JOSHUA

Joshua had said his piece. The group could either choose to believe in Deborah and her group, or they could leave. If God gave them their free will, who was he to try to take it away from them?

At least he felt confident Tristan would stick around. Joshua was really starting to like the kid. He kind of reminded Joshua of himself when he was that age.

He looked up to find Noah but realized his friend was gone. Joshua needed a break from Adam, so he decided to explore the camp some more. He wandered over near the soldiers.

Joshua was befuddled. They didn't look like soldiers preparing for war. Instead of practicing with their swords, they were reciting scripture and praying. He remembered Marcus saying that the group was a little too religious for their liking, but Joshua found it energizing. He felt alive around these people, and their presence provided him with a sense of safety.

Joshua laughed at himself. Maybe Adam was right. Maybe he was just so tired of running that he was willing to believe anything, especially after witnessing firsthand what they were up against.

Joshua studied the soldiers and what he saw amazed him. They showed no sign of fear. They were calm, focused, and confident. The Army of Angels dressed in all white. Joshua found that odd. He wondered why they didn't wear dark clothing to blend into their surroundings.

One soldier in particular caught his attention. Her piercing, dark brown eyes locked on to his. Her radiant smile sent a million butterflies loose in his stomach. She walked over to Joshua, and for the first time in his life, a woman's presence was making him nervous.

He had never been nervous around Emma. At first she had just been Noah's twin sister, and then slowly over time their attraction for each other grew. It was such a natural progression, from childhood friend to lover, that they had skipped all the awkward moments most couples experience. Then, after losing her, he had never found anyone he was interested in. There were plenty of attractive women he had met, but that was all they were to him – beautiful women. There was never an inner connection.

The woman offered Joshua her slender hand. "Hi, I'm Rebekah." As they shook hands, Joshua was surprised to find that her lovely, caramel skin was so soft. He expected it to be rough from living out here. Her dark hair hung over her right shoulder in a loose braid.

Joshua wanted to laugh at the irony. All these years, and nothing. But now that the world was coming to an end, he meets her – a woman who had the power to make him feel like a twitterpated school boy. "Good one, God," he thought to himself.

"I'm Joshua. Can I ask you a question?"

Rebekah nodded. "Sure."

"Aren't you scared out of your mind? You all seem so relaxed. I have seen the Army of Darkness. I know what they can do. How can you be so calm?"

A smile formed at the corners of her mouth. One of the other soldiers called out to her. "Hey Rebekah, we're ready."

She nodded at her fellow soldier, then turned back to Joshua. "I gotta go, but to answer your question, it's because we know what God is capable of." She gave him a playful wink before joining her comrades.

Joshua thought about Emma and her sister Anna. "Yeah, well, I know what he is capable of too," he said to himself.

NOAH

Deborah placed a gentle hand on Noah's shoulder. It was the same shoulder he had injured while playing football in high school. The physical strain of the past few weeks had caused it to ache more than normal.

Her smoldering blue eyes bore into him. "I can't force you to believe in what I am telling you," she said. "You have to decide that for yourself. But I am begging you as the leader of your people that tonight you take refuge in the grove."

Noah realized that the pain in his shoulder had subsided. He looked at her in amazement. He didn't know what to think. Was she completely mad? Deborah's head tilted toward him slightly. Her gaze appeared to be filled with genuine compassion for him and his followers. She proceeded to speak to him in a way that left him unnerved.

"Noah, please listen to me. Tonight a horrific assault from the darkness awaits, one the likes of which you have never seen. The battle you witnessed with Marcus and his men pales in comparison to what is coming. The battle will end at daybreak with the coming of the light. Until then, the enemy forces will bring an unending tide of evil against us. I beg you to stay hidden within the grove. My soldiers and I have prayed a hedge of protection over you and your people. As long as you follow my instructions, you will be safe. I hope to see you alive and well when this siege is over. I must hurry, there isn't much time left."

Before Noah could respond, Deborah had landed gracefully on the ground below and was running toward her warriors, who were already gathering in the middle of the clearing.

With the familiar pain in his shoulder returning, he fumbled down the tree and headed off toward his group. Due to their close proximity, he had only minutes to think about what he would say to them. Noah was forced

69

to make a rash decision, something he had always tried to avoid.

The members of his group were busy talking as they sat around the campfire. Many of them were debating whether the tall, muscular, black soldier was the famous Lucious Washington, a former football star. Noah had to raise his voice over the din.

"Listen up. We need to gather our belongings and head down to the grove. It's imperative that we move quickly."

He didn't miss the concerned looks on their faces, but was impressed with how quickly they followed his orders. The only two who seemed to be at peace with his decision were Joshua and Tristan. Noah sighed heavily as he heard Adam begin to question his authority.

"I don't agree, Noah. Why the sudden change of heart? Even you said earlier that the cave is our best source of shelter and protection. How will that grove protect us? You're leading us into a trap. We will all die by your hand. Is that what you want? Are you now in league with the enemy? Tell us, why are you listening to that little imp?"

Noah's teeth clenched. He was astonished to discover that not only was his pride ruffled due to the accusations Adam had made against his leadership, but that he was also offended by the harsh words he had spoken against Deborah.

It had not been an easy decision. Everything in his head was telling him to choose the cave, but everything in his gut was telling him to choose the grove. He knew there was a chance that Deborah and the men and women who fought with her were luring them into a trap, but he couldn't get Joshua's question out of his mind. If they were part of the evil that was being unleashed on earth, why didn't they wear the mark?

"Why would you question Deborah's leadership? We were the ones hoping to find them, not the other way around. Or have you forgotten that? Not to mention that they are the only ones we know of who have survived a battle against the Army of the Dead, which is on its way here as we speak. Or have you forgotten that as well?"

Adam continued to argue. "Maybe that is how 'your Deborah' wants it to appear. What if the reason she and her soldiers are the only ones to have survived is because they are secretly conspiring with the enemy? Maybe they're setting the snare as we speak. Use your head, Noah. How do you explain that scrawny group of so-called warriors surviving the Army of Darkness when Marcus and his 80 men were slaughtered? You have become soft ever since you laid eyes on that little sprite!"

Anger and doubt warred within Noah. Could it be true? Hadn't he accused Joshua of the same thing earlier? Had he really become soft because of his unspoken attraction to Deborah? Noah had been so sure and confident that Deborah was telling him the truth when it was just the two of them up in the pine tree. But now he was standing alone, facing questions that caused him to wonder why he had felt so confident just moments earlier.

Noah glanced over at Deborah, and her eyes pleaded with him to follow her instructions. His eyes traveled back toward the cave. In all practical senses, the cave was their best line of defense. What was the truth? Without thinking about it, Noah found himself talking with God inside his head, just like he would have spoken to his father if he were still alive.

"God what is the truth? Are you real? If so, please show me what I am to do. I am so lost and confused."

At that very moment, as Noah looked at the cave, his stomach lurched and twisted into knots. He was speaking before he realized it.

"I can't explain how or why I believe in Deborah, but something leads me to believe she is telling the truth, and it is not for the reasons Adam implied. If Deborah's words are true, we are running out of time."

Hatred oozed from Adam's lips. "That's not good enough for me. You have failed to be the leader Parker believed you to be. You are not thinking with your head, but with your heart, or whatever you want to call it!"

Adam looked around at all the members of the group. "Anyone who wants to is welcome to join me in the cave." Adam shot Noah a challenging look as he led his family toward the cave. Noah's heart sank as he watched the others follow Adam's lead. Jack let out a sad whimper.

Joshua and Tristan were the only members left standing with Noah. Joshua gave Noah a firm pat on the shoulder. "What can you do? They can't say you didn't warn them."

As the three men turned to leave, Noah caught a look of sorrow and regret on Deborah's face. It was if she were mourning them already. Noah's hand jerked up awkwardly as he offered her a clumsy wave. There was so much he wished he had said. He hadn't even wished her luck, or thanked her for all they were doing.

The three men barely had enough time to take cover in the grove before a thunderous crack resonated over their heads. Noah squinted into the darkness, trying to locate the source of the ominous sound that was still ringing in his ears. Their surroundings were so dark that no one would have been able to see a thing if not for the campfire that burned near Deborah and her comrades.

Seconds later, Noah, Joshua, and Tristan stared in complete shock. Deborah and her warriors had become enveloped in the most magnificent pure light any of them had ever seen. The soldiers looked intimidating as they stood poised in a battle stance, ready to fight to the death. There wasn't a single sign of fear or doubt among them. Men and women, standing 12 feet tall and clothed in pure white, had joined Deborah's ranks. These beings were blindingly bright. Noah was unable to see the glow of the campfire because the light they emitted overtook everything.

In what seemed like mere seconds, another thunderous clap violently shook the mountainside. Jack let out a vicious snarl as more than 100 dark soldiers, the same he and Joshua had seen in Jefferson National Park, appeared atop the dusty rubble that had previously been the roof of the cave. Noah knew that Adam and all those who had entered it had been crushed.

Noah looked over at Deborah. How had she known? Noah recalled her warning to the group, when she tried to explain how a thing could appear to be one thing when it was really something else entirely. She had told them that they needed God's help to discern the difference. Instead of offering protection from the enemy, the cave had become their tomb.

The battle now taking place before them was swift. Skillful maneuvers were executed at lightning speed. It was near impossible to keep up. Noah, Joshua and Tristan caught their breath as the towering beings that fought next to Deborah and her warriors shifted their bodies during the battle, revealing gorgeous, powerful wings that were tucked in behind their backs.

Noah heard the awe in Joshua's voice as he spoke, "They must pull them in tight so they don't get injured during battle."

Noah felt a wave of relief wash over him. "So you can see them, too? I'm not losing my mind?"

Joshua shot Noah a quick glance and then returned his attention to the battle. "No, you are not alone, my friend. Either we are both going crazy, or we are both witnessing a miracle. To tell you the truth, I don't know which one scares me more."

DEBORAH

Deborah knew her enemy's tactics. They had fought the same way each time, yet she still spent all of her free time gearing up for battle. The majority of her prep time was spent in God's Word. Deborah knew that these battles were won by the power of God.

The sound of clashing steel rang in her ear as she blocked the enemy's attempted blow to her head and opened his throat with a blindingly fast swing of her axe. Two more dark soldiers ambushed her from behind, but Deborah nimbly ducked under the first soldier's sword before plunging her short sword deep into his abdomen. She spun to avoid the second soldier, pushing him off with her powerful legs and gaining time for her to reposition.

She recited scripture unceasingly. She did not just simply cry out, "God help me!" inside her head. No, Deborah shouted the words, sending them up as fervent prayers to heaven. She thanked God for his victories and prayed that his will would be done on Earth, as it is in heaven.

As Deborah and her company proclaimed the words of the Bible, Noah and his two loyal friends could not help but notice how it caused the snarling demons to lose their footing, over-swing their heavy weapons, and stumble and fall to the ground. If that wasn't enough to get their attention, the proclamation of scripture appeared to make the beings in white grow stronger.

The current battle was nothing like the one Noah and Joshua had observed when only a handful of dark soldiers had slaughtered Marcus and his 80 trained men. The sight before them gave Noah, Joshua, and Tristan hope. They experienced such relief as they watched, for the very first time, good conquering evil.

Noah could deny it no longer. These beings had to be angels. Now it all made sense. Everyone had speculated as to why the Army of Angels went by such a silly name. Now, after witnessing how truly amazing these wonderful creatures really were, "silly" was the last word Noah would have used to describe them. They were breathtakingly beautiful and at the same time downright terrifying. Now Noah understood what Deborah was trying to tell him when she said she did not fight with her own strength, but through God's power.

The three survivors watched in awe as the 13 white warriors delivered deathblow after deathblow, not once missing their mark. Their accuracy was astonishing. Of the 13, there was no denying that Deborah was the swiftest and fiercest warrior. Noah wondered if this had something to do with her level of faith.

The demonic soldiers did their best to steer clear of the majestic beings flanking Deborah's company. Not once did they take on an angel by themselves. The minimum number of soldiers from the Army of Darkness that Noah saw fight a single angel was seven, and even then they lasted mere seconds.

Just as the three of them thought the battle was about to end, another wave of dark soldiers descended from the mountain, running full speed at Deborah and the Army of Angels. Deborah's words could be heard clearly by all.

"The Lord is the everlasting God, the Creator of the ends of the earth. He will not grow tired or weary, and his understanding no one can fathom. He gives strength to the weary and increases the power of the weak. Even youths grow tired and weary and young men stumble and fall; but those who hope in the Lord will renew their strength. They will soar on wings like eagles, they will run and not grow weary, they will walk and not be faint."

One of Deborah's soldiers also shouted, "The Lord will march out like a mighty man, like a warrior he will stir up his zeal."

"Give us aid against our enemy, for the help of man is worthless!" another shouted out. "With God we will gain the victory, and he will trample down our enemies."

Joshua heard Rebekah chime in. "His heart is secure, he will have no fear, in the end he will look in triumph on his foes."

A broad, husky, redheaded warrior joined in the rally. "You who fear him, trust in the Lord – he is their help and shield."

The scriptures being recited were unending, and the three newcomers who remained safely in the grove bore witness to the strength and endurance these priceless words gave to the Army of Angels.

The battle raged for what seemed like an eternity. Noah couldn't believe what he was seeing. It was not humanly possible. Deborah and her band of warriors, along with their mighty angels, had crushed more than 300 dark soldiers. He was certain they must be exhausted. He had been squirming the entire time, expecting someone to be wounded, but none had. He was amazed by their persistence. They never stopped shouting scripture toward the heavens, as if it powered their bodies. It certainly appeared to be fuel for the entities of light. Noah felt worthless and yearned to help somehow.

Finally, all of the angels and warriors proclaimed, "Let there be light!"

Slowly, from behind the grove, the sun began to rise, bringing the bright birth of a new day. As the light filtered through the trees and into the field of battle, painful shrieks emanated from the dark soldiers, and they retreated to the hell from which they had come.

The warriors fell to their knees, praising and thanking God. Even the angels knelt alongside Deborah and her companions. Not one of Deborah's warriors or the fearsome angels had been harmed. Suddenly, another thunderous clap shook the earth, and Deborah and her 12 warriors were left to themselves.

Noah found himself pondering Deborah's words from the previous night. This war was different from man's wars. How could he, Joshua, and Tristan stand against these supernatural creatures? Noah intently observed everything that had transpired during the battle. Clearly the power and strength that offered victory in this battle was not sheer strength and the strategic planning of men. It was something far greater, something that Noah did not yet understand.

MARY

Mary sat up in her bed, breathing heavily. She had been haunted by the same nightmare nearly every night for at least a week. In it, she is confronted by the repulsive creature Angela had described the night Luke's sister had been killed.

Her mind was racing, consumed with the talk among their house guests about an army of evil soldiers who were supposedly even more dangerous than the patrol unit she and Martha had run into at the roadblock weeks ago. No one could stop thinking about the so-called Army of Darkness – or as others referred to it, the Army of the Dead.

Mary shuddered and pulled the covers higher. She found herself secretly returning to her faith. One day she had snuck out to the treehouse, where she asked God to forgive her. She had brought along her old Bible, and when she opened it she felt a sense of peace come over her. She wasn't sure if it was a sign from God, or just nostalgia.

Until her mother's death, being a Christian was all she knew. Her life had been filled with church services, Christian music, and family devotions. But one thing seemed to be the same: God always spoke to her through scripture. There, staring up at her, were his words: "Have I not commanded you? Be strong and courageous. Do not be afraid; do not be discouraged, for the Lord your God will be with you wherever you go. Joshua 1:9"

Mary had decided to commit this scripture to memory, hoping the truth of these words and the promise she had received of having eternal life in heaven would alleviate her fear of death. But deep down she was terrified of dying, especially at the hands of the evil beings that threatened her and her family.

Mary pulled her knees up to her chest and rocked herself back and forth in a futile attempt to calm her nerves. She longed to be more like Martha, who was brave and courageous. Martha lay in the bed next to her, fast asleep, her soft, feminine snore giving her away. Martha had abandoned her own bedroom and began to sleep in Mary's room since all the terrible events had started. Mary was comforted by her sister's presence, but apparently it was not enough to stop the incessant nightmares.

Mary let out a deep sigh. She would give anything to have her parents beside her again, especially now. There wasn't a day that went by that she didn't think of them. Everyone had always said the pain would slowly subside with time, but that was a lie – at least it was for Mary.

Mary's thoughts drifted to her mother. Death never had any control over her mom. Even when she fought a long, tough battle with breast cancer, Anna did not fear dying.

Mary started replaying one of the last memories she had with her sister and mother. Her mother's words were forever etched in her memory. It had been a beautiful summer day. The three of them were laying in the hammock. They were snuggled up tight, Anna in the middle, Mary and Martha on each side of her. As the evil disease slowly consumed her flesh, Anna had never been more beautiful in Mary's eyes. Her face was beaming with joy as she soaked in the beauty of her English garden and the precious love of her daughters. To her, that was what life was all about: family.

Martha, bothered by the reality of their situation, asked their mother, "Why are you so happy? Don't you love us? Aren't you afraid of dying and never seeing us again?" Tears poured down Martha's face as her words cut through the beauty of the moment.

Anna gently wiped away her daughter's tears. "Of course I pray for life, because the thought of leaving my family is painful. But if God decides to bring me home, that means my work here on Earth is done, and I trust that he will watch over and protect you girls should it be his will that I leave."

Anna gave them each a quick peck on their cheeks. "You girls are a precious gift from God and I thank him for the blessing of being your mom every day. But you belong to him first. He knows the plans he has for all of us, and we need to trust him and believe in him even when life seems cruel and does not make sense to us."

Mary wished to be as steadfast and strong in her faith as her mother, but she feared that was impossible. She was still hugging her knees in the dark, contemplating whether she should make another attempt at a peaceful night's sleep, when Rascal jumped up from his bed near the door and ran to the window. His growl was low, but Mary saw the hair on his back begin to stand up.

The commotion woke Martha. She grabbed the shotgun from under the bed and was peering through the curtains into the yard below when she caught her breath. Moments before dawn's light broke through the sky, she saw them. About a dozen uniformed soldiers were running into the forest.

Martha sat down on the bed, a horrified expression on her face. Both she and Mary jumped as Luke entered the room. From the look on his face, he had seen the soldiers as well.

Martha's hands were shaking. "Did you see what I saw?"

Luke looked as pale as a ghost. "Do you mean the men or the swords they carried?"

Martha was unnerved. "Both!"

Luke nodded. "This settles it. No one is to leave the house after dark, ever. Our chores will just have to wait until the sun rises. I can't even fathom what might have happened to us if we hadn't overslept this morning." He looked at Martha. "I know you don't want to hear this, but someone was watching out for us today."

Martha was too rattled to protest. Then that steely determination set in. "From now on, everyone is to carry a weapon whenever they go outside. Who's to say they won't return during the day?"

Luke nodded. "I agree."

Mary felt her insides trembling. She had been continually praying for her Uncle Noah's return, but so far her prayers appeared to fall on deaf ears, much like her prayers for her mother.

Martha had dressed and was heading out of the room. "Hey, you. You okay?"

Mary nodded. But the truth was she was anything but okay. "Yeah, I'll be there in a minute." She gave her sister the most reassuring smile she could muster. Martha returned her smile. "Okay, see you in a bit."

Once she was alone, Mary began to speak to God. "Okay, I seriously need you to give me something here. Anything. My faith is hanging on by a thread. Please, please, please give us something that we can hold on to. I need to know that you are real and not some fairytale we make up to give ourselves hope so we can make it through our miserable lives. Lord, if you are real, please bless us with your awesome power."

DEBORAH

They had fought for hours on end, yet Deborah felt invigorated. God's words never failed to energize her during battle. She knew death was a possibility, but death didn't frighten her. She knew God would have the final victory, thus Deborah had defeated every foul being that had crawled out of its dark pit and into her path.

As she opened her eyes and surveyed her surroundings, her gaze fell on Noah. She let out a deep sigh. She had been so engrossed during the battle that she had forgotten about the newcomers. Deborah offered up a silent prayer. "God, please forgive me. I know I'm not perfect and that I too am unworthy, but give me strength. I find Noah to be highly irritating and I just really want to punch him sometimes."

Rebekah had a wry smile on her face as she approached Deborah. "So, what are we going to do with the three stooges over there?" She nodded toward Noah, Joshua, and Tristan.

Deborah shook her head. "I don't know. I have prayed about it, and if I am understanding the big guy upstairs correctly..." She patted Rebekah on the back as she continued, "It looks like you may have an admirer in the camp."

Rebekah feigned shock. "Why, whatever do you mean?" she said jokingly. She studied Joshua for a moment before adding, "You know, he is pretty cute."

Deborah rolled her eyes. "Seriously? We barely survive an epic battle, during the Great Tribulation no less, and you're standing here gushing over some stranger?"

Rebekah shrugged her shoulders. "He started it."

Deborah gave her a look of disbelief as Rebekah chuckled and said, "Oh look, here comes Mr. Wonderful."

Deborah turned, expecting to find Joshua heading in their direction. But as she saw Noah marching toward her, she instantly understood the sarcasm in Rebekah's voice. Deborah braced herself. "Great. Nothing like jumping from the frying pan into the fire," she muttered under her breath.

To her relief, Noah appeared to be humbled. He threw his hands in the air.

"Okay, you have our attention. What you all did was amazing. And it goes without saying that the three of us are so thankful that we heeded your warning and stayed out of the cave." She couldn't help but notice the sheepish look on his face. "I have to ask you," he continued, "how can we learn to fight like that? As I told you earlier, I have two nieces back at our family farm – or at least I am praying that I still have two nieces – and I need to learn how to protect them."

Deborah noticed the tenderness that appeared in his eyes when he mentioned his nieces. Maybe he wasn't as big a jerk as she had originally thought.

She was about to respond when a slight commotion in the camp interrupted her. She turned to find the company's scout, Matthew, entering the clearing. Deborah let out a sigh of relief. She knew she was supposed to trust God and accept whatever fate their Heavenly Father had in store for them, but whenever Matthew was out there all by himself, Deborah couldn't help but worry.

It felt like a continuous battle. First she would leave her concerns with God, but before long she would find herself dwelling on all the "what ifs." Realizing that she had failed, she would vow to give her troubles completely over to him again. She seemed quite well rehearsed at this dance. Two steps forward, one step back.

Matthew had willingly joined the Army of Angels and had proven himself a valuable asset, but the fact still remained that Matthew was her little brother, and she would always feel responsible for his well-being.

Her face glowed with happiness as she turned to Noah. "Please excuse me."

Noah nodded as Deborah ran off to join the rest of her troops, who were gathering around the young man who had just entered the camp. Everyone seemed excited to see him. Noah noticed that Joshua and Tristan were strolling over to the group. Jack was glued to Joshua's side. Noah decided that he should probably join them as well.

Deborah and her soldiers appeared deeply engrossed in whatever the newcomer was sharing with them. When Noah was a few feet away, he thought he overheard the young man mention "Gatlinburg," and Joshua turned to Noah with an alarmed expression.

MARTHA

Martha mindlessly dabbed her bacon into the bright yellow yolk of her fried egg. Luke nudged her as she nibbled at her breakfast. "You okay?"

She left her thoughts as Luke's words abruptly brought her back to the present. "Hmm?"

Luke rolled his eyes and chuckled to himself. "I said, are you okay?"

Martha nodded. "Oh, yeah, yeah, I'm good."

Luke knew her far too well. "A penny for your thoughts," he said with a quizzical look.

Martha looked around at all of the people crammed into their kitchen and living room. She leaned over and whispered in his ear. "I'll tell you later when we have a little more privacy."

Luke nodded. He caught a light scent of her perfume, which sent his head spinning. It reminded him of more intimate times between the two of them. He knew he should be remorseful for their behavior, but deep down he found himself fighting his desire to be with her again. He knew they were too young to be together in the eyes of most of society, but he didn't care. He loved her. Martha was the only one for him. He knew that the divorce rate was high, but in his opinion you are either committed to making it work and have the determination to stick it out through the rough times, or you will eventually crash and burn, no matter how long you have known each other, or how old you are.

Now it was Martha's turn to tease him. "Hello? Anybody home?" She laughed.

Luke looked up at her. "Sorry, did you say something?"

Martha shook her head. "Yeah, I asked if you were ready to get started. The sun is out and if the sounds coming from the barn are any indication, I would say the natives are getting restless."

Luke nodded. He jumped off of the bar stool and grabbed their coats. "Come on, slow poke, we haven't got all day," he teased.

The two of them walked toward the barn with their guns drawn, their eyes scanning the horizon for any sign of the enemy. When Luke pulled open the heavy barn doors, Martha jumped in and raised her sawed-off shotgun. Luke instinctively did the same with his pistol as he peered into the barn. His heart was pumping hard, and it took a moment for his eyes to adjust to the darkness. Several figures were crouching down in corners throughout the stables.

His voice was deep and intimidating. "Freeze! If I see the slightest movement, I will blow your brains out!"

Martha slowly walked over to the nearest intruder. As she pointed the shotgun at the trespasser's head, she suddenly lowered her weapon and broke out in her familiar nervous laugh. Luke looked at her as though he was trying to read her, not quite sure if he should relax as well.

The tension slowly ebbed from his body as he heard a familiar voice. It belonged to his father's closest friend, Ernie Pike.

"Sorry guys, we didn't mean to scare you. It's just so dark in here that we couldn't tell if the sun had come out yet or not."

Members of Ernie's family crawled out from their hiding places. His youngest daughter, Lizzy, was crying softly. Her father wrapped her in his arms. "It's okay, sweetie. We're all safe now."

The words the child spoke next unnerved Martha and Luke. "I thought the bad men had found us and were going to do to us what they did to Tommy and his family."

Ernie's wife stroked her daughter's strawberry blonde hair. "Shh, it's alright, sweetheart. Look, the sun has risen. The bad men are gone now."

Martha forced her voice to sound confident and cheerful. "Hey, who's hungry? I know Mary has some warm breakfast that needs to be gobbled up. Anyone interested?"

Lizzy's eyes lit up. "I'm so hungry I could eat a whole cow." Everyone burst out laughing as Bessie, their milking cow, let out a loud rebuttal.

Luke and Martha escorted Ernie and his family into the kitchen. There was still plenty of food left over. Mary shot Martha a puzzled look when the group walked through the back door into her kitchen.

Lizzy ran over to Mary and threw her arms around her. Mary had been Lizzy's favorite babysitter. "Well, what an awesome surprise, and you're just in time for breakfast."

Lizzy's voice was filled with excitement as she asked Mary, "Do you think you can put peanut butter on my waffle before you add the syrup? You know, how you always do when you fix me waffles for dinner when you babysit me?"

Mary let out a dramatic sigh. "I don't know, I will have to see if I have any peanut butter... do you wanna help look for it?"

Lizzy nodded eagerly. Mary took Lizzy into the pantry, attempting to distract her from the adult conversation Martha and Luke were having with her father.

Ernie was explaining to them the events that had taken place and landed them in the barn on the girls' farm. He kept his voice low.

"I don't know how much you guys hear way out here, but there is another division of the World's Army that has been dispatched. These guys are menacing. I am dead serious when I say they have some sort of supernatural powers. So far they only come lurking around at night. The next morning, poof! Families who refused to take the mark are gone. We don't know if the soldiers are taking them somewhere and holding them, torturing them, or killing them."

Martha was confused. "Why were you hiding out in the barn? Why didn't you come up to the house?"

Ernie's voice trembled slightly. "We thought we had more time, but they are moving faster now. I was upstairs tucking Lizzy into bed, dusk was turning into night, when I saw a few figures dressed like Mainyu's men slowly moving out of the forest. They had our neighbor's house, the Galiers, totally surrounded. Their weapons were drawn and they moved in like they were on some kind of covert operation.

"I panicked. We threw on our heaviest coats, scarves, and boots and snuck out the back door. We made our way through the forest and headed here. We had heard that some of the other townspeople had headed out this way. We thought there might be safety in numbers. But when we squeezed through your gate, I thought I saw some movement across the yard just beyond the forest. If we had headed to the farmhouse, we would have been in clear sight. So we crept around to the back of the barn and I lifted everyone through one of the windows before I shimmied through it myself. I made sure to close the window behind me."

Ernie quickly looked around and whispered. "There were people wandering around your property last night. I had everyone bury themselves under the straw, but I am almost certain it was Mainyu's guys. Their voices are raspy, not quite human." Ernie shuddered at the memory.

When he continued, he looked directly at Martha. "I overheard them talking about your uncle and Josh Hansen. I couldn't make out exactly what they were saying, but I definitely heard them mention their names, and then... then I heard them saying something about it not being the right time to take her yet, that their master had insisted they wait."

Chills ran down Martha's spine. "Did they ever mention a woman's name?"

Ernie shook his head. "Not that I could hear. But it sounded like they are staking out the farm for something."

Their conversation was brought to a halt as Lizzy crawled up onto her dad's lap. She looked up at her father, smiling from ear to ear. "Guess what, guess what?"

Ernie chuckled. "I don't know, what?"

Lizzy bounced up and down on his knee. "We found the peanut butter."

Martha gave Lizzy a big smile. Her mind was wandering, frantically trying to make sense of the information their newest guest had provided. Well, if they were talking about Uncle Noah and Joshua, that was a pretty good sign that they were still alive, unless they were talking about... no, she wasn't going to go there. It appeared that the soldiers were planning something, but what? Were they waiting for reinforcements? And who was this "her" they were talking about?

PERSEPHONE MILLER

Persephone walked into the Oval Office wearing a wry smile, obviously quite pleased with herself. President Mainyu didn't bother to look up. Her perfume preceded her.

"I hope you have good news," he said.

Persephone was getting tired of his attitude. He was getting a little too big for his britches. She settled down on the couch in a seductive pose. She looked at her nails as if she were bored, refusing to respond until he offered her the respect she deserved.

Mainyu took a deep sigh and reluctantly met her gaze. "Well...?"

"Our agent has made contact. He has confirmed that Admiral Marcus and his band of rebels have been eliminated," she said proudly, almost bragging.

Mainyu looked pleased. "Well done." Then his voice turned. "And?"

Persephone assumed he was referring to the so-called Army of Angels. "Angra, he will let us know about this little band of renegades, if they actually exist, when he finds them."

Mainyu shook his head. "That is another matter to discuss, but I am referring to the agent you told me not to worry about. Remember? Hansen? The one you assured me you had under control?"

Miller winced. She had done so much for him, and this was how he was going to show his appreciation? Without her, he would be a nobody.

"Angra, maybe it would be best for both of us to focus on the positive. Our soldiers are rounding up anyone who refuses to take the mark. We have taken Marcus and his men out of the equation. I would say that we are on a pretty good roll. It's just a matter of time before Hansen and his reporter friend meet the same fate as Marcus. In fact, I have plans in motion as we speak to deliver you our fugitives."

Mainyu was furious that Hansen had escaped in the first place. How was he supposed to rule an empire with such incompetent fools working for him? He knew the extent of damage Agent Hansen could cause should he leak any confidential information he had had access to. Mainyu had harped on this fact on several occasions to Miller. He wanted to do so again, but he still needed her. He could sense her hostility growing toward him. She was not someone he wanted as an enemy.

As much as it repulsed him to do so, Mainyu sat down next to Persephone on the couch. He leaned in and passionately kissed her supple lips. He could feel her recoil from his touch. Her body was taut with tension, evidence that he needed to change his approach if he wanted to keep her on his team. He pulled away, his voice low and husky as he whispered in her ear.

"I'm sorry, my darling. You're right. You have done an excellent job, and I need to appreciate you more. Please forgive me."

Miller was no fool. Angra Mainyu was full of crap and she knew it, but it stroked her ego a little to see him grovel. He was obviously smarter than he looked. They both knew she could take him down with a snap of her fingers. "I suggest you tread lightly, my dear," she thought to herself.

NOAH

Noah was breathless. "Did you say the Army of Darkness is headed for Gatlinburg?" He scanned Matthew's face for an answer.

Matthew nodded. "Yes. It's a small community not too far from here. What's weird is why Satan would send his army there. It's a well-known Christian community. There shouldn't be a lot of unbelieving souls lingering around that town. So why this group of people, I don't know."

Noah was baffled. He turned to Deborah. "What is he talking about? Satan? Unbelieving souls?" Noah then turned back to Matthew. "And who are you?"

Deborah interjected. "Noah, Joshua and Tristan, would you guys please come with me? We don't have a lot of time, but I can see the three of you need to be brought up to speed." She looked at the rest of the group. "I need everyone else to get ready to clear camp. It looks like we are headed back to the farm."

She led the three men over to a group of small boulders. "Please have a seat." She gestured to the large rocks, and once they had sat, she began.

"As you have seen, we fight for God. We believe that according to the book of Revelation, President Mainyu is the Antichrist and his advisor, Persephone Miller, is the False Prophet. We also believe that the mark is the sign of the devil. Once you agree to take the mark, you have sold your soul to the devil. Period. From what we have witnessed, it is our impression that Satan's demons possess the souls of those who take the mark. It doesn't happen all at once."

She turned to Noah. "You have witnessed firsthand the gradual change."

Noah looked surprised. "Me?"

She nodded. "Yes, you. You had stated that during your visit to

Andrews Air Force Base, the soldiers there seemed off, not quite themselves. Correct?"

Noah nodded.

She continued. "Then you have witnessed what the final outcome is, the dark soldiers we warred against last night."

The three men looked at each other, astonished by Deborah's last remark. Joshua interjected.

"So you are telling us that everyone who takes the mark will eventually turn into those supernatural, diabolical creatures you guys fought last night?"

Deborah nodded.

"Holy smokes," Tristan said under his breath.

Noah noticed Deborah fight off a faint smile before she resumed. "The Army of Darkness has been sent to acquire the souls of unbelievers. Satan doesn't want to give them the opportunity of turning away from their sinful nature and accepting Jesus into their lives."

Deborah called the rest of the group over. Once everyone was gathered around, she spoke up.

"I am at a loss as to what he wants with these people. Maybe he is changing his game plan," she said. "Perhaps he wants to try to steal Christian souls. That would be an even bigger boost to his ego, but it still doesn't make any sense. We need to come together and pray for God's guidance."

Fear seized Noah's mind. "What are you talking about? We don't have time to sit here and pray! We need to act now! My nieces live in Gatlinburg. Joshua and I grew up there. If we leave now, we should be able to make it there by morning. We can't just abandon them. Please, listen to me. We have to help them!"

To Noah's surprise, it was Rebekah who responded. "We will pray and seek God's will, as we do in all situations."

Noah's blood was boiling. They could sit here and pray to their god, but he was not about to waste any time. He had to get to his family's farm as soon as possible, with or without them. He was about to depart on his own when Jack let out a friendly bark.

Noah looked up to see a tall, slender woman with short auburn hair walking down the rugged hillside. She never missed a step as she glided effortlessly down the steep terrain. Noah instinctively reached for his gun, but failed to pull it from its holster. Deborah did not appear worried to see this woman approaching them, and the warriors remained at ease.

To his surprise, the stranger walked right past Deborah and the rest of the company. Without saying a word, she walked straight up to Noah. Her intent stare bore into his skull. He could see every little fleck of her green eyes. Noah didn't know what to say, so he just stood there, feeling like an idiot.

Finally she broke the awkward silence. "Hello, Noah."

Noah was startled. How did she know his name? He wondered if she was some kind of psychic, but from what he remembered, Christians didn't believe in psychics. Of course, that was assuming that she was part of their group.

The woman's voice was soothing. She directed her next statement to Deborah. "It is God's will that you leave immediately. The enemy will not leave the remaining residents of Gatlinburg alone."

Noah interrupted her. "Why, what have they done to them? What does he want with them?"

Her face remained composed. "They have been chosen by God to help him defeat our enemy, but that is not the purpose of enemy's presence there tonight."

Even Deborah seemed confused. She turned to the woman who remained, in Noah's opinion, too close for comfort. As he took a subtle step back, Deborah asked, "Then what are they doing there?"

The woman looked at Joshua and then at Noah. "They have been deployed to eliminate the two of you. They are to bring back your heads as proof that their mission was carried out successfully."

Noah shuddered. "But I'm not at the farm, so why attack there?"

The woman gave him a knowing expression. Noah thought he was going to be sick. "No! They are going after Mary and Martha to get to me?"

She nodded. Noah felt dizzy as waves of fear and rage collided inside his mind. Joshua ran to his side. "Don't worry, we will reach them in time. It'll be okay. We won't let anybody hurt them!"

Noah nodded his head, wanting to believe Joshua was right.

Jack stood next to Noah, offering his support in the form of wet kisses. Noah patted the dog's soft head with appreciation. "Thanks, buddy."

Noah couldn't help but smile when Joshua responded. "Anytime."

Rebekah and Tristan joined them as Deborah wandered off with the strange woman. Tristan asked Rebekah, "Who is she?"

Rebekah chuckled at the expression on the three newcomers' faces. "A little intimidating, isn't she?"

Tristan nodded. "Yeah, just a little."

"Her name is Danielle. She is part of our group."

Noah interrupted Rebekah. It was a bad habit of his. "Then why didn't she fight with the rest of you guys last night?"

"Because she is not that kind of a warrior. She is a prophet. In fact, she is the last prophet on earth."

Noah's face lit up. "Then she can tell us if my nieces are safe."

Rebekah grabbed Noah's arm as he started after Deborah and Danielle. "I said she is a prophet. I didn't say she is a psychic. Besides, Danielle only reveals to us what God wants us to know, nothing more."

Noah was irritated. "Well, why wouldn't God want me to know that my nieces are safe?"

Rebekah offered him an exasperated look. "This isn't going to come easy for you, is it? God uses trials and tribulations to build our character and, more importantly, our faith."

This did not sit well with Noah. "What kind of bull is that? God wants us to suffer so he can be sure that we serve him?"

Rebekah rolled her eyes as Joshua and Tristan exchanged a knowing look. Her voice was calm and civil.

"No, that is not what I'm saying. Whether we like it or not, all of us will perish from this life. Our souls do not belong here; they belong with God in heaven. The enemy loves to trick us into believing that all the chaos and mayhem he creates is God's fault, and not his. If he succeeds, he is able to turn us against God, which is his ultimate victory. If we do not turn back to God and ask for forgiveness before we die, then he has gained possession over our soul."

Noah was annoyed. "You still didn't answer my question."

Rebekah let out an exasperated sigh. "Yes, I did. Look, God uses trials to build our character. When we face difficult situations and remain firm in our faith, we in turn build our trust and faith in him. We are not guaranteed that everything is going to be perfect and a bed of roses. We are guaranteed that he will be there for us, and should we remain steadfast in our faith, his promise of eternal life is our reward. Basically, you can choose life, or you can choose death. The choice is yours to make."

Before Noah could offer up another argument, Rebekah excused herself. Noah looked at Joshua and Tristan. "Are you guys buying any of this?"

Tristan gave Noah a sheepish look. "Well, kind of..."

Noah exclaimed. "Are you serious?" He turned to Joshua. "What about you? You aren't buying into this load of bull are you?"

Joshua braced himself for Noah's protests. "Look, it kind of makes sense to me. How else can you explain all this bizarre craziness?"

Noah shook his head. "I can't believe you."

Joshua shrugged. "All I am saying is, I think there might be something to what they are saying. I mean, can you explain what happened to Marcus and his men compared to what happened last night? It is kind of like a David and Goliath thing. And it is something that we both witnessed with our own eyes."

Noah glared at Joshua. "So that's it? Now you trust in God? You are just going to forgive and forget? Did my sister's life mean that little to you?"

Noah saw how much his words hurt Joshua, but he was on a roll, his anger had a hold of him and his words spewed out like poisonous venom.

"Do you really think I don't see the way you look at her?" His eyes drifted toward Rebekah. The thought of his twin sister laying in her grave was more than he could bear. "What I want to know is why didn't you do anything to save her? You were all about being the hero for Marcus and his men. Well, why weren't you Emma's hero?"

Everyone was staring at them. Noah's voice had reached a higher decibel level than he'd realized. Noah saw the tears welling up in Joshua's eyes as he turned and joined the rest of the group. Jack let out a whine before he left to follow Joshua.

Tristan's face was filled with shock as he turned to Noah.

"Dude, Joshua would lay down his life for you. And like it or not, if it was your sister's time to go home, there wasn't a thing Joshua could have done to stop it. You might be okay with letting the anger that consumes you destroy who you are, but you don't have to use it to try and destroy those who care about you."

Tristan shook his head as he slowly turned his back on Noah and joined the others.

For the first time, Noah felt completely isolated. His eyes traveled over to Deborah. He found her looking at him with a pitiful expression. He was curious to know what she and Danielle had been talking about. All he knew was that they weren't leaving camp fast enough. He didn't know what he would do if he lost Mary and Martha.

Noah thought to himself. "Okay, God, you have my attention. If you are real, show me what you can do."

MARY

Dusk was starting to fall across the property, forcing all who had taken up residency at the farm to abandon their chores and file into the farmhouse. With all the new arrivals at the farm, Mary had a small crew of helpers she oversaw to assist her with her increased kitchen duties.

Tonight they were having minestrone soup, lasagna made with homemade pasta, and mouth-watering garlic bread. Naturally, there was a beautiful salad for those who enjoyed their greens. There was one thing you could always count on when you lived on a farm: People are going to be hungry.

Everyone was lined up for the buffet-style dinner, chatting about their day, when Ernie ran up to Mary. "Have you seen Lizzy? I can't find her anywhere." A slight sense of panic etched his voice.

Mary shook her head. "I haven't seen her since lunchtime. Have you checked the bathrooms?"

Ernie's eyes relaxed. "Ah, I bet that's where she is. I'll send her mom to go check."

Once everyone else had served themselves, Mary made herself a plate and joined Martha and Luke. "What was that all about?" Martha asked, nodding toward Ernie.

"Oh, he couldn't find Lizzy. I asked him if they had checked the bathrooms. Sara went to go check."

Mary barely had time to finish her sentence when Sara ran in with a grim expression. She looked straight at Ernie and shook her head. Mary instinctively looked out to see how much light they had left. There was just a faint glow of light left in the sky.

Mary and Ernie jumped to their feet and rushed to the door. Ernie ran across the yard, hollering out for Lizzy. Rascal did not leave Mary's side, but before she could clear the last step of the back porch, Luke had grabbed her.

"Let me go! I have to find her!" Mary yelled as she fought to free herself. "Lizzy!"

Sara was clutching the banister. Tears streamed down her face as she frantically scanned the horizon for her baby girl. "Where could she be?"

Martha's eyes lit up. "Ernie, check the treehouse."

Ernie was in the barn, checking all the stalls, unable to hear Martha. That was when Luke flew off the porch and bolted toward the treehouse. Mary did her best to restrain Martha, and just before she lost her grip on her sister, Luke's mother came to Mary's aid as Martha fought feverishly to free herself.

Martha's voice rang out across the yard. "Luke, no!"

Moments later, Mary felt a sense of relief to see Luke climbing out of the treehouse with Lizzy clutching on to him for dear life.

All the commotion had gotten Ernie's attention. He emerged from the barn and was running toward Luke and Lizzy when a dark figure suddenly appeared from the shadows and moved in with startling speed. There was no mistaking the fact that it was the enemy, as a blaze of fire danced on the tip of its sword. Steel glinted in the moonlight as Satan's soldier swung the weapon, cutting down Ernie as he ran toward Luke and Lizzy.

Luke paused for a moment as shock and disbelief overtook him. Now two of the enemy's soldiers were closing in on them, but Lizzy was oblivious to their approach as she screamed at the sight of her father's dead body. She somehow wrestled herself free from Luke's grasp and ran as fast as her little legs could carry her. But before she could reach her father, a soldier ran her down, taking her young life with a single swing of his sword.

Mary grabbed onto the banister to keep from falling. She could not believe what she was seeing. Realizing she was free from their hold, Martha raced to Luke's side. She reached out and retrieved a hoe as she ran by one of the gardens.

One of the dark soldiers let out a raspy laugh as he stood over Luke, first knocking him to the ground with a glancing blow and then raising his weapon to deliver a two-handed death strike. "Say your prayers, Christian," he hissed.

Martha desperately moved in to block the soldier's sword with her garden tool, and without realizing what she was doing, began shouting at the top of her lungs. "Behold, I give you the authority to trample on serpents and scorpions, and over all the power of the enemy, and nothing shall by any means hurt you."

Strangely, it appeared that Martha's words had caused the enemy to wobble, and he stumbled under the weight of his upraised sword. Taking full advantage, Martha brought the hoe down with all her might, lopping off the dark soldier's head and causing the shocked onlookers to let out a simultaneous gasp.

Martha bent down to help Luke up. Blood ran down his arm where he had received a nasty laceration from the attack.

It was at that moment Martha saw Luke's eyes open wide and heard Mary's voice shouting from the porch. Looking behind her, she saw a flood of dark soldiers emerging through the tall pines that encircled their home.

"Heaven help us," she said.

NOAH

Noah's heart beat like a drum. He ducked to avoid another scrape from the low-hanging branches that covered the narrow dirt trail. His right cheek still oozed a little blood from a branch that had snagged his face earlier. He had secretly worried that Satan's soldiers might be attracted to the smell of blood like sharks.

His nerves were eased a little by the nonchalant attitude the rest of his traveling companions displayed regarding the nasty gash that was sure to leave a rugged, manly scar across his face. As much as he wanted to believe that women bought into that machismo malarkey, he didn't buy it. He knew his thoughts were silly, but focusing on the trivial outcome of his minor wound helped him control the anxiety that threatened to overtake him at any second.

Deborah's company, which now included Noah, Joshua, and Tristan, had embarked on their mission right after Noah had publicly humiliated himself in front of the entire group. It felt as though they had been weaving their way through the untamed wilderness for hours. Staying off the beaten path added time to their journey – time they didn't have.

Noah had been surprised to discover that Danielle would travel alone. According to Deborah, Danielle always resided on the outskirts of their camp. Supposedly, the solitude created a tranquil environment that assisted her being able to hear from God.

Noah was impressed. He was a man, traveling with God's army, and he would be lying if he said he wasn't scared. The fact that this slender, nonathletic woman traveled alone, unprotected from predators, astonished him.

When they had first set out, Noah had unsuccessfully attempted to pry information out of Deborah regarding her conversation with Danielle. His trained eye had picked up on the grave expressions that both women had worn during their private discussion.

Noah desperately desired confirmation that his nieces were safe and out of harm's way, and his frustration grew when Deborah fell silent to his queries. As he walked, he kept replaying their conversation over and over again in his mind.

"Deborah, please don't ignore me. Why won't you tell me what Danielle said? Has something happened to Mary and Martha? Are they in danger? I know you know."

She appeared to be mulling something over. It felt like ages before she finally responded. "Danielle did not tell me the outcome of this battle. She never does." She paused for a moment, then continued. "Some of my people were opposed to you joining us."

Noah burst out. "What? Why? We are traveling to my family's farm where my nieces are. It doesn't make sense for me not to be there."

Deborah nodded her head. "You have a valid point, but then again, so did they."

Noah tried to gain control over his emotions. He took a deep breath before calmly asking, "Which was?"

Deborah hesitated before answering him. "Their number one issue with you joining us is the fact that you can be a tad bit obstinate."

Noah's face burned with anger, even though it wasn't the first time someone had said something similar. In fact, Abigail brought it up rather frequently. His obstinance is what helped him win awards as an investigative reporter, but Abigail failed to ever see that side of it.

Noah nodded his head. "Go on."

"And, they argued the fact that you still have so much to learn."

He looked puzzled. "What do you mean?"

Deborah let out a deep sigh. "I guess now is as good a time as any to start filling you in. When we fight, we are not concerned about the outcome."

Noah was even more confused. "Why would you fight if you're not interested in winning? And why wouldn't you want to win?"

"Because, we fight so that God will obtain victory over Satan. If we must die to bring about that result, then that is the cross we must bear. We go into battle ready to give our lives for his cause."

Noah shook his head. "But how can God achieve victory with fallen soldiers?"

Deborah smiled. "Good question. One which I do not presume to know the answer. God has a plan for each and every one of us. This plan is not to benefit us, but to benefit his kingdom. Look at Jesus. He saved us by sacrificing his life on the cross for our sins."

They walked in silence for a while as Noah thought about what she had shared with him. It didn't take long before he had another question. "How do we know what his plan is for us?"

Deborah let out a low chuckle. "Unfortunately, we don't." She could see from his expression that this bothered him. "God gives us just enough light to see the step we are on, not the entire path. That is how he builds our faith, for if we knew the entire journey, especially the final result, it wouldn't require us to use our faith."

She let out an exasperated sigh. "I'm sorry. Am I making any sense to you?"

Noah was panic-stricken. Since meeting the Army of Angels, it had never occurred to him that they could have their lives taken from them. Noah was not the only one adept at reading people.

She placed a gentle hand on his sore shoulder. "Don't worry. As believers, our home is not here on this planet. Our home is in heaven with him, and one day when we are sitting up there, we will wonder why we ever cherished this ghastly place."

Noah looked at her sideways, unsure of what to think. Deborah's voice was confident. "Heaven is a reward, not a punishment. But, if that doesn't sound enticing to you, you can always take the mark and become a slave to the master of the underworld."

Noah knew she was teasing him, but he shuddered at the thought. "Nah, I think I'll pass."

Noah bumped into the soldier in front of him. He had been so lost in thought that he failed to notice that the company had come to an abrupt halt. Deborah motioned for everyone to be quiet. Noah followed suit as the warriors pressed themselves firmly against the side of the hill next to them.

Noah's heart sank as he heard a familiar sound in the distance, a sound that caused his spine to tingle. He heard the clash of steel, as a fierce battle apparently was unfolding nearby, but what really turned Noah's gut was the fact that he could hear voices shouting scriptures. Only one army could be defeated by the Word of God. Noah watched as Deborah dispatched Matthew to go on ahead of them and scout out their best approach. The rest of the company silently waited for his return, mentally preparing themselves for war.

DEBORAH

Deborah's face clouded with concern. This was the first time she had commanded untrained soldiers in her ranks. In the past, everyone had been required to endure a rigorous training program before Danielle would determine whether they were qualified to be accepted into the fold. In order for a person to pass, Danielle would have to receive affirmation from God that their heart was sincere and true to him. From there they would proceed through the formal initiation ceremony before ever acquiring a weapon.

Danielle had assured Deborah that Joshua and Tristan were up to the task, but Noah... she had forewarned Deborah that he would be her biggest challenge yet.

Deborah had questioned her. "Even worse than Lucious Washington?"

Danielle laughed. "Yes, I'm afraid so... but, if Noah chooses to return to his faith and can overcome his trials, he will be a mighty man of God."

Deborah shot her friend a look. "Oh, wonderful. The infamous 'if.' And I don't suppose you would be willing to bless me with a little insight as to what lies ahead for him?" Deborah's expression pleaded for help with the situation.

Danielle shook her head. "Now where would the fun be in that?" she chided.

Sarcasm oozed from Deborah's lips. "Well, I'm glad that one of us is having fun."

Deborah remembered the inner struggle Lucious had fought to overcome his pride. Before the Rapture, Lucious had been a star player in the NFL. There wasn't a receiver in the league who could match his skills on the field. People would say that he had hands of Velcro, not to mention his ability to outmaneuver and outrun every opponent he had ever faced.

But Lucious' God-given talents were also his toughest challenge when it came to the battle for his spiritual life. He had a tendency to take full credit for his achievements, forgetting about the one who had knit him together in his mother's womb, blessing him with such astounding physical gifts.

Now God had deemed Deborah up to the task of mentoring and shaping another soldier for his army. But this time the elected soldier's pride had not been a result of God's gifts, but of the enemy's wicked schemes to destroy a strong Christian family.

Snuffing out the lives of sisters Emma and Anna before their brother was ready to say goodbye had left Noah bitter, broken, and wanting nothing to do with the only one who had the power to repair the wounds the enemy had inflicted upon him.

Deborah rolled her eyes and looked up toward heaven. "Yeah, sure thing. I've got this," she uttered sarcastically under her breath.

Lost in her prayers, Deborah was startled as Matthew suddenly appeared before her. He was breathing heavily. He had run the entire way. "From what I saw, a small group of townspeople are engaged in fighting the dark soldiers at the edge of the property while other members of their group are clustered on the porch. I think we should leave our three newest members at the farm with the others, and the rest of us can relieve the townspeople who are fighting."

After revealing his findings to the group, they headed out along the shore of a nearby river. It was not long before the river led them right behind the farmhouse.

The company's stealthy movements would have put the Navy SEALs to shame. Within seconds, they were skirting the sides of Noah's childhood home, weapons unsheathed and ready to face their foe once again.

MARTHA

Martha grabbed Luke's good arm as the two of them sprinted toward the farmhouse. They were approaching the others when they ground to a halt.

Mary yelled. "What are you doing? Come on, hurry!"

There, right in front of them, white-clad soldiers with swords, axes, and daggers raised for battle were charging straight toward them. Martha surveyed the distance between this new group of soldiers and the ones closing in on them from behind. Realizing that they were sandwiched between them with no place to go, she looked at Luke.

"We don't have a choice. We have to fight."

She broke the long handle of the hoe over her knee, holding up the two pieces for Luke to choose from. He rolled his eyes at her as he left her the piece with the metal blade and chose the broken stick. They braced themselves against each other's back, prepared to fight to the death, when to their surprise the new group of soldiers raced past them and toward the advancing dark soldiers.

Some of the men and women in their group had picked up farm tools and were doing their best to fight off the enemy. Seeing the effect scripture appeared to have on Satan's soldiers, Martha's actions had inspired them to emulate her behavior, and so far no one else had been killed.

Overwhelmed with relief, Martha burst out in her nervous laugh. Luke leaned over and gave her a soft kiss on her cheek. "Thank you for saving me. You are my knight in shining armor and I will forever be in your debt."

Martha shoved him away. "Knock it off, you goof ball." Her eyes fell on his wounded arm. It was bleeding and smelled horrible. "Come on, we need to bandage you up."

Before Martha could finish her sentence, Luke stumbled, nearly falling over. Martha and Mary cried out in unison as Noah suddenly appeared out of nowhere, catching Luke before he hit the ground. Martha was exhilarated and relieved to see her uncle, but consumed with fear for Luke.

As the battle behind them raged, Noah carried Luke into the house and up the stairs, putting him down on Anna's old bed. Martha and Mary were close on his heels, with Mary peppering him with questions. "Where have you been? What in God's name is going on? Why are all these evil soldiers attacking us?"

Luke's mother and his sister Margo had been right behind them, and both were as pale as a ghost.

Mary and Martha jumped, startled by Joshua's voice. They hadn't seen him or the strange young man who was with him come into the house. Rascal, however, was already very aware of Jack's presence. The two dogs circled each other, doing the familiar "get to know you" dance dogs are known for.

"We came here with the Army of Angels, and if you believe them..." Joshua's words were interrupted by a thunderous crack in the sky. Rascal and Jack both cowered to the unpleasant sound. "We have entered into the Great Tribulation."

Both girls' mouths dropped, but not because of Joshua's shocking words. They were staring past him, out the large bay window at the enchanting light that filled the night sky.

Mary was transfixed. "What are those things? They're gorgeous!"

The three men smiled amongst themselves, but it was Tristan who responded. "That's exactly why they're called the Army of Angels."

Tristan kept Mary busy by introducing himself and sharing with her the story of how they met Deborah and her company of soldiers while Noah called Joshua over and pointed out Luke's wound.

Noah asked Martha to tell them what had transpired before their arrival. When she told them that Luke had been grazed by the dark soldier's sword, both men shot each other a knowing glance.

Martha tried to fight back the panic that was welling up inside of her. "What? What did that look mean? What has happened to him?"

Noah sat Martha down on an oversized chair. "Relax. I am sure there is something we can do for him."

Martha shook her head. "But why has he collapsed? He didn't lose that much blood."

Noah leaned in close to Martha, not wanting to frighten Luke's mother and sister. "You need to remain calm and be strong for Luke and his family. Can you do that?"

Martha felt the blood rush from her extremities. She slowly nodded her head.

Noah gave Martha a comforting smile. "We believe the enemy's swords possess some type of poison."

Martha let out a quiet gasp. "What? What do we do?"

Tears welled in her eyes. She couldn't lose Luke, not now. She fought back the urge to curse God.

JOSHUA

Joshua wandered over to the bay window where he found himself searching for Rebekah in the midst of all the fighting. The men and women who had taken up their yard tools to defend themselves had slowly been trickling back to the house once Deborah and her company arrived.

Joshua was deeply concerned for Luke; he didn't know how much longer the young man had. He prayed that Luke would be able to hold on long enough, until Deborah or Danielle could be consulted. There had to be something they could do for him.

Martha did her best to clean the wound with warm water as Luke's mother and sister prayed over him. Joshua sent one up on Luke's behalf. He doubted God really wanted to hear from him. They hadn't been on the best of terms over the past few years, which reminded Joshua of his and Noah's last few words together. They hadn't really spoken since Noah revealed his insulting opinions of Joshua to the entire camp.

Joshua mindlessly watched the battle as he stood in front of the bay window sulking. He felt helpless as he stood there while Rebekah and the others fought on. It made him feel like a heel, but Deborah had made the three of them promise that they would not engage the enemy unless they were attacked and could not escape. Just in case they should find themselves face to face with one of Satan's demons, Deborah had given each of them a scripture to memorize, instructing them to use it should such an incidence occur.

Lost in his thoughts, Joshua hadn't seen Danielle approach. Her words caused him to startle. "Satan's forces are becoming stronger. Our people are not going to be able to keep this up without help."

Joshua looked at her eagerly. "Put me in coach. I'm ready."

Danielle smiled. "Slow down, turbo. You and your buddies need to have more than one scripture under your belt before you take on these bad boys, but you can gather everyone else and lead them in prayer."

Joshua looked confused. "Should we pray for Luke?"

Danielle nodded. "I would strongly advise it. I would also advise praying that God continue to supply our soldiers out there with strength and endurance. It is going to be a long night."

All of a sudden, Joshua leaned down and squinted. In the distance it appeared that there was some kind of wild beast lurking in the top of a pine tree, watching over the battle and the house. Joshua figured his mind must be playing tricks on him when he noticed Danielle staring in the same direction.

"Do you see it, too? Do you know what it is?" he asked.

Danielle simply smiled as she turned and walked across the room.

DEBORAH

Deborah could not believe the size of Satan's force. She had ordered her soldiers to fight in a circular formation, guaranteeing that no one was left with their back exposed to the enemy. While she was fighting off the most aggressive soldier she had come across, her eyes flew up to a dark figure that was hunched in one of the trees. Her heart did a flip-flop at the sight of the beast. It was the very same creature that had haunted her dreams since she was a child. She had never expected the beast to be real.

A maniacal laugh pierced her ear drums as the dark soldier she was fighting nearly knocked her off her feet. A disgusting stench filled her nostrils as its breath hung in the air. "Oops, you should be more careful. You wouldn't want to give me a chance to lop off your pretty little head," it hissed.

Rebekah shot her a concerned look. "Are you okay?"

Deborah nodded. "Yeah, I got this," she answered as she silently scolded herself. "Focus girl, focus."

Deborah looked the demon in the eyes as she recited, "And when He had called His twelve disciples to Him, He gave them power over unclean spirits, to cast them out, and to heal all kinds of sickness and all kinds of disease."

The demon snarled as her words weakened his resolve and made him vulnerable. As she had done hundreds of times, Deborah took advantage and pierced his side with her short sword seconds before she split his skull with her axe.

Deborah saw the strain that was weighing down on her comrades and the angels that fought alongside them. She sent up a silent prayer.

"Thank you, God, that you have provided us with the strength to hold off the enemy. I ask that you increase your favor upon us, and I claim your promise that states we will not grow weary. Lord, we need your spirit to lift us up so that we can continue to do your work on earth as it is in heaven. In Jesus' precious name, I pray. Amen."

Deborah found herself wondering what or who was at the farm that Satan so desperately wanted to get his hands on, or kill. Noticing that the beast perched in the tree still held his post caused her to wonder just why he was there? Why hadn't he joined the soldiers? What was he after?

MARY

Danielle carefully inspected Luke's wound before turning to Martha. "The poison would have killed a lesser man. It appears he has more faith than he lets on."

Martha looked surprised. "Who are you?"

Danielle smiled. "I am Danielle. I am with the company that is protecting you." She sat down next to Martha. "Do you know what spared your life out there tonight?"

Martha shook her head. "No, I just remember being terrified. I can't imagine life without him." Martha nodded to Luke. "It is my fault that he is still here. If it weren't for me, he would have been spared all of this and would have been swept up with everyone else in the Rapture."

Danielle's voice was gentle. "No, child. You are not the reason he remains here on earth. You all are here because you have a role to play in overthrowing Satan and his minions. Your life was spared because you instinctively returned to what you know deep down within yourself to be true. You called upon your heavenly father out there, and he responded to your plea."

Martha snorted. "Believe me, he doesn't want a thing to do with me."

Danielle shook her head. "That's where you are wrong. Stop listening to the words of the enemy and start listening to the words of the one who made you."

Martha was becoming a little annoyed. Who was this Danielle woman? Martha responded. "That is where you are wrong. You say these words, but you don't know who I am or what I have done."

Danielle disagreed. "God has not cast you out. You turned your back against him, but he is waiting with open arms for the day you realize how important you are to him. You have a monumental role to play during these

107

last days. The time has come for you to choose whose team you are going to play for. The fact that you have not taken the mark, and your actions tonight, tell me that you have already made up your mind. Luke will not die tonight, but even if he did, he has a place in heaven waiting for him. God does not expect us to be perfect. If he did, he wouldn't have had his only son die such a gruesome death for our sins. He only asks that we continue to seek him. His grace and his mercy are there for us no matter how many times we have to ask for his forgiveness."

Danielle stood up to leave but paused. "Oh, I almost forgot. Mary, would you please come join us."

Mary was a little intimidated. "Uh, me?"

Tristan laughed. "Don't worry. She is awesome, I promise."

Mary gave Tristan a sideways glance. "Oh-kay."

As Mary approached the side of the bed, Danielle stepped aside. Danielle looked at Mary. "I want you to use the power God has given you to heal Luke."

Mary let out a scoff. "Me? Um, I'm sorry, but I don't know what you are talking about. I'm not a doctor."

Danielle calmly guided Mary. "Place your hand on his wound."

Mary was hesitant but did as Danielle instructed. Danielle smiled. "Very good. Now close your eyes and shut out all the noise around you and speak the words you hear inside."

Martha looked at Danielle like she was crazy. Her voice was irritated as she spoke. "Look, Luke is a good person. He needs real help, not some hokey pokey... whatever this is."

Danielle ignored Martha and focused her attention on Mary. "You can do this. God has given you authority. Now use it."

Mary nodded. She would give it her best shot for Luke's sake. It took her a while to shut out all the noise, especially the doubt that ran rampant in her mind, but once she did she heard a still, small voice. At first she thought she was just imagining things, but she heard it again, and this time she repeated the words out loud. "By his stripes, you are healed."

Danielle smiled. "Very good. Now say it louder and with authority, like you mean it."

Mary took a deep breath. As she exhaled, she firmly pronounced her words. "By his stripes, you are healed."

Mary heard a collective sigh fill the room as the wound on Luke's arm slowly closed and began to heal. Mary couldn't believe what she was seeing.

As she stood there, blown away by what was happening, Luke blinked a couple of times before his eyes finally opened. Martha flung her arms around him, wrapping him in a full embrace. Tears ran down her face. "Oh, thank God. Thank God you are okay."

Noah stood there scratching his head. He looked directly at Danielle.

"Can you tell me what just happened here?"

Danielle let out a soft laugh. "I think it would be better if Mary explained it."

Mary was taken aback. "You want me to explain it? I don't even know what happened myself."

Danielle looked Mary straight in the eye. "Yes you do. It is just that the answer is so simple, it is difficult to comprehend. Our human minds want a more complicated answer. We don't do 'simple' very well."

Mary cleared her throat. "Okay. Well, all I can say is that Luke's injury was not due to the fact that it was time for him to return to heaven. It was a vicious act of the enemy in an attempt to deplete God's forces."

Mary looked around at all of the faces staring intently at her. Her voice began to shake a little. She was not comfortable speaking in front of large groups.

Danielle encouraged her. "You are doing just fine. Carry on."

Mary closed her eyes to shut out all the faces. "God has given us power and authority over the enemy. That is why I was able to cast out the poison by using the promise of God in his word. We have power over all things that are not of God when we proclaim his word over them."

Mary opened her eyes again. "There. That's it. I'm done."

Tristan was the first to catch on. "That is why the warriors proclaim the word of God while they are fighting. They are claiming his promises."

Danielle nodded. "If you recall, when Jesus was alone in the wilderness, Satan came along in an attempt to convert Jesus to 'Team Satan.'"

Danielle's eyes fell on Martha. "If Satan is bold enough to approach the son of God, we should not for one minute think that he will not aggressively go after us. And, unlike Jesus, there will be times when we will stumble and fall. But the trick is learning to get back up. God forgives us as soon as we ask. The hardest part is learning to forgive ourselves."

Martha squirmed uncomfortably as Danielle's words pricked at her heart.

Danielle looked around at all the individuals in the room. "The important thing to remember is that Jesus cast down Satan by using the words of his father. He repeatedly responded by saying 'It is written.' That is why we emulate his example that he left for us by fighting with the one tool capable of defeating Satan, God's Word. It is fuel to our minds, bodies, souls, and our spirits. It unleashes God's power to assist us in our time of need. That power can come in many forms. It can come as a source of supernatural power, a host of heavenly beings, a cure, or even a timely word or hug."

The group couldn't help but notice that the sounds of battle were growing closer. Mary and several others ran to the window. Their eyes widened as they saw the enemy's men pushing Deborah and her company back, gaining ground on them as they moved closer and closer to the farmhouse.

Mary looked around with a sense of panic. Her uncle put his arm around her shoulder. He attempted to reassure his youngest niece. "It's okay, Lil M, Deborah won't let anything happen to us."

Joshua's eyes fell on Rebekah. The enemy's forces were overwhelming. The warriors and the angels continued to fight with everything they had. Scripture was being shouted from every direction, but it wasn't enough.

Danielle looked at Joshua. He nodded his agreement then raised his voice so all could hear him. "It is time that we do our part. We need to start offering up our prayers of support for our fellow soldiers out there. Like it or not, we are now part of God's army, so let the praying begin."

Mary ran and grabbed her Bible out of her room. When she returned, she looked up at her uncle. "Will you recite this scripture with me?"

Noah never could resist her sweet smile. "Sure."

Together they read Mary's highlighted verse. "...that through death He might destroy him who had the power of death, that is, the devil, and release those who through fear of death were all their lifetime subject to bondage."

As they finished the verse, Noah's heart melted. Mary desperately wanted to be free from her bondage. Noah wrapped her in his strong arms. "Oh Lil M, I pray that by his stripes you are healed from your fear of death. That you are forever set free from Satan's grasp."

Tears ran down Mary's face. "Thank you," she whispered.

NOAH

Noah could not measure the level of humiliation that was coursing through his veins. How ridiculous he must appear, a grown man standing in front of the entire group, holding a puny stick as if it were a mighty weapon. Some of the younger children who had taken up residence on the farm had picked up sticks of their own and were emulating Noah's movements. When he had agreed to follow the Army of Angels' strict initiation and training policies, this was definitely not what he had envisioned.

Deborah stood in front of him with a look of full-blown exasperation. "Seriously, Noah, if you don't suck up your pride and focus, something far worse than your precious ego will be hurt when you face your demons on the battlefield." Without warning, she jabbed his ribs with her stick to bring her message home. He jumped back, scowling as he clutched his side.

"Ouch! What the heck was that for?"

A smirk crossed Deborah's delicate face. "You think the demons are going to be polite about their intention to kill you? Buck up, sissy pants, and learn to take it like a man."

A playful laugh escaped her, and many of the onlookers joined in. Deborah had a fun, lighthearted side to her that leaned toward being downright mischievous when she was not caught up in her responsibilities. Noah often found himself wondering what she had been like before the Army of Darkness existed.

"Oh, really? That's how you want to be, huh? Okay, two can play this game. I suggest you watch out, little Miss Bossy, for you are about to encounter the wrath of Noah."

Before he completed his last sentence, he lunged at her, hoping to catch her off guard. His pathetic attempt to gain an unfair advantage failed miserably. She counterattacked without even giving him her full attention. Then Noah attacked as though Deborah was one of his mortal enemies, hell-bent on snuffing out his last breath. She countered every one of his moves with ease, but he noticed the glint in her eye that showed him she approved.

He was learning at an accelerated pace, which was no small feat. It was not easy to memorize all of the scriptures and then recall them while someone was trying to pummel you to death. Most soldiers were regarded in high esteem just for mastering their weapon and employing it in the heat of battle. But Noah had found that when he succumbed and allowed his heart to soften toward the teachings of the Bible, he was able to fight more effectively without having to focus so much on his movements. The more scriptures he committed to memory, the more natural and advanced his skills became.

After a long, tedious session of sparring, Deborah finally signaled that it was time to stop. "Let's take a break and watch Joshua and Rebekah for a while."

They walked over and sat under a tall tree, resting their backs against its wide trunk. Noah had found himself wanting to apologize to Joshua for the spiteful comments he had made earlier, but every time he tried to bring up the subject, a wave of anger would wash over him. There was a part of him that resented Joshua. Not that he would admit it to anyone, but deep down Noah was angry with his best friend for being able to move on, for being able to forgive God, and for leaving him to suffer all alone in his misery. It wasn't that Noah didn't want to believe and forgive; he really did. But every time he began to embrace the faith of his youth, his mind would replay the horror that had ripped his world apart, and anger and doubt would seep back into his soul. Poor Mary wasn't the only one suffering from a severe case of bondage.

Noah watched Joshua and Rebekah. He hated to acknowledge it, but they did complement each other quite nicely. Noah sat there contemplating Joshua's attraction to Rebekah. He found his friend's response to the formidable female soldier odd. She was absolutely stunning, there was no denying that, but she was so different than Emma. Rebekah boasted exotic features and carried herself in a sophisticated manner, where Emma had been the typical girl next door. Emma had been gorgeous, but her beauty had more of a natural origin, and her allure came from her playful, tomboy antics and her sharp mind.

Joshua was excelling under Rebekah's tutelage. He and Tristan had become more open-minded and accepting of what was happening around them. Noah noticed how Rebekah's approach to teaching Joshua was subdued compared to Deborah's assertive approach with him.

Danielle had been very astute at reading their personalities when she had assigned their trainers. Joshua was much humbler and gentler than Noah. Noah needed Deborah's fiery spirit to keep him in check. He would have walked all over Rebekah, or maybe not. She might be quiet and demure, but she skillfully tossed her weapon around as though it was a mere twig. Noah had observed how fierce and noble a fighter she was during battle. Her skills were intimidating.

Noah caught Deborah watching him. Her smile indicated that she was on to his thoughts. She gave him a quick wink.

"Come on, you, let's go practice with the real weapon now."

What she meant was, it was time to pull out the Bible and study the Word of God. As he turned to leave, Noah saw Tristan training with his instructor, Reuben. Reuben was a stocky, red-headed soldier who was no joke, either.

The truth was, there wasn't anyone in this camp with whom Noah would rather have as his instructor. To his complete irritation, his feelings for Deborah were blossoming the more he spent time with her. She was complex, and that just spurred his attraction even more.

Before he picked up his Bible, Deborah stopped him.

"Without looking I want you to recite Psalm twenty-three."

Noah felt a flood of panic wash over him. "You mean the entire thing?"

She nodded. "Yep."

"You can't be serious. That's a lot!"

She shook her head and rolled her eyes. "You are the biggest whiner I know. You can do it! Stop doubting yourself. Negativity is your go-to response. Replace it with hope and belief." The uplifting tone in her voice turned to a demand. "So come on, let's hear it."

She was right, of course, but he sure as heck wasn't going to admit it.

Looking into her face, he saw such boldness and encouragement. It gave him confidence.

"Okay, here goes ... 'The Lord is my Shepherd. I shall not lack.

He makes me lie down in green pastures; He leads me beside the still and restful waters.

He refreshes and restores my life; He leads me in the paths of righteousness for His name's sake.

Yes, though I walk through the valley of the shadow of death, I will fear or dread no evil, for You are with me; Your rod and Your staff, they comfort me.

You prepare a table before me in the presence of my enemies.

You anoint my head with oil; my cup runs over.

Surely goodness, mercy, and unfailing love shall follow me all the days of my life, and through the length of my days the house of the Lord shall be my dwelling place.' "

Noah let out a sigh as he watched Deborah's face, searching for a clue as to how he had done. She shook her head slowly as though she was disappointed. Noah's heart sank. He thought he had nailed it this time. Suddenly, she let out a joyous laugh.

"Noah, you have got to stop being so gullible. You were awesome! You didn't miss a single word."

She gave him a good-natured shove. He wasn't sure if she was just being playful or if there was a flirtatious undercurrent hidden in the gesture. Secretly, there was a part of him that hoped there was.

"Great, that's just wonderful. The world is supposedly coming to an end and for the first time in your life you decide to develop some secret attraction to this bossy, Bible-preaching lunatic who can take your life in her sleep," he thought to himself.

Noah reached over and gently swept the hair out of Deborah's eyes. It wasn't the first time he had noticed the thin scar that marked her forehead, but it was the first time he had felt comfortable enough to question her about it.

"How did you get your scar? Was it during one of your encounters with the Army of Darkness?"

The somber expression that washed over her face caused him to regret his decision to ask her about it. She shook her head. "No. That scar, ironically, is the source of both my spiritual doubts and my confirmation that God is real and has a plan for each and every one of us. It's my Emma." Deborah smiled knowingly at Noah.

Noah was blindsided. "You know about my sister?"

Deborah nodded. "And Anna."

Noah was confused. "But how?" His eyes narrowed as they wandered across the yard at Joshua, who was sitting too close to Rebekah, probably studying his scripture verses. Jack laid his head on her lap as she laughed at something Joshua said. Anger seethed through Noah. How dare he share such information without consulting Noah first?

Deborah read the misunderstanding on Noah's face. Her voice reeled in his anger. "No, no, you have it all wrong. Joshua didn't say anything to me; in fact, he isn't even aware that I know."

Noah was becoming frustrated and his tone failed to mask his feelings. "Then how?"

His eyes fell on Mary and Martha, who were sitting with Luke and Tristan. From the looks of things, Tristan had taken a liking to Mary. Noah chuckled to himself, "At least she attracts the good guys."

Deborah followed his gaze. "No, not the twins either." Noah turned and looked at her before she continued. "God shares things with Danielle, who in turn shares bits of information that she believes are important for me to know."

Noah was still annoyed. "And Emma was something she deemed

important?"

Deborah nodded. "Of course. If the four of you are to be under my command, I believe it is pertinent that I understand your weaknesses."

Noah cut her off in mid-sentence. "And you think my sister Emma is a weakness for me?"

Deborah's eyes narrowed. Her patience for his prideful outbursts was wearing thin.

"Yes, as a matter of fact, I do. We all have weaknesses, areas where the enemy has worn us down over the years. Areas he has been using time and time again, in an attempt to harden our hearts against God. Do you honestly think that you are the only soul here that has suffered unbearable loss and pain? Are you that much of a narcissist that you believe you are the only soul that is important to God? If we weren't precious in his sight and worthy to his cause, do you really think Satan would be going to such extreme efforts to strike us down?"

Deborah's fuse had finally been lit. "You know, sometimes you allow me to see these brief glimpses of who you really are, and I have such admiration for you, but then you inevitably turn into this arrogant, egocentric jerk, and I just want to..." Deborah took a deep breath before walking off, leaving Noah alone once again.

As he watched her disappear behind the farmhouse, Noah's pride stung from Deborah's harsh but honest words. For the first time, the thought occurred to Noah that maybe Deborah and the other soldiers had experienced sorrow and loss. He just assumed that the members of the Army of Angels had led pristine, perfect lives, and that such people never had to deal with the cruel realities of this world. It had never dawned on him that life had also dealt them some heavy blows.

As Deborah's words sunk in, and he realized the error of his thinking, he found himself desperately wanting to know what kept them true to their beliefs when he had faltered?

MARY

Mary remembered the first time she met Deborah. The commander and her men and women had shifted the tide of the battle once the group inside the farmhouse had begun to lift the warriors and their angels up in prayer. The results raised the spirits of both those on the ground fighting and those who eagerly wished to do their part while tucked away in Anna and Joel's old bedroom.

As an earth-shaking, thunderous clap ripped through the heavens and sunlight filtered down through the sky, the possessed beings were swiftly called back to their den of darkness and the heavenly hosts took a knee beside their human comrades before their father called them to return to their posts.

As Mary observed Deborah, kneeling, with her hands and clothing splattered with blood, her face lifted to heaven, Mary felt a sense of peace that she hadn't experienced for quite some time. She was drawn instantly to Deborah. There was something familiar about her. She reminded Mary of her mother. Her faith was vibrant and mighty like Anna's had been. She looked a lot like her mother, too. Mary wondered if her uncle and Martha saw it as well.

Mary was determined to join the Army of Angels if God ordained it. She liked having them around, so when Mary overheard Deborah instructing the army to search the town for a place to make camp, a light went off in her head.

She quickly spoke up. "Excuse me, but why not use our farm? It's a perfect location, and we have plenty of supplies to feed and house everyone. Not to mention the fact that this is sacred, holy ground that has been blessed by God's followers for generations. We can pray a hedge of protection around the farm and even ask God to send his angels to guard

116

the property."

As Mary waited for Deborah's response, Noah jumped in. "That would be perfect. We can use the barn as shelter, too, and there is plenty of land here for our training exercises."

A huge smile spread across Deborah's face. "We would be honored and blessed to accept your proposal. You are right; this is a perfect answer to prayer. Almost makes me think God had this planned out the entire time."

Deborah gave Noah and his niece a playful wink. Deborah eyeballed Mary for a moment. "You must be Mary."

Mary nodded. She gave her uncle a questioning look. He let out a sly chuckle as he shook his head. "Don't ask me. They always seem to know things that most people wouldn't."

As the individual members of the company left to set up camp, they made sure to express their gratitude for Mary's generous offer.

Deborah noticed how Mary's offer of using their property seemed to ignite a fire in her. It had given herself, her uncle, and her sister a purpose. They no longer seemed to view themselves as victims, but as warriors – at least for now.

Deborah knew the war for their faith was far from over, but she sent up a silent prayer thanking the Lord that at least they had won this battle. She asked God to provide them with victory in all the battles the enemy set in front of them. She prayed that all of her friends would come to know just how much they meant to their Heavenly Father. The fact that they were precious and dear to God meant that they were living, breathing targets. As long as they were still alive, Satan would never cease his attempts to steal their souls.

A short while later, Mary approached Deborah as she was wandering through the flower garden. Her mother had loved flowers and was enchanted by the beauty of lush English gardens since she was a little girl, so their father, Joel, had seen to it that Anna had her very own English garden right in her own backyard. The bench that sat next to the custom water feature her father had meticulously created made for a perfect spot to spend one-on-one time with God. It was like a little slice of heaven on Earth, or at least that is what her mother used to say.

Remembering her mother's frequently spoken words brought a sparkle to her eyes, as well as some salty tears. It was a bittersweet moment, and Mary knew she would have to brace herself for many more such moments in the days to come.

Mary found Deborah sitting in her mother's spot. Her eyes were closed and her lips moved silently. Mary was about to leave when she heard the woman's voice call out to her.

"It's okay. You're not intruding. Come sit with me." Deborah patted the spot on the bench next to her.

Mary was not expecting the surge of relief she experienced at those words. She spun around and planted herself right next to her new friend.

"I was wondering if you would be open to sharing with me how you stay so strong and steadfast in your belief and actions," Mary said.

Deborah nodded slightly: "I am no expert on how to be a Christian, that's for sure, and please believe me when I say, 'I am human and far from perfect and make a great deal of mistakes!' But what helps me is staying in constant contact with God. I talk with him about literally everything, but not out loud when I am around other people, of course."

They both let out a hearty laugh at that image.

"But there isn't anything I don't talk with him about. I have resigned myself to the fact that nothing else in this world matters. God is it! If it doesn't please him or isn't part of his will for my life, then I don't go there. It's not always easy, but I have learned that nothing good ever comes from following my own will. Yes, at first it may seem awesome, but it always comes crumbling down and is never worth the consequences."

Deborah took in Mary's demeanor, looking for a way to offer her something solid that she could take away from this conversation. "I also am a firm believer in reading my Bible every day, no matter what, and memorizing scripture. As a member of the Army of Angels, it's mandatory."

Deborah scanned Mary's face to read her reaction. When her face lit up, Deborah knew she had heard God correctly just moments before Mary had entered the garden.

"So, how about I give you one of my scriptures I turn to when I'm feeling beat up and bruised by the enemy, and one I turn to while in battle as well?"

Mary nodded, her eyes wide with anticipation.

"Okay, I often turn to Psalm 145:14, which says 'The Lord upholds all those who are falling and raises up all those who are bowed down.' You may feel defeated, as though God has abandoned you and the enemy has won, but that is exactly what Satan wants you to believe. But you need to know that every time you deny Satan and seek God's truth, no matter the circumstances, you defeat the enemy. We cannot allow our emotions to lead us, including fear! We must deny them, which is extremely difficult! But every time we do, we lift ourselves up a little closer to heaven. Our ultimate goal is to join God and all of our loved ones there, not stay trapped in this literal hell hole. We know from this scripture that God has promised to sustain us and raise us up."

Deborah paused for a moment before God put it in her heart to share one last thought with Mary.

"Another thing that helps me is knowing that sometimes I have to give God and his angels a little time. The enemy doesn't want us to receive what

God has intended for us, so he sends out his demons to fight God's angels who deliver his will to us. As you witnessed last night, Satan always sends multiple demons per angel. Although the angels are always victorious, they do have to put up a good fight, and that can take a little while, but our prayers and our ability to recite the scriptures helps fuel God's warriors. So if you ever find yourself in dire need of heavenly support, turn to the one thing that can defeat your foe: God and his Word."

Mary was engrossed with everything Deborah had to say. She felt such a desire to be part of the Army of Angels. She felt such peace and a sense of belonging when she was in their company.

Mary timidly voiced her request. "Deborah, do you think that maybe I could join your army?"

She looked Deborah straight in her eyes like her father had taught her to do when she was a shy young girl. She was afraid that Deborah would sense her fearful spirit and deny her, but she refused to allow her fear to paralyze her, so she followed her mother's advice and did it afraid. Her mother used to listen to Joyce Meyer, and was known to quote Joyce from time to time. One of those quotes that she often shared with Mary was, "Do it afraid." Mary thought to herself, "Well Mom, I listened to you, now let's see what happens."

Deborah smiled radiantly. "First of all, it's not my army. The Army of Angels is God's army. I am merely the earthly commander. God is the true commander-in-chief."

Deborah had to let out a little chuckle at what was, at least to her, a witty analogy. "Second, you are not accepted automatically. There are steps you must take. We have training requirements, and if you pass all your training, you will still have to declare your vows to God before the entire army at the initiation ceremony. Does this sound like something that might interest you?"

Mary could barely contain her excitement. "Yes, yes I am very much interested. Can I start today?"

Deborah paused for a moment. Then, after what seemed like an eternity to Mary, she delivered her decision.

"Yes, you may begin your training today. Your first assignment is simple, but it's not going to be easy. I want you to stay in constant communication with God. You are to start talking to him all the time, as if he were your best friend. I also give you the responsibility of praying vigilantly for your sister Martha and your uncle Noah. I sense they are having a harder time accepting their loss than you are. I am not implying that you loved your parents any less, just that you have found a new direction and have accepted God's plan a little sooner than they have. We need to pray for them. They are weak right now, and the enemy is well aware that this is an opportune time to pounce. He likes to hit us when we're down. So pray constantly for their souls and find scripture to proclaim the promises of God over them and yourself. God has honored you with a great task, and the enemy is privy to this information." Deborah looked Mary straight in the eye. "Do you accept these responsibilities?"

Mary nodded. "Yes! Oh, and Deborah, thank you."

She leaned over and placed a soft kiss on Deborah's cheek before she left to oversee the lunch preparations. She was secretly relieved. She had expected her training to involve learning how to fight with a sword. It seemed God was not going to test her faith that severely after all.

MARTHA

Martha tossed and turned under her covers. She couldn't help but notice how intensely bright the full moon was as it penetrated her bedroom windows. How in the world was Mary sleeping so peacefully?

Martha tried to fight off her feelings of jealousy, but she couldn't help it. Mary was an entirely different person since the Army of Angels arrived. Martha had not seen her sister so alive and focused since their mother's death.

Martha was in love with Luke and she didn't want to be with anyone else, but she still enjoyed the attention of other men. She needed the reassurance that she still had what it took to turn heads. She knew it was absolutely ridiculous, especially given the events that were taking place in the world around them, but she was still a girl, and she still wanted to know she had feminine charm.

Martha had always been the one to draw the boys' attention. Even though she and Mary were identical twins, there was something about Martha that made them take notice. Mary never really seemed to care much about that sort of thing. She had always delved into her studies, determined to follow in her Aunt Emma's footsteps. In fact, she too had been accepted to Harvard, but then the Rapture happened and Mary no longer wished to pursue that path. It was as if she knew her time here on earth was limited.

But now Tristan and Deborah's brother Matthew were staying with them, and all their attention was being showered on Mary. Even Rascal seemed annoyed by their constant presence at Mary's side. Martha knew she shouldn't be jealous of the attention Mary was getting, particularly since Mary seemed oblivious to their advances. It was as though she had been cast in the "friend" role for so long that she didn't see herself as anything else.

Martha stared out the window at the source of her insomnia. The dark beast that had perched itself high in a tree the previous night had returned. So far it had not attempted to enter the barn or the farmhouse, but Martha dared not close her eyes while it was still out there. She didn't want to fall asleep, only to wake up with the hideous monster standing over her, or worse.

She kept repeating, "Be still and know that I am God" to herself as she listened to her sister's rhythmic breathing. Eventually, her eyelids grew heavy and sleep found her, but it was nearly 4 a.m. before her body finally gave in to its desperate need for rest.

NOAH

Noah and the rest of the men took up residence in the barn while the women made themselves at home in the farmhouse. Noah hadn't slept out in the barn since the girls were in elementary school. He and Joel would camp out here with Mary and Martha every now and then during the summer. They stayed up late telling ghost stories and eating homemade desserts Anna had baked especially for the occasion.

Noah had hoped his faith in God would remain steadfast and strong, but once the moon rose overhead and everyone found their places for the night, the angry thoughts and feelings started to gnaw at him.

Why did God allow bad things to happen? His spirit-filled self knew the answer, but his human heart was wounded and bitter. Deborah was the only person other than his sister Anna to possess what he would call the spirit and heart of God's disciple John. Noah remembered his Sunday school teacher telling them that the other disciples always said that John was Jesus' favorite – or at least that was what he remembered.

Anna had been like John, and Deborah was like John, but Noah always found himself relating to Peter, whom Jesus was always correcting. It was so confusing to Noah. God's ways seemed so foreign and unnatural. Tonight was especially difficult. Noah had not been home since Anna died, and being back here rekindled all the anger inside him.

"God, please, I am begging you, please lift me up out of this pit," he prayed. "Place my feet on the path of righteousness and lead them directly to you. I need you now more than ever! Give me a sign. Let me know that you are here with me and that you have not forsaken or abandoned me. I can't feel your presence. Is my sin so great that you refuse to forgive me? I feel lost and alone. Save my soul, Jesus, please save my soul."

Noah must have stayed up half the night pleading with God to give him peace and joy in the midst of his suffering. His mind and body finally succumbed to its primal need for rest, but as he drifted off to sleep, rest would be the last thing he would encounter that night.

MARY

As Martha's emotional torment finally relinquished its control to her body's overriding need for sleep, Mary began to stir. Her peaceful spirit diminished as an ominous nightmare took over her dreams.

Mary saw her mother being escorted by two angels. It was unclear where they were headed or what their mission was, but as they traveled in the dark, massive emptiness of space, several menacing creatures attacked the trio. These hideous beings were far more terrifying than any of the soldiers who fought for the Army of Darkness, and they were increasing rapidly in strength and numbers.

To Mary's surprise, her mother knelt down suddenly between the two angels and began to pray with power and authority. Mary could not make out everything her mother was saying over the din of the battle, but she was almost certain she heard her mention the name "Michael." As Anna knelt there praying, not a single trace of fear emanated from her. In fact, she prayed with such fierce determination that the angels appeared to become stronger and swifter. In less than a minute, the most breathtakingly beautiful angel appeared next to them, causing many of the demonic forces to screech as if they were in tremendous pain and flee.

Pure fright caught Mary's breath when the vilest of Satan's beasts loomed out of the darkness. At that very moment, Mary's mother opened her eyes and spoke calmly to her, "Mary, pray."

Mary bolted up in bed, gasping for air. She wiped the perspiration from her brow with a trembling hand. Now wide awake, she still heard her mother's voice inside her head. "Pray!"

Panic shook Mary to her core as she realized this was more than a bad dream; it was some kind of supernatural reality. She jumped out of bed, grabbed her robe and hurried out of the house.

When she reached the bench in the middle of her mother's garden, she realized that she had run from the house without knowing where her feet were taking her.

She knelt on the dewy ground in front of the bench and prayed with every ounce of her being. Her dream was fresh in her mind. She found herself praying in a tongue she did not know, but the words flew out of her mouth as though she had spoken this foreign language her entire life.

A loud crack that sounded like thunder rumbled somewhere in the distance behind her. For a moment, fear entered her heart. She knew the foreboding, thunderous crack would fill the air moments before the beasts of hell were set free on Earth. Were the beasts on their way? Should she wake Deborah and the others? Mary's entire body shook uncontrollably when the still small voice repeated its instruction.

"Pray, pray without ceasing."

So that is precisely what Mary did. She closed her beautiful hazel eyes and refused to give in to the fear that threatened to overtake her. Instead, she prayed and allowed herself to trust God no matter what the outcome. When her phobia crept up, choking her trembling voice, she pushed it back by reminding herself of her favorite female role model in the Bible, Esther, and her real-life hero, her mother. Both had demonstrated the importance of answering God's call, no matter the cost. So she remained on her knees, uttering strange and unfamiliar words, refusing to turn and look behind her.

NOAH

Noah woke up soaked in sweat. His heart was racing and goose bumps covered his body. He shook his head as if he were trying to shake off what had just happened. He headed outside to see if some fresh air would help clear his mind.

Noah found himself walking along the babbling creek that led straight to their childhood treehouse. As he climbed through the trap door, he nearly lost his footing. The sight of Joshua sitting on one of the giant pillows his mother and Anna had made specifically for their fort startled him. He looked around, half expecting to find Rebekah with him, but Joshua was alone and seemed just as surprised to see Noah.

"What are you doing up here?" Noah asked.

Joshua shook his head. "The weirdest thing happened. I was sound asleep, lost in a wonderful dream, when I was jarred awake by what sounded like Anna's voice telling me I needed to pray. It was the oddest thing, but it wouldn't leave me alone, so I headed up here and started praying until just a few minutes ago. I don't even know what I was praying about, because I was praying in some foreign language. It was such a trip. To tell you the truth, I'm still a little confused by the whole thing." He paused. "So what brought you out here? Did you get the same message?"

Joshua gave Noah a hopeful look. If Noah had had the same bizarre experience, then Joshua wouldn't feel as though he were totally losing it.

"Nope. My trippy experience was awesome, but it left me thinking that I was hallucinating until you told me your story."

Joshua let out a chuckle. "Well then, by all means, please share with me."

Noah took a slow, deep breath. "I was sound asleep. I don't think I was even dreaming at that point, just sleeping, and then an explosive noise broke the silence and this magnificent light filled the space around me. I was alone in this healing glow when I heard Anna call my name. A moment later, she was standing at the foot of my bed. Three magnificent angels, who must have accompanied her, stood guard around us. One angel in particular was so impressive and mighty in stature that I kept finding myself staring at him. All fear left me while I was in his presence. He was extraordinary! Then Anna began to speak to me."

Noah noticed Joshua's eyes grow big as he leaned in, eager to hear what Anna had shared.

"Tears trickled down her face as she pleaded with me to hold tight to my faith in God. She told me that God has sent his angels here to protect us, but that it is crucial that we lean on God and remain steadfast."

Noah paused a moment, "But what took me by surprise was when she told me that God and his army need our help, that this is just the tip of the iceberg. We have not witnessed Satan's worst followers yet. Anna insisted that before this is over, the enemy will open the deepest and darkest doors of the lake of fire, and foul, menacing creatures will roam our lands day and night."

Joshua nervously ran his hands through his hair as Noah continued. "And according to Anna, these sadistic creatures will roam the Earth seeking to devour and consume the souls of both unbelievers and believers alike. No one will be safe from their wrath. She said that one has already entered our realm. He is here on a reconnaissance mission while he awaits his fellow companions."

"Holy crud!" Joshua exclaimed.

Noah nodded. "Exactly. On the bright side," Noah laughed uneasily, "she also said that the cliché was true and that she was in an amazing and awesome place. She told me to never fear death, for once you have been to heaven, you will never wish to return to this Sodom and Gomorrah. Anna also said how sorry she was that we have been left here to deal with all the sadistic and terrifying horrors that will soon be let loose upon us!"

Noah paused. His voice became husky with emotion as he continued. "She made me promise that I would not only keep myself strong in my faith but that I would watch over Martha and Mary, too. She said that God has crucial roles for us in his strategic plan and that he is counting on us."

Noah stopped himself, unsure if he wanted to share his sister's final words.

Joshua studied Noah's face. "What? What else did she say? I can tell you are holding something back."

Noah tried to think of something to say to squelch Joshua's curiosity, but finally relented to his best friend's inquisitive look. Joshua knew him too well, and he would see right through any fib Noah tried to tell anyway. "She also said that she approves of Deborah. What the heck? I have no idea what she was talking about."

Noah blushed, turning his head away from Joshua. "She begged me to let go of past pain, to let God heal my wounds so that I could open my heart to love again. She insisted that Emma's accident and the disease that took her mortal life were vicious schemes of the enemy designed to attack my faith. According to her, the enemy knew I would be a vital player for God and an integral part of his master plan, so Satan hit me below the belt, counting on it to ruin my faith and destroy my relationship with God.

"She also instructed me to form a group of prayer warriors from our followers. This war will not be won by our physical strength but by our spiritual strength. All will be tested severely, but we are to be like King David and constantly remind God of his promises he made to us by quoting his words from the Bible. She quoted Philippians 4:13, 'I have strength for all things in Christ who empowers me. I am ready for anything and equal to anything through him who infuses inner strength into me; I am self-sufficient in Christ's sufficiency.' "

Noah looked at Joshua, humbled by his past behavior toward him. "Dude, you have been my closest friend since I can remember. You have tolerated my very worst, and for that I am truly sorry. But right now I need your honest opinion. Am I losing it? Do I miss Emma and Anna so much that I'm creating these illusions in my head?"

Before Joshua had a chance to answer, a loud commotion in the distance caught their attention. They hurried down the tree and headed toward the farmhouse, from which the noise seemed to be coming.

Noah looked at Joshua and rolled his eyes as he took a deep sigh. "What now?" he uttered.

JOSHUA

As Joshua and Noah ran toward the farmhouse, they realized the uproar was actually coming from the gate at the entrance of the farm. As they approached the crowd, Rebekah joined them.

"A little late to the party, I see," she said with a smile.

Noah bit his lip. He could not miss the glimmer of attraction that danced in her eyes as she looked at Joshua. Joshua shot her a subtle look of caution. He did not wish to reignite Noah's anger. The two men were on speaking terms, but there was an underlying tension that had not completely subsided. Joshua didn't want to offend Rebekah, but he did not think it was wise to flaunt their feelings for each other right under Noah's nose.

Noah struggled to sound nonchalant. "What's up?" he asked her.

Rebekah rolled her eyes. "Politics," she scoffed before continuing. "Matthew discovered some strange man lurking around the perimeter of the farm. He claims he's running from Mainyu's men and is requesting to take refuge here with us. And, of course, we are divided. Some believe it's our duty to protect those who cannot protect themselves, while others believe it foolish to let just anyone enter our camp. Personally, there's something about him that doesn't sit well with my spirit, but Matthew has checked and he hasn't taken the mark."

Noah moved in closer so he could examine the stranger. He couldn't help but notice Jack's protective demeanor. The Great Pyrenees was standing next to Tristan, snarling and baring his fangs at the stranger.

Joshua nodded toward the man. "So, what do you think?"

Noah shook his head. "It doesn't feel right. One, he's not from here. If you are not from these parts, the chances of stumbling across the farm are extremely low." Joshua nodded in agreement. "Second, I am sure you have already seen Jack's response. In my opinion, dogs are a darn good judge of character." Noah smiled at his friend, remembering how Jack instantly took to Joshua.

Joshua narrowed his eyes. "I agree. It all seems a little shady to me. And did you notice all his fancy equipment? Tell me, if you were fleeing for your life, would you have time to pack up all your camping gear?"

Noah shook his head. "Nope."

Joshua pulled Noah away from the crowd. "Do you remember me saying that Persephone had mentioned having an agent they had sent out to locate the Army of Angels?"

Noah's eyes widened as the recollection of that conversation registered. Joshua stared at the stranger. "What are the chances he's their guy?"

MARY

Deborah purposely stayed back so she could observe the entire scene. She smiled as Danielle's familiar gait entered her peripheral vision. "It's about time. I was beginning to think maybe a bear had got ya," Deborah chided.

Danielle let out a soft laugh. "Not this time."

Deborah nodded toward the chaos. "So, what do you think of all this?"

Danielle shrugged her shoulders. "It's a little disappointing. They stand there arguing amongst themselves, but have they taken time to ask God's will? Humans... we are so quick to jump in and pronounce our thoughts and opinions. When will we learn to silence our tongue, and lift up our voices before God before making up our minds on matters we have so limited knowledge of?"

Deborah rolled her eyes. "Probably never."

Danielle nodded her head as she slowly walked to the front of the group. "Good morning. I see we have encountered a bit of a dilemma. I suggest that we have a civil, organized, formal meeting in the barn." She looked at the stranger. "My name is Danielle, and who might you be?"

Tension ebbed from the man's muscular body. Danielle saw his jaw relax as he answered. "My name is Caleb."

Danielle offered him a warm smile and gestured for him to lead the way. "Welcome, Caleb. After you. The barn is to your right."

Noah and Joshua ran up to Deborah, and Noah gently grabbed her by the arm. "Deborah, wait. We need to talk to you. It's important."

Noah breathed a sigh of relief when she stopped and gave them her full attention. "What's the problem?" she asked.

Noah cleared his throat. "There is so much I need to tell you, but some of it can wait. The most important thing is that we are almost certain this man is a spy for President Mainyu and Miller."

Deborah looked alarmed. "That is a pretty serious accusation. What evidence do you have to back up this claim?"

Joshua spoke up. "We don't have proof. But we both have been trained to read people, and our surroundings. The day I was nearly captured back at the White House, I overheard Mainyu and Miller speaking about an agent they had dispatched to locate the Army of Angels. His orders were to locate you, if you were even real, and if you did turn out to be more than just some Christian fairytale, he was to infiltrate your ranks and learn all there was to know about how you operate. This man did not just flee his home in a desperate attempt to outrun the enemy. Look at the clothes he is wearing, the gear he brought with him. He was prepared to be out here a while. None of the families who fled to the farm had time to pack all their camping equipment."

Noah jumped in. "And you know that Jack is an excellent judge of character, and he seriously dislikes this guy."

Deborah nodded in agreement. "Okay. You both have made some valid points, but let's see what Danielle has to say about him before we jump to conclusions."

As everyone found a place to sit and quieted down, Mary and Rascal quietly entered the barn. Tristan was sitting next to Noah, anxiously waiting for Mary, and he noticed that Caleb's eyes lit up when he saw her. Since Joshua and Rebekah had become an unspoken item, he had felt too much like a third wheel. But he didn't mind because it allowed him to spend more time with Mary. Before the Rapture, Tristan had been studying at MIT, so he found Mary's intelligence stimulating in more ways than one.

Tristan caught Caleb's attempt to hide his expression at the sight of Mary. He whispered under his breath. "That son of a ..."

Noah shot Tristan a quizzical look. "Who the heck are you talking about?" Noah was shocked by Tristan's behavior. He had never heard a foul word come from the young man's lips. Not that he was judging. He just didn't know what to make of it.

Tristan smiled at Mary. She and Rascal sat next to him as he leaned over and whispered in Noah's ear. "Caleb. I don't trust him. I didn't trust him before, but..." Tristan looked around the room to see if anyone was paying attention to them. "Just now, when Mary walked in, his eyes lit up like he just found a room full of hidden treasure. He's up to something, and the way he looked at Mary, well..."

Noah trusted Tristan and he believed his young traveling companion, but what he said didn't make sense. "What could he want with her? If he is who we think he is, he is after information on the Army of Angles, and possibly Joshua and myself. What would Mainyu and Miller want with Mary?"

Tristan shook his head. "Beats me. But I know what I saw."

Mary leaned over. "What are we whispering about?"

Noah and Tristan gave each other a quick look when Noah piped up. "We were discussing how we are going to run out of pigs soon if you keep fixing all that bacon with breakfast. I think you are trying to kill us off before the Army of Darkness has a chance to do it."

Mary looked at them sideways with a skeptical expression. "Whatever."

Noah looked up to see Deborah watching them closely. Her eyes traveled from Caleb to Mary and back to Caleb. Had she witnessed the same thing Tristan had?

Danielle's voice broke the silence. "I would like to give everybody who has something to say about our guest, Caleb, a chance to speak their mind."

Several warriors stood up, one after the other, expressing their opinion on the matter. Many claimed that the man was not to be trusted. Joshua stood up and shared his and Noah's take on the situation, but Noah was surprised when a few people argued that he should be allowed to stay. They claimed that it wasn't our position to judge the heart of a child of God, that judgment and punishment belonged to God and God alone. Noah couldn't believe what he was hearing.

But what shook him totally senseless was Martha's actions. She stood up and boldly spoke before the group. "We stand here and proclaim our faith in God, yet we contradict our words by acting in fear of this person. What can he do to us? If God is for us, then who can stand against us?"

Lucious rebutted. "Do not underestimate a conniving human. Our enemy uses humans to bring about his devastating schemes with one sole purpose, to destroy us." He looked around the room. "Are you really going to listen to this young, inexperienced girl who has not even stepped foot onto a battlefield?"

Danielle's voice rang out. "Enough. I have made a decision. Caleb will stay. He will train with Deborah and Noah."

A hushed sigh of disbelief filled the air. Noah looked at Deborah. Did they really expect him to train with a suspected spy? Noah saw a brief look of concern cross Deborah's face before a look of determination set in. First and foremost, she was a servant for her Father in Heaven. She would do what she was told to do, no matter what her personal feelings on the subject may be. Noah shook his head. "Great,." he muttered.

Tristan's brain was analyzing the situation. "This might not be a bad decision."

Noah shot him a death look. Tristan chuckled. "No, listen. If Danielle sets him free, who knows what he will do. Think about it. Keep your friends close and your enemies closer."

Noah still wasn't buying it.

"Dude, Danielle isn't an idiot," Tristan said. "She has strategically placed him with our commander, allowing her to keep a close eye on him. This also works in our favor. You too will be able to keep your eyes on the guy." Tristan gave Noah a wink.

Many people had started protesting Danielle's decision. She raised her hand to silence them. Danielle looked around at everyone in the room, including Noah. "We are here to bring God's lost sheep back into the fold so that they may enjoy eternal life with their Heavenly Father. God is not asking for your feelings on the matter. If you are not up for this calling, then step down now, but do so knowing that your very soul is at stake. You were not placed here to sit in judgment over others. God can handle that without any help from us, and our sins are no less painful for God to endure than those of his lost children. Sin is sin, my friends, and we are all full of it. So swallow your pride, because we are in the business of saving souls, not judging them."

Danielle's voice was solid and firm. Her eyes pierced the souls of every soldier who dared to meet her gaze.

"Not all of our soldiers are called to fight with a physical weapon in their hand, and those who are need our assistance." She gestured to Martha. "Please stand up."

Martha looked stunned, but stood before the group. "I am placing Martha in charge of training and organizing a group of prayer warriors. All those who are not able to fight on the battlefield will join Martha in sharpening your arsenal against our enemy. You will use scripture, song, and prayer to add strength to our soldiers, and glorify our Father in Heaven."

Martha spoke up. "But I am capable of fighting alongside the soldiers." She looked at Luke for support. "Ask Luke. I am strong and athletic." She nodded toward Mary. "My sister Mary, she would be perfect for this position."

Danielle offered Martha an apologetic smile. "I'm sorry if this decision troubles you, but I do not call the shots. This is where you are most needed."

Martha nodded and sat back down next to Luke. "What is she thinking? I am the one who stopped the stinkin' soldier before they even arrived. I'm not some wimpy little chick who's afraid to break a fingernail."

Luke rubbed her shoulder. "I had always envisioned us fighting side by side together. It will be weird being out there without you. But Danielle does not make this stuff up. You know she simply shares God's will with us. Maybe the prayer warriors are going to need someone who is capable of defending them. Who knows what he is thinking, but you can count on him having it all worked out for our benefit. Remember, his ways are not our ways."

Martha shot Luke a look. "Whatever."

As she sat, half-listening, Mary felt cheated and hurt. She missed her mother so much. Her heart ached continually since her mother's absence. So why hadn't her mother come to visit her, as she had Martha and Noah? Had she done something wrong? Was her mother disappointed in her for some reason?

Mary was lost in her thoughts until she noticed a figure standing before her. She looked up and realized it was Danielle. She was also surprised to discover that the room had emptied and they were alone.

"Oh, I'm sorry, I'll go join the others right away." Mary was ashamed that she had allowed her feelings to take her attention away from the task at hand.

Danielle shook her head. "No, I want a private moment with you." She settled down on a milking stool next to Mary. "I have a message for you."

Mary looked surprised. "Me?"

"Mm hmm." Danielle placed a slender hand on Mary's knee. "Do not allow the enemy to turn what was meant for good into something harmful."

Mary was befuddled. "Come again?"

Danielle offered a gentle smile. "Your mother loves you so much, and she is incredibly proud of the woman you have become."

Mary smiled, pushing back the tears welling in the corners of her eyes. "Well, circumstances would lead one to believe otherwise."

Danielle shook her head. "No, that is a lie planted in your mind by Satan. Your mother wanted so desperately to be able to visit with you, too, but time did not permit her that luxury. You saw the demons that the angels and your mother had to fight off so they could reach your uncle and your sister."

Mary nodded her head, but she was still feeling neglected.

Danielle continued. "You are stronger than you know. God's spirit resides in you, and he always sends strength to those who are in need of it. That is why your mother's spirit visited Martha and your uncle. God needed your strength and your faith to be proclaimed in your prayers so that your mother and the angels were able to come and hopefully renew their spirits. Without your prayers, and Joshua's, they would have been tied up in battle with the enemy, unable to spend time with the ones whose faith was shaken and weak. You were not neglected; you were needed. Does that help you to understand?"

Mary nodded. "Yes, that helps tremendously. Thank you so much!" Mary could not control her relief as she wrapped the prophetess a big hug.

To Mary's surprise, a robust and hearty laugh escaped Danielle.

"How I miss being surrounded by human contact. Thank you, Mary!"

Mary pulled back and looked at her, confused. "What do you mean? Are you saying you don't live a secluded life by choice?"

Danielle shook her head. "No, sweetheart. My calling requires it of me.

It allows me to hear from God and God alone."

Mary's heart sank for her new friend.

"Oh, sweet child, do not feel sorry for me. I accepted my calling. Remember, God always gives us free will. There are many blessings I receive because of my calling, but there are also sacrifices. Then again, we all have to make sacrifices for God."

Danielle's face turned somber as she lowered her voice. "Speaking of callings, I haven't told you what yours is."

Mary interrupted without thinking. "Oh, that's okay. I already know. I am called to be a prayer warrior."

Danielle gave her a serious look. "Well, that is correct, but that is not the full story..." Her voice was barely louder than a whisper as she proceeded to reveal Mary's full and complete calling.

Minutes later, Mary walked through the broad barn doors to find Deborah and report for training. Her face had lost all color, and she was fighting to wrap her mind around Danielle's words. She hoped and prayed with every fiber of her being that Danielle had heard God incorrectly.

PERSEPHONE MILLER

Persephone sauntered across the room in her silk negligee to the president's personal liquor cabinet. She retrieved two rocks glasses, added a couple pieces of ice, and poured two generous glasses of bourbon.

Mainyu looked up as she handed him a glass. "And what are we celebrating?"

Persephone seductively crawled onto his lap as she took a slow sip of her drink. She threw her head back, allowing her long blonde tresses to fall in a disheveled manner.

Mainyu had to admit to himself that she was pretty much irresistible like this. He pulled her down on top of him, gently kissing her neck, pleased with himself as he heard her moan softly. Their lips met as their desire for one another escalated. He bit the fullness of her lip, breaking the skin just enough to cause her to bleed slightly.

She sat up and retrieved an ice cube from his drink, placing it on her lip before she drew it down along her long, slender neck. Mainyu threw her on her back and hovered over her. "You haven't answered my question," he said. His voice was low and husky, alluding to his state of arousal.

Persephone gave him a sly smile. "Am I not enough? Are you implying that you need more?" she said with a sultry tone.

"Don't tease me, woman. I can tell when you are pleased with yourself, so why don't you share your little secret and let us both be pleased with you?"

She taunted him further. "I don't know. You have failed to mention what kind of reward I will receive for all my hard work."

Mainyu let out a low chuckle as he pressed himself firmly against her. "Don't you worry. I promise you will be fully compensated for your service."

"Well then, I guess I should tell you that I have received word from our agent," she paused for effect. When Angra raised his eyebrow, implying he was intrigued, she continued. "And it just so happens that he has been accepted as a soldier with the Army of the Angels."

Angra was annoyed. "So they really do exist."

Miller purred. "Yes, my darling, they do exist, and we have been deploying your forces against them for quite some time now."

He looked surprised. "I wasn't aware of this."

She smiled at him yearningly. "No, there was no need to bore you with such trivial matters, but now we have confirmation that Agent Hansen and his reporter friend are aligned with these rebels."

Mainyu pushed himself off of her. "I don't see how this is supposed to please me."

She slowly began to run her delicate fingers across his chest. "Oh darling, don't you see? We not only have the Army of Angels, but we have our two fugitives as well. Our agent is in the process of discovering their secrets so we can use their tricks against them. And I happen to have something else up my sleeve I think you will be very pleased to hear about," she purred.

Mainyu rolled the ice around in his drink. "I'm listening."

Our master has assigned me with the task of finding a certain female he requires to win this nasty little war," she said. "And guess what?"

Mainyu shrugged his broad shoulders. "I don't know, why don't you tell me?"

She sat up and began to trace the tip of her tongue down his ear. As she reached his earlobe, she wrapped her lips around it and gently scraped it with her teeth, knowing full well the effect it had over him.

"Our agent has located her as well. It seems that everything we have been searching for has been hiding out on a little farm in the middle of nowhere."

When he didn't respond, Persephone pulled away. "What is it? I thought you would be pleased," she pouted, pursing her full red lips together.

"Why wasn't I informed about this woman? And what does he need her for?"

Persephone shrugged, bored with all the talking. She reached over and swallowed the rest of her bourbon. She sighed before responding.

"How am I supposed to know why he didn't tell you? He probably assumed you wouldn't be interested. And as far as what he plans to do with her, well, he hasn't shared any of those details with me. All I know is that he supposedly has struck some kind of deal with the man upstairs. He appeared quite confident and pleased with himself."

She was still pouting as she slowly lowered the straps of her negligee. "I'm bored. Are we going to drone on about some frightful little girl, or are things going to get interesting?"

Angra laughed. "I suppose I do owe you some kind of compensation."

DEBORAH

Since Caleb's arrival, the camp had been divided. Those who were opposed to his presence followed Danielle's order, but the tension was so thick you could cut it with a knife. Before Danielle had left to occupy an abandoned cabin in the woods behind the farmhouse, Deborah had pulled her aside.

"You do know that the chances of this guy being a spy for Mainyu are exceptionally high, right?"

Danielle nodded her head. "I'm almost certain that he's some kind of a spy. He appears extremely interested in Mary. You need to keep a close eye on her."

Deborah stared in bewilderment at Danielle. "Then I don't get it. Why are we allowing him to live, let alone spy on us?

Danielle shrugged. "Good question. I wish I knew." Deborah could see the apprehension in her friend's eyes.

"Deborah, things are going to get real hairy, real soon. It will feel as though the tides are turning in Satan's favor, but we cannot lose faith in God, or his plan. Remember, things are not always as they appear." Deborah nodded at Danielle. "We have to step up our game. I need you to push our people. Double their training time, and we have to bump up the initiation ceremony, too."

Deborah's eyes widened. "How? With the enemy out there, we can't train once it gets dark."

Danielle smiled at her. "You'll find a way. You always do." The prophetess gave her friend a quick hug before she returned to her life of isolation. She cast her eyes up to heaven. "Hey God, you there? I could use a little company."

Deborah turned to gather her soldiers when she heard a ruckus on the other side of the house. She ran to see what was going on, rolling her eyes in exasperation and sending up a quick prayer. "God give me strength."

Tristan had Caleb pinned up against the side of the barn, his hands clenched around his neck. As she approached, she could hear Tristan threatening the newcomer. "If you dare lay a finger on her, so help me God..."

Matthew jumped in, trying to diffuse the situation. "Tristan, just take a deep breath. I detest Danielle's decision as much as you do, but remember, she's not speaking for herself. She is speaking for God."

Jack stood at Caleb's feet, baring his teeth at the man. Tristan shot Matthew a look of contempt. "Stuff it, choir boy. This man is a spy. How many of us will die because of him? And considering your affection for Mary, I'm surprised you didn't notice the way he reacted when he first laid eyes on her. It was like a dog drooling over a bone, but not for the obvious reasons a man would drool over a woman. No."

Tristan cinched his grip as he stared into the man's eyes. "No, you have some malicious intent for her, and I for one will not allow you to fulfill that threat."

Deborah's voice was low and firm. "Enough!"

Her words silenced Tristan, but they were not enough to get him to loosen his grip. Deborah walked over to the young man. "Release him," she demanded.

Tristan looked at her skeptically. "Whose team are you really on?"

Deborah shook her head. "Don't go there, Tristan. Have you ever wondered why God would allow this man to join our ranks?" Deborah's eyes narrowed as she looked at Caleb.

Tristan shook his head. Deborah nodded. "Exactly. This is his fight, his war, his children he is trying to save. We are merely instruments. The moment we take matters into our own hands is the moment we bring all hell upon us. You are not God, so do not presume to think that you know more than he does."

Tristan was not convinced. "So I should just let him go? And what happens if I do? What happens to Mary? Don't you care about her?"

Deborah let out a deep sigh. "You know darn well I do." She tried to reel in her anger. "But you also know that when we fight for him, we are not guaranteed our lives here will not be spared. He guarantees us eternity in heaven. Matthew 16:25 tells us, 'For whoever wishes to save his life will lose it; but whoever loses his life for My sake will find it.' "

Deborah shot Caleb a look of disdain, then looked back at Tristan. "Do not let the enemy steal that from you. You can pass this test. You are stronger than this."

Tristan's hands were shaking as he loosened his grasp from Caleb, who bent over gasping for air. Deborah leaned in close to Caleb. Lowering her voice, she warned him, "You may feel pleased with yourself right now, but no matter what you do to us, if you follow the path of destruction and folly, you will never escape the Lake of Fire."

Caleb snarled back at her. "What do you know? You and your pretty little friend out there all alone in the forest are a joke. You are certain of my intentions, yet you spared me. Your weakness will cost you this war."

Deborah scoffed. "What you call our weakness is what God calls obedience, and even if you take our lives, you will not take away our reward – his gift of eternity."

She turned and walked away, but paused and turned back at him. "Oh, and about your question, 'what do I know?' Well, I know that Miller purposely kept you from taking the mark so you could infiltrate our forces."

Caleb was caught off guard, but quickly composed himself. "So?"

Deborah gave him a smirk. "So, you still have a choice."

NOAH

The sun had long set behind the majestic pines that surrounded the farm. The moonless sky was set ablaze with countless stars. Noah marveled at how close they appeared. It felt as though he could reach up and grab a handful of them.

Even if he could manage such a feat, he didn't think they could make the farm appear any more magical. The property had a whimsical sensation that lifted his spirits. It was as if he had stepped into an old fairytale his grandmother used to read to him and his sisters.

Delicate lights hung just overhead, and freshly picked flowers decorated various displays. The women in the group had done a phenomenal job of creating a mystical environment that, for at least a moment, made everyone forget about the dire times they were facing.

Tonight marked a significant and life-changing event. After what seemed like an eternity, but which was in reality only a couple weeks of training and studying, Noah and the rest of the newcomers were about to be initiated into the Army of Angels. Deep down, Noah knew that their lives were about to change forever.

Danielle stood next to one of the angels that had descended from its heavenly realm to guard and protect God's earthly soldiers. Her senses happily soaked up the intoxicating sights and aromas. It filled her heart with joy to see this band of strangers come together and form a strong community – well, with the exception of one. Even though Caleb had chosen to partake in the initiation process, the rest of the group still distrusted his motives.

Danielle's heart grew heavy as she thought about the trials that lay ahead of them, when she heard the Holy Spirit reminding her that there is a time and a place for everything and that tonight was a time of celebration and joy, not sorrow. "Hmm, you are so right, God," she prayed quietly. "And it is time for the ceremony and the celebrating to begin."

Danielle raised the largest bell from the local church's bell choir high above her head and brought it down three times. The deep sound rang across the yard, signaling the commencement of the ceremony.

As everyone gathered, Noah was impressed with what he saw. The entire group looked stunning, dressed all in white. Over the past few days, several members had snuck into town and looted several abandoned homes in order to bring back enough apparel to clothe the new members in white, just like every other warrior had done before them.

Noah had been one of the members chosen for the mission, along with Joshua, Martha, and Luke. Lucious and a couple of the other veteran soldiers had accompanied them, while Deborah and Rebekah stayed behind at the farm to watch over Mary.

Noah turned to find Mary. As his eyes fell upon her, a smile crossed his face. Mary looked breathtakingly beautiful. She was a spitting image of her mother Anna, but the part that amused Noah was the fact that she was flanked by her two most loyal companions. Rascal and Tristan appeared to be in some sort of competition for her affection. Even young Matthew had been vying for her attention, but true to her nature, Mary was oblivious to their affection for her.

As Noah looked around for Martha, he saw Deborah standing underneath the arbor where so many of his family members had stood while taking their wedding vows. Noah's heartbeat quickened as he took in the sight of her. He couldn't help but notice that the white dress she wore fit her a little too well. "Darn that woman," he thought to himself. There was something about her that was so infuriating.

His attention was brought back to the present as he and the rest of the initiates formed a crescent shape in front of the arbor. Deborah's voice floated through the air like a gentle song, as all who were present recited with her.

"Blessed are the poor in spirit, for theirs is the kingdom of heaven! Blessed and enviably happy are those who mourn, for they shall be comforted! Blessed are the meek, for they shall inherit the earth! Blessed and fortunate and happy and spiritually prosperous are those who hunger and thirst for righteousness, for they shall be completely satisfied! Blessed are the merciful, for they shall obtain mercy! Blessed are the pure in heart, for they shall see God! Blessed are the makers and maintainers of peace, for they shall be called sons of God! Blessed and happy and enviably fortunate and spiritually prosperous are those who are persecuted for righteousness' sake, for theirs is the kingdom of heaven! Blessed are you when people revile you and persecute you and say all kinds of evil things against you falsely on my account. Be glad and supremely joyful, for your reward in heaven is great, for in this same way people persecuted the prophets who were before you."

A sense of alarm ran through Noah's entire body as he caught Caleb staring at Danielle as he recited the last sentence. Caleb's action did not go unnoticed by the prophetess, but to Noah's surprise she simply returned his steady gaze with a beautiful and peaceful smile.

"You are the salt of the earth, but if salt has lost its taste, how can its saltiness be restored? It is not good for anything any longer but to be thrown out and trodden underfoot by men. You are the light of the world. A city set on a hill cannot be hidden. Nor do men light a lamp and put it under a peck measure, but on a lamp stand, and it gives light to all in the house. Let your light so shine before men that they may see your moral excellence and your praiseworthy, noble, and good deeds and recognize and honor and praise and glorify your Father who is in heaven."

As the voices of all who were present finished proclaiming this scripture, Noah looked around him. He was not surprised to see that many initiates as well as veteran soldiers had tears in their eyes. The ceremony moved its participants through a gamut of emotions.

Deborah spoke directly to the initiates. "I must now speak to you about the power of living in agreement. Our company pales in comparison to the uncountable legions of demonic forces Satan has at his disposal. However, these forces are no match for the holy power that stands alongside us. We do not fight as men and women of the flesh; rather we fight with the power of God and his multitude of angels at our sides."

Deborah's eyes fell on Caleb. "Our strength builds as we stand in agreement and put the needs of our fellow human beings, whether they are believers or not, above ourselves. If we attempt to lift ourselves up, we will surely fall and fall hard, but if we allow God to lift us up in his timing, his glory will be magnified forever. As a soldier for Christ and his army, whether you fight with sword, hammer, or the Word of God in prayer, you have forfeited your will and your life to him. You no longer belong to yourself, but vow to honor God in all that you say and do. We are called to 'live in harmony with one another; not to be haughty but readily adjust ourselves to others and give ourselves to humble tasks. Never overestimate yourself or be wise in your own conceits.' So says Romans 12:16. I cannot stress this enough. We all put our faith and trust in each other. We are a team."

Deborah's attention subtly turned to Martha, causing her to blush. "No one is exulted or lifted up above another! We are all equal in his sight. Although we rely on each other, our ultimate and complete faith is in our Heavenly Father, for without him our efforts are futile and we would all perish. This road is not an easy one. All of human-kind is under siege, and the enemy seeks to steal as many souls as possible at any cost. He is deceptive and a master at what he does. Be alert at all times. He loves to play mind games with us. I pray for your eternal souls. Our earthly existence is fleeting, but his promises stand for all eternity!"

Danielle raised the bell above her head and rang it once, signaling the beginning of their vows. The new members knelt before the senior members.

"My soul, wait only upon God and silently submit to him," Deborah and her fellow soldiers boldly proclaimed, "for my hope and expectation are from him. He only is my Rock and my Salvation; he is my Defense and my Fortress, I shall not be moved. With God rests my salvation and my glory; he is my Rock of unyielding strength and impenetrable hardness, and my refuge is in God! Trust in, lean on, rely on, and have confidence in him at all times, you people; pour out your hearts before him. God is a refuge for us, Selah!"

A deep silence filled the night sky. The presence of the Holy Spirit penetrated the grounds as a profound reverence exuded from the souls of all who were present.

"What say you, initiates?" Deborah and the soldiers asked, their voices stern.

The initiates rose simultaneously. Noah stood tall among them. Mary and Martha flanked him, with Joshua, Luke, and Tristan proudly alongside them. In his wildest dreams Noah had never imagined such a moment. He found himself desperately wanting to fully believe the words that Deborah and the others spoke in regards to God, but there was that nagging voice of doubt he had yet to control. He privately envied his fellow initiates. Their faith seemed to return to them so easily – well, everyone but Caleb. Noah never would understand Danielle's decision when it came to him. It was obvious to all of them that he was a bald-faced hypocrite, a wolf not even attempting to wear sheep's clothing.

Noah shuddered as he recalled Deborah's words to both Noah and Caleb during their last training session together. "I am giving both of you full warning. If you know that in your heart you do not believe in the teachings of God's Word, I implore you to refrain from taking part in the initiation ceremony! God's Word is very clear on this matter. Hebrews 10:26 clearly cautions us of what will happen. It states, 'For if we go on sinning deliberately after receiving the knowledge of the truth, there no longer remains a sacrifice for sins.' Christ's blood can no longer redeem you."

Noah sent up a quick prayer. "Please God, keep me strong. My faith is weak. I desperately want to believe, but I am constantly plagued with doubt. My anger and my tongue continually get the best of me. I don't understand why you would pick someone like me to serve you. Do not let me fail you. I pray that you will strengthen me so my thoughts, actions, and words will bring you glory."

The silence was broken as the initiates' voices resonated through the night air. "'God, you are my God, earnestly will I seek you; my inner self thirsts for you, my flesh longs and is faint for you, in a dry and weary land where no water is. So I have looked upon you in the sanctuary to see your power and your glory. Because your loving kindness is better than life, my lips shall praise you. So will I bless you while I live; I will lift up my hands in your name. My whole being shall be satisfied as with marrow and fatness; and my mouth shall praise you with joyful lips when I remember you upon my bed and meditate on you in the night watches. For you have been my help, and in the shadow of your wings will I rejoice. My whole being follows hard after you and clings closely to you; your right hand upholds me. But those who seek and demand my life to ruin and destroy it shall go into the lower parts of the earth. They shall be given over to the power of the sword; they shall be prey for foxes and jackals. But the king shall rejoice in God; everyone who swears by him shall glory, for the mouths of those who speak lies shall be stopped.' As Jesus is our Savior we so vow that our lives are solely devoted to him to do with as he so chooses to bring about his victorious plan. May our service to him bring honor and glory to his name. So help us, God, to remain true and steadfast to your will no matter the cost. In Jesus' name, Amen!"

Then Danielle spoke. "Initiates, each one of you has a torch with your initials on it. Take the wick from your personal training soldier and find your torch. As you stand before it, wait until all members have located their positions. When I instruct you to do so, speak the following words in unison: 'So it will be done on Earth as it is in heaven.' Then you will light your torches together."

Noah took his lighted candle from Deborah, who still maintained a reverent posture, and then found his torch. As he waited silently for the other initiates to locate their torches, an unexplainable sense of peace washed over him. He felt lightheaded and euphoric. Then Danielle's gentle voice echoed around him.

"Now you may proclaim your faith to your Heavenly Father and let this torch be a symbol of your ever-burning light that is to shine upon the earth for all to see and witness the glory of our almighty and powerful God."

The multitude of voices rose to heaven. Seconds later, a whoosh of light filled the night sky. As the fire danced about, causing glorious shadows to play across the land, Danielle spoke one last time.

"We welcome you as honored brothers and sisters into the holy and mighty Army of Angels. May your service bring honor and glory to God."

With Danielle's last words signaling the end of the initiation ceremony, a thunderous sound of rejoicing erupted throughout the congregation. Smiles and laughter emanated from all. Noah was smothered immediately as Mary and Martha squashed him with giant bear hugs from both sides.

Mary looked up at her uncle with adoring eyes. "Thank you for being our strength. God is using you in a mighty way to lead us and comfort us."

Martha was crying so hard that all she could manage was a nod of agreement and a "Ditto!"

Noah thought about the absurdity of the moment – that even though they had all lost so much, he had never been happier. He chuckled.

"Now listen to me, Thing One and Thing Two." These had been his nicknames for them since birth. "I have needed you more than you will ever know." Noah looked over toward Caleb, and his face hardened. "And I promise I will do everything in my power to protect the two of you."

As Deborah approached them to offer her congratulations, she couldn't help but overhear their conversation. She warmly gave Noah a look of caution. Feeling as though he had just been scolded, he sheepishly added, "God willing."

Noah was astounded by the transformation both Martha and Mary had demonstrated over the past few weeks. It flooded him with feelings of happiness and concern. He worried about the consequences that that kind of faith could bring upon them. The enemy was not going to permit their contagious convictions to go unchecked.

He knew Deborah had taught him that fear and worry are a sin, but how was he supposed to control his feelings? They just showed up unannounced and uninvited. He remembered Deborah telling him to cast his fears and worries at the foot of the cross so that God could deal with them. His job was to hand his concerns over to the big guy upstairs, trusting him to work out everything for the good of all. Easier said than done; at least that was how it was for Noah.

Mary and Martha ran off to join Luke, Tristan, and Matthew. Noah headed over toward Deborah, who was busy laughing with Danielle and Rebekah at something Joshua and Lucious had said, when he saw Caleb out of the corner of his eye. He was off in a corner by himself, obviously feeling rejected.

That was when Noah heard a small voice prompting him to go over and talk with Caleb. "Oh, no, not me, Noah silently argued. "Why can't you have someone else do it?" He rolled his eyes as Hebrews 10:26 popped into his mind, reminding him of the consequences of deliberate sin.

"Not fair. Fine... I'll do it," he grumbled to himself.

As Noah approached, Caleb scoffed. "What are you doing? Believe me, I don't need your pity. Especially from someone like you."

Noah was taken aback. "What is that supposed to mean?"

"Oh, please. You know darn well that you don't belong here. You are as tainted, hard-hearted, and bitter as I am."

Noah nodded. "You're right. This doesn't come easy to me. My human nature messes me up all the time, but it doesn't mean that I am not worthy. It just means God has to work a little harder," he said with a laugh.

Caleb looked at Noah. "So, you are trying to tell me that you are buying into all of this malarkey?"

Noah took a deep breath. "All I know is that I have seen what happens to those who take the mark, and I don't want anything to do with it. Is the world spinning out of control? You bet. Am I scared? Absolutely. But from the looks of things, we have two choices. The middle ground has disappeared. You are either on Team God or Team Satan. The world as we knew it has vanished and it has been replaced by a lot of bizarre and crazy sh-."

Noah winced at his word choice. He sent up a silent apology to heaven. "Sorry, God."

Caleb shook his head. "You guys are doomed. I know what is coming, and you guys don't stand a chance."

Noah felt a wave of panic travel through him, but then something unfamiliar took over.

"This world is passing away. I am not fighting for my existence, I am fighting for my soul's survival." Noah looked the spy up and down. "Tell me this, why are you still here? You know our secrets, and you have already relayed your findings to Mainyu."

Noah saw Caleb shoot him a quizzical look. Noah smiled at the outcast. "So why stay here? Why not take Satan's mark and join his ranks?"

Caleb remained silent, looking off in the distance. Just as Noah turned to walk away, he heard the stranger's voice. "Because my work here is not finished."

DANIELLE

Danielle had thoroughly enjoyed this enchanted evening with those she had come to care for deeply in such a short amount of time. Facing the end of the world can do that to a person. Danielle longed for things to stay just as they were at this very moment, but the ebb and flow of life could not be stopped.

It was going to be very difficult to pull herself away and return to the empty cabin, alone in the wilderness. It was not merely the loneliness, but the fact that she knew what God's plans entailed for her in the very near future that made it extremely distressing.

God had shared with her in vivid detail that first his survivors must walk through the darkness in order to conquer Satan's hold on mankind, so that God could bring them into the light of salvation.

The enemy repeatedly tortured the poor souls who rightfully belonged to their Heavenly Father by tricking them into returning to the misery of death instead of living the life of freedom that Christ had purchased so painfully for them on the cross.

Danielle called a final meeting in the barn. She sat on a couple of hay bales so all could see and hear her. She used what might possibly be her last opportunity to prepare them mentally and spiritually for the unthinkable trials that lay ahead. Words would not be sufficient, but with the help of the Holy Spirit, she would do her best to imprint the magnitude of what was lurking just around the corner. She would leave specific names and details out, including her own fate. She wanted to prepare them, not scare them to death – a challenging feat.

She looked out over the group, committing every face to memory before she cleared her throat to speak. "I must leave you now, but I want to thank you for the wonderful memories. I have enjoyed every moment that I have had with you."

Her gaze settled on Caleb. "All of you. It is with a very heavy heart that I say goodbye. I must leave to face the trials and tribulations that God has chosen for me. I will not lie to you. I would love for my cup to be taken from me, but deep down in my heart I yearn to see my Heavenly Father face-to-face one day. And when I do, I want to be able to hear him speak the words, 'Well done, my true and faithful servant. Welcome home.' So I choose to confront whatever burdens he has chosen for me."

Danielle paused to regain her composure before she continued. "I have the affliction of knowing what I must face. The rest of you, with the exception of one, will face your trials blindly. But do not fool yourselves into thinking your task will be light. All of us will confront evil and be tested by this dark force. If any of you are still struggling with your faith, I beg you to renounce your doubt and return to him before it's too late. The enemy is approaching. His hour has come. Mankind has turned its back on God! We have cruelly and arrogantly rejected our Father. But God is loving and steadfast, and he is offering every soul left on Earth another chance to return to him."

This time her gaze fell on Lucious. He rolled his eyes in response. "He loves us, and God disciplines those he loves. Think of our human parents. They would neither take the time nor have the emotional investment to discipline a child they did not love. So it is with our Heavenly Father. We are now facing the consequences for our reckless and disrespectful behavior."

She paused for a moment, once again praying that God would continue to speak to his children through her. "I implore you to stand tall and firm in the promises of Abba, and answer his call to you. This is his last call. I beg you to sit and read Isaiah Chapter 5 together. We cannot run from the wretchedness that is coming for us, but we can remain steadfast in God's Word. Remember your vows. You are elite and mighty soldiers in God's army. Do not fall prey to deception. Stay the course. Our time here is short. I pray that I will see all of you again! You are my dear friends. Until then, I leave you with much love."

She purposely let her eyes connect with Mary's, knowing that Mary would have to endure the most grueling and challenging fate of anyone. Both women gained an abundance of encouragement and strength from their brief connection before Danielle turned from her fellow believers and strode toward what awaited her in the wilderness.

The worst part of knowing what was coming was not knowing the exact timing of it. She took a deep breath and inhaled the comfort of God's spirit that had filled the barn. Her voice was barely audible, though no one was there to overhear her.

"Abba, give me strength and calm my nerves. Yea, though I walk through the valley of death, I will fear no evil for thou art with me! Don't leave me, Lord! Your word promises that you are with me. I am holding you to that one! Please keep my feet firmly on your path of righteousness so that I can finish my race and be there for Mary when her time arrives."

Then a disturbing thought came to Danielle that she had not considered. "What if Mary meets her fate before I meet mine?" Danielle shook her head. No, that didn't make sense. The timing would be off. God had already shared the sequence of events with her. The enemy was already on his game, trying to get inside her head and weaken her resolve and faith in God's plan.

"Heavenly Father, strengthen me..."

MARTHA

As Danielle spoke to the congregation, Martha couldn't help but notice the slight tremble in Mary's hands. Martha began to wonder if Mary was the exception that Danielle referred to in regards to knowing what fate lay ahead.

Martha had discerned that as her sister's faith grew, so did her courage. Seeing Mary's subtle sign of fear piqued her concern. Now that she thought about it, she had noticed that Deborah or one of the other elder members of the group had constantly been by her sister's side for quite some time now. Did they know something she didn't?

Once again, she found herself questioning Danielle's decision to place her in charge of the prayer warriors. Unlike Mary, Martha had always been the calm, cool, collected one who had been blessed with nerves of steel – which was precisely why she should be wielding a physical weapon, especially if Mary's life was in danger. How was she supposed to protect her armed with nothing but a bunch of words?

Martha stopped herself. "Get out of my head, Satan! I am a child of God, redeemed by Jesus' blood that he shed on the cross for my sins. You have no authority over me. In the name of Jesus Christ my lord and savior, I demand you to leave me alone!"

Martha's thoughts drifted back to her mother's visit. She remembered how beautiful her mother looked, and the angel she called Michael. His presence was overwhelming, and the sword he carried had to have been forged in heaven by their Creator.

But what really stuck with Martha were the words her mother had spoken to her. "I beg you to accept the role for which you have been chosen. You have been asked to step out of your comfort zone so that you will learn two very important lessons. One, that there is power in the name

154

of Jesus. Two, that your strength does not come from your human abilities, but rather is a gift from God. He has blessed you with superior athletic talents, but those talents cannot defeat our enemy. Events are about to take place that the human mind cannot comprehend. Lives are at stake, and the only true weapon designed and capable of achieving victory over the master of the underworld is in your Bible. You have excelled in your physical training; now it is time to work a different muscle group. I implore you to build up your spiritual arsenal. Many lives are depending on it. Without it, there will be no victory."

Her mother paused, leaning over and kissing Martha's cheek. "Stay true to your faith. Do not waver! I will be watching over you and your sister." A tear rolled down her mother's face. "I must say goodbye now. Your father and I will be waiting for you and your sister on the other side."

Martha wrapped her arms around her slender torso, remembering her mother's gentle embrace before she vanished back to her heavenly realm. She took Mary's hands in hers and silently spoke with God. "Okay, if this is your plan, then I am all in! I will praise you without ceasing, no matter what sort of terrifying chaos is surrounding me."

As the meeting ended and Danielle was turning to leave, Martha noticed a split-second connection between the prophetess and Mary. She also noticed that in that moment, Mary's hands steadied and her breathing settled.

"Thank you, God," Martha prayed. "I don't know what this is all about, but you do and you are seated on the throne and you are in control! You rock! I don't know what my sister faces, but I do know that as long as I still have breath and my mind is still functioning, I will be praying for her. I will not let her down!"

Martha looked up to see Caleb watching them from across the barn. She shuddered as an ominous sensation traveled through her, causing chills to run down her spine. Mary's gaze settled on the suspicious stranger.

Mary turned to her sister. She spoke under her breath, causing Martha to lean in close to hear her. "Marty, I need your prayers. I need them big time! I don't know if I have the courage to face what God has asked me to do. It is imperative that I succeed, but I'm scared to death! I can't do this without your help."

Martha heard the tremors of fear in Mary's voice, and a sense of alarm seized her as she watched her sister's flushed face turn white and her lips take on a bluish hue. She knew that Mary would have revealed her trial to her if she could, so she didn't even bother to question her about the details. Instead, she asked Mary to make a list of exactly what she needed her to pray about. Martha would carry that list next to her heart.

"Okay, Satan, if you think I am going to let you take out my sister without the fight of your life, you are sadly mistaken! You are going to have to go through me and the entire Army of Angels. So take that, you low-life snake!"

Martha squeezed Mary's small, delicate hand. "Don't you worry about what that swindling blow-hard has up his sleeve. Do you hear me?"

Mary nodded.

"You belong to God! God will take this punk and make mince-meat out of him. You have the Army of Angels, Mom and Dad in heaven, Uncle Noah, and, of course, yours truly on your side. If God is for you, then who can be against you? He has your back. No matter what, don't you dare forget that. Promise me?"

Mary couldn't help but chuckle. "Yeah, I promise. And you need to promise me that you will watch your back. If you think the devil is going to let you weaken his forces through scripture so that our warriors can annihilate his army without trying to kill you, you're naïve. He'll do everything he can to strip you of that power. Remember, you wield the only weapon capable of defeating Satan and his Army of Darkness."

In truth, Mary was more than concerned for her sister. She knew all too well how powerful the Word of God was against Satan, and she knew he would try to silence Martha. Mary wasn't sure what was worse – knowing what lay in store for her, or not knowing what was coming down the pike for her sister. At least she could attempt to prepare herself, but how was Martha supposed to prepare herself? But then, that was part of the plan, wasn't it? It caused both of them to place their trust in God.

NOAH

A deep, somber feeling filled the barn when Danielle departed. It was an eerie sensation that caused Noah to feel unsettled and nauseated. He looked up at Deborah, who had been sitting on one of the hay bales near Danielle. She motioned for him to join her. He wondered what was running through her mind. It was difficult to read her expression.

Deborah looked up at him. "I believe that you are meant to read this passage to the congregation. Will you?"

Noah nodded.

Deborah smiled up at him as she rose to her feet. She stood perfectly still, not saying a word as she scanned the members of their group, bringing the hum of conversation to a halt.

"I believe it is vital that we follow Danielle's advice," she said. "Therefore, I have asked Noah to read Isaiah Chapter 5 to us, and he has graciously agreed."

She handed Noah the Bible. It was already open to the passage. Noah nodded and then read the scripture. The solemn feeling lingered, and his voice was low and somber.

After Noah finished reading the passage with all of the "woes," he felt sick to his stomach. The chapter was written to God's chosen people centuries earlier, but how telling it was. The similarities between the Jews of Isaiah's time and the people and the events of modern day were more than uncanny. Why did we continue to repeat the sins of our fathers? Even after Jesus sacrificed his life on the cross for our sins, we continue to nail him back up there through our inability to rise above our flesh.

As Noah stood there with the taste of bile in his mouth, he heard Deborah's voice ring out strong.

"Yes, human-kind has not risen above its sinful disposition since the

157

time of Isaiah. However, we must stand strong in the fact that we have Jesus Christ on our side. He has conquered the cross, and by the blood he shed on the cross for us, he has saved us from our sins and an eternity in hell. Our time has come. We must take a stand. Take up your cross and follow Jesus' example. Your works will not save you, for all have fallen short of the glory of God, but your faith will conquer the grave. It will conquer the call the enemy has placed on your soul."

A smile emerged on Deborah's radiant face. She chose her words carefully, wishing to lift the dour spirits of everyone in the barn. "Your faith in your Heavenly Father has purchased you a one-way ticket to paradise. Do not lose your boarding pass. Saint Peter stands at the gates of heaven, and he has your name on his list. You have made it to the VIP section. The enemy wants to deny you entry."

She paused as a slight chuckle rippled through the crowd. Then her face grew serious.

"By nightfall, we will dance with Satan's forces. He is a serpent who lies in wait, ready to strike at our heels. He strikes when our backs are turned, and where we lack defense. We must protect ourselves and gird ourselves with the Armor of God. We must prepare ourselves for a battle like no other. The deepest cells of Sheol have been unleashed. No matter what transpires, do not lose hope and faith in your Almighty Father in Heaven! In all circumstances, you must trust in the Lord. By nightfall, you shall assume your posts and stand your ground. May God be with you and bless you!"

MARTHA

Martha and her band of prayer warriors were just inside the hedge of protection that she and Danielle had put in place the night before. The two of them had wandered around the farm for what seemed like hours, searching for the right location, until Danielle reached out and grabbed Martha's hand.

Martha's heart quickened as she realized that Danielle was confirming the deep sense of knowing that she had just experienced. Yes! This was the spot. The two women laughed with a sense of reassurance. The location was smack dab in the middle of the pond.

The twins' great-grandfather had insisted on building an oversized gazebo on the small island that rose above the surrounding water in the center of the enormous pond. It had been a favorite spot for childhood adventures.

Martha reflected on the numerous escapades she and Mary had conjured up with their wild and vivid imaginations over the years. Her favorite was when they pretended they were princesses hiding in a remote castle in order to protect them from the evil neighboring king who wished to smite them so he could become ruler of their kingdom. The water that surrounded the castle was a moat that contained dangerous beasts and magical spells of protection. Oh, to be young and innocent again!

Martha could not help but discern the eerie similarities between their make-believe world and the supernatural reality of their current existence. Only this time Mary would not be securely hidden away with her. Martha fought to push back the feeling of dread that accompanied that last detail.

The last prayer warrior was just climbing out of the small dinghy they used to get to the island when the commotion started. The night had been peaceful and calm until they heard the warning sound of a conch shell being blown.

Tristan and Luke ran to grab their binoculars. They had been chosen by Danielle and trained by Matthew to keep a watch over Martha and her circle of warriors. They were assigned to be the eyes and ears of the group, freeing the others to be able to focus on their duties. Martha was thankful God had provided Danielle with such forethought.

She promptly took her position on a folded blanket. It was one of many that formed a large circle on the ground. Martha lifted her face to heaven, and the other warriors followed her lead.

Luke stood next to Martha as he relayed what he saw taking place across the pond. His voice was steady, but there was no denying the anxious undertones. "Our soldiers are emerging from all directions, and it appears they are convening in the barn."

Tristan and Luke kept their eyes peeled for any sign of the enemy. Nerves escalated as they waited for further news. Was this simply a drill, a false alarm, or had the vile creatures crawled out of the Lake of Fire, finally reaching the farm's perimeter?

The suspense was unbearable. Martha fought to focus on her conversation with God as the harrowing silence warred for her attention. It was vitally important that she and her fellow warriors remain alert and focused. Satan was trying to divert their attention from their prayers.

Luke's voice finally broke the silence. "The soldiers are exiting the barn now." There was a slight pause as Luke's voice caught in his throat.

Tristan spoke up, his voice ominous. Our soldiers are all armed. They are carrying a variety of weapons besides their swords. A soldier is heading across the farm toward us, but I can't make out who it is..."

Tristan left the group and walked closer to the island's edge to get a better look. He shouted back toward the others. "I believe it's Matthew. From what I can see, it appears as though the majority of our soldiers are leaving the property, but it looks like Deborah has left a small unit behind with us."

When Matthew reached the edge of the pond, Luke sent the boat back to retrieve him. Martha waited anxiously for him to reach the island. Her heart pounded in her chest. It seemed to take forever for Matthew to cross the water. He did not bother to get out of the dinghy.

She looked back at her warriors. "Hold your positions. Continue to pray. I will be right back."

Martha went to Matthew. It was only then that she noticed his wounds. His face was cut, and he wore a blood-soaked bandage around his left arm. Martha's breathing quickened. This was the first time that the heavens had allowed a soldier of the Army of Angels to be harmed.

"So, Danielle's prophecy was being fulfilled. Wonderful!" she thought to herself. And this time her uncle and her twin sister would be among the soldiers fighting the demonic forces that, until now, had been locked away in the darkest, deepest parts of hell.

Luke placed a reassuring hand on her shoulder as a shudder crept down her spine. Luke's presence comforted her. His loving gesture reminded her of her mother's visit. She recalled how peaceful and alive her mother had been. She had promised Martha that life here was nothing compared to the wonders of heaven. What did she have to fear? Death? Well, maybe for a moment as her spirit felt the pain of her human shell suffering, but then it would be set free, free to travel to its true destination. She almost welcomed death when she thought about what awaited her on the other side. But she knew she feared being left behind without her loved ones more than she feared death.

Matthew wore a grim expression, and his deep, raspy voice spoke with the authority of one who had witnessed the terror firsthand. "You and your warriors must raise your petitions up to our Holy Father now! Do not delay. Every soul on this earth needs your prayers and intercessions. You must unleash the legions of heavenly forces before it is too late. Do not cease praying until either our soldiers come home, or the world comes to an end. The greatest evil ever to exist now walks among us! Satan's forces will soon have us surrounded. We need the entirety of God's forces here on earth. Without them we are sure to perish. The Army of Angels is headed to Knoxville. Pray that they make it there in time, for it is under siege as we speak. The believers who live there are putting up a fierce and courageous effort, but without the power of your prayers and the reinforcement of our army, they will not last long."

Matthew's voice had been shaky and weak. He paused for a moment. The fight had drained him of his strength, and yet, rather than being consumed with his own well-being, Matthew was here pleading for the souls of others.

Martha was deeply concerned for him. "What happened to you?" she asked.

"As I was heading back to camp to inform my sister of what I had learned, a savage beast ambushed me from behind. He had been hiding high up in a tall pine tree. God's heavenly hosts must be in the middle of a fierce battle because it took longer than usual for my guardian angel to join me. It took the two of us fighting together to defeat the beast. My angel accompanied me for the remainder of my journey back to the farm. She is standing guard just outside the gate… If my angel hadn't arrived when she did, I would have died."

Matthew lifted the paddles, ready to return to the farm. Martha held out her hand. "Wait, let us heal your wound."

Matthew smiled. "Thanks, but Mary has already promised to do so as soon as I return to the farmhouse."

Tristan felt a rush of jealousy surge through him. Martha was caught off guard by Matthew's mention of her sister. "Wait, what? Isn't Mary with Deborah and the rest of the soldiers?"

Matthew shook his head. "No, Deborah insisted that she stay back with the unit that is assigned to protect you."

Martha was silent for a moment as she tried to collect her thoughts. "But then shouldn't she be here with us on the island? She shouldn't be left all alone, unprotected." Martha felt a sense of panic rise up in her.

"No, Danielle warned her against it. The likelihood of the Army of Darkness coming to attack you and your warriors is extremely high. Without your prayers interceding on our behalf, we are defenseless, and Satan is well aware of that. You, my dear friend, wear the largest target on your back of any warrior left on Earth. If he can take you out, he takes us all out!"

Martha's face turned white as the truth of his words sank in.

Matthew smiled at her. "Don't worry. The Holy Spirit led you and Danielle here to this very spot. The enemy will try to penetrate God's defenses, but God will not be defeated. You are in capable hands."

Martha was caught up in her human way of thinking. "If that were the case, then this would be the perfect place for Mary."

"One would think so, but Deborah had her orders. You know how this stuff works. It's almost like the more you feel like you are in the dark, surrounded by decisions and events that don't make sense, well, that's when you know you're working in his will."

Matthew gave Martha a quick hug as best he could with his wounded shoulder and then departed across the water. Luke and Tristan used a rope to pull the dinghy back onto the island after Matthew hopped out. He gave them a wave before he turned and ran off.

Martha turned to rejoin her fellow warriors when she saw the concerned expression on Tristan's face. She and Luke had witnessed the growing attraction that had blossomed between her sister and their new friend. They had also watched Matthew's pain as he clumsily tried to conceal his feelings for Mary. The only one who seemed to be oblivious to his attraction to her was Mary herself.

Luke attempted to alleviate Tristan's stress. "Hey, don't worry, man. God has her back. He's not going to let the enemy harm her. Have a little faith."

Tristan shot Luke a look. Luke nodded. "Okay, a lot of faith. But we all need your A game, including Mary. Don't let him get in your head."

Tristan nodded. "You're right. I got your back." He was determined to stay focused, even if he couldn't shake off the uneasy feeling that gnawed at him.

NOAH

Noah was one of the soldiers Deborah had chosen to accompany her to Knoxville. He felt a slight sense of guilt at his hidden pleasure that Rebekah was staying behind to help protect the farm. He missed Joshua's company. Between all the time they spent training and the time Joshua spent with Rebekah, Noah didn't get to spend as much time with him as he once did.

Noah had been spending a lot of time with Lucious. The two of them spent hours discussing the "good old days" when Lucious had played for the Chicago Bears. Many people compared his athletic style to that of Walter Payton.

Noah remembered Lucious' response when he had asked him how it felt to be compared to such a revered legend like Payton. Lucious had shaken his head. "Man, you just don't know how much pressure that puts on someone. I know I had been blessed athletically, but I was never able to come close to matching Walter's personal character. He was 'Sweetness,' ya know? There was a reason people loved and admired him, even if they hated the Bears."

Noah related to his new friend. They both had excelled at what they did career-wise, but had the tendency to see their success as something they had accomplished rather than a gift from God. Each of them had to continually wrestle with their ego to keep it in check.

Noah's nerves were tingling. He tried to not think about the fact that this was going to be his and Joshua's first battle with the Army of Darkness. Since the company had to travel by foot through rough terrain to avoid Mainyu's patrolling soldiers, Noah worried that they might not make it there in time. He wasn't anxious to go toe-to-toe with the dark soldiers, but at the same time he didn't want to walk up on a bunch of innocent dead bodies.

Deborah was leading them at an even pace. He knew her well enough to realize she did not want her soldiers exhausted before they arrived at their destination. If that were the case, they wouldn't be any good to anyone. The path had been slippery as they scaled down steep hillsides, which was more perilous to Noah than when they had to hump over steep hills. He was more balanced trudging up a hill then he was trying to keep his footing on the uneven vertical slopes.

Noah wondered if the other soldiers were also reciting their favorite scriptures for battle.

"God, please keep my spirit calm and my mind at peace so that your word remains at the tip of my tongue, ready to be shouted out to all the earth. Please do not let me seize up in terror!"

That was the last thing he needed, even though Deborah had reassured the unseasoned soldiers that if this happened, they were not to panic. Martha and the rest of the prayer warriors were praying fervently on their behalf. So even if they froze up and forgot to pray or recite scripture, prayers were being sent up to heaven for them.

Noah's thoughts were interrupted as they reached the summit of the hill they had been climbing and a shallow gasp escaped from many of his fellow soldiers. The city below them was ablaze. Dead bodies were scattered about the empty streets, and in the center, a horrific and terrifying battle was taking place.

Deborah motioned for her soldiers to duck down out of sight. All remained silent as she worked her way over to a tall tree nearby. Within seconds, she was perched on a branch so she could get a better look at the gruesome sight below. Noah looked up at her even though he knew what he would see. Deborah sat gracefully on a thick limb with her eyes closed and her soft lips barely moving.

Suddenly, Noah was overtaken with the urge to pray for her. He asked God to give her wisdom, discernment, and favor. Lost in his conversation with the Almighty, he failed to notice the despicable beast that had silently approached his flank. A rancid stench filled his nostrils, causing him to look up. At that very instant, Deborah called for an attack.

Noah lost his balance and fell onto his back. The blood-stained demon raised his axe over his head. It was as though everything was happening in slow motion. Noah heard scriptures being shouted all around him and steel ripping into flesh. He scrambled to his feet as words flew from his lips.

"Hear my prayer, O Lord, and let my cry come to you. Hide not your face from me in the day when I am in distress! Incline your ear to me; in the day when I call, answer me speedily. The Lord will protect him and keep him alive; he shall be called blessed in the land; and you will not deliver him to the will of his enemies."

The enemy took his shot, but missed as Noah rolled. The blow was close, chopping a few hairs from Noah's head, but he was in one piece. Praise God!

Now standing firmly on his feet, Noah executed the moves Deborah had spent hours teaching him. He watched as the gnarly being stumbled backwards, but before Noah could breathe in relief, the demon was swinging his weapon at him as if nothing had happened. It was such a blur that it seemed as though the demonic creature had six arms, each holding a weapon of some sort.

"Okay, Lord, here we go. 'The Lord lives! Blessed be my Rock; and let the God of my salvation be exalted. The God who avenges me and subdues peoples under me. Who delivers me from my enemies; yes, you lift me above those who rise up against me; you deliver me from the man of violence. Therefore will I give thanks and extol you, O Lord, among the nations, and sing praises to your name. Great deliverances and triumphs gives he to his king; and he shows mercy and steadfast love to his anointed, to David and his offspring forever.'"

Noah wasn't sure how long he had been swinging and stabbing at Satan's soldier before he realized that a glorious, bright being was fighting alongside him. Noah was in such awe of the angel that he almost lost his concentration. It took everything in him not to stop and take in the splendor of the heavenly warrior. The sharp thud of a hatchet that narrowly missed Noah's foot jolted him back to the present danger that consumed him.

"Hey, God, do me a favor and don't let me do that anymore, okay?"

Noah's heart was beating so hard that he was concerned he might have a heart attack. He was tired and a little unsteady on his feet, but he fought on.

"As for God, his way is perfect! The word of the Lord is tested and tried; he is a shield to all those who take refuge and put their trust in him."

That was it. With that final scripture, his foe was defeated by a mighty blow from the angel. The demon's head went tumbling down the steep slope, and its body collapsed in a noxious heap.

Noah turned around to evaluate how the battle was going for his comrades. To his relief, the last few remaining demons met their deaths and all of his fellow warriors remained standing. This had not been the way Deborah had intended to join the battle of Knoxville, but blood-splattered and fatigued would be the way they would descend upon the prevailing fight below.

Their commander gathered the company and the angels formed a defensive circle around them as Deborah led them in their battle cry. Their voices shouted to the heavens. "Be strong, courageous, and firm; fear not nor be in terror before them, for it is the Lord your God who goes with you; he will not fail you or forsake you."

Noah was astonished to find how refreshed and invigorated he felt after he and his fellow men and women had all come into agreement and prayed together. It seemed that there was strength in numbers when it came to prayer, too. He felt encouraged as the light that radiated from the angels grew brighter with every word they spoke. Now that they were spiritually rejuvenated, the next step was to face the Army of Darkness, which awaited them with bloody fangs and claws.

Noah raised his eyes toward heaven, "Wonderful," he uttered. "Well, God, at least you didn't make me suffer through a boring and uneventful life."

MARTHA

The night was pitch black, typical of a new moon. Martha felt as though a swarm of butterflies had been set loose in her stomach. Evil always seemed to come in droves during the new moon, and although she couldn't put her finger on it, Martha had an awful feeling that something of grave importance was about to happen.

It was the same nauseating and foreboding sensation that had overtaken her the night her mother had died. She had an unshakable feeling that something dark and evil was lurking around the corner. She felt its terrifying presence somewhere in the shadows. She found herself on edge, not knowing exactly when it would strike. It was waiting for the opportune time to make its move.

The fact that her uncle and several of the other soldiers she had come to care about were miles away facing their own set of demons didn't help. She didn't agree with the decision to divide their forces. To her, there was safety in numbers.

Luke had notified Martha when Rebekah had relieved Mary of her watch, which should have offered her a sense of comfort. But relief was the last thing she was feeling tonight. Something told her they needed to take their praise and worship to a whole new level.

Martha rallied her warriors. "We need to dwell completely in the presence of the Lord! It is imperative that his Holy Spirit abides in us, lifting up all who fight for him!"

Martha glanced around the island. A sigh escaped her lips as she took in the sight of the heavenly hosts standing guard, prepared to defend their human comrades to the death. Martha nodded to their worship leader. He nodded back and immediately began to lead their worship team in praise.

As their voices sang out, "Holy, holy, holy," an indescribable peace fell upon God's servants. A collective gasp filled the air as the warriors looked over their heads. They were awestruck by the vision of two magnificent creatures descending onto the roof of the gazebo. Martha immediately recalled her Uncle Noah reading about them when he read a section of the book of Isaiah to everyone in the barn. They were the seraphim.

They too were signing. "Holy, holy, holy is the Lord; the whole earth is filled with his glory!"

Martha knew without a doubt that something huge was about to go down. Why else would God send such heavenly creatures to earth?

NOAH

Noah was surprised and a little shocked to discover that Deborah was not leading them directly into battle. Instead, she had them hold their ground on the hilltop. She ordered them to stay low and to pray harder than they had ever prayed before. Then Deborah returned to her post up in the tree. Noah was confused by her decision, but he trusted her and knew there had to be a good reason why she was not marching them into combat.

He took the opportunity to pray for himself, his loved ones, and his fellow soldiers, but he found himself unable to concentrate due to the hushed voices he heard in the distance. His senses were on high alert. No one knew exactly where the enemy was. They could be hiding anywhere, and Noah was determined not to allow his foe to sneak up on him again. He turned and followed the disturbance, only to find Lucious engaged in a heated argument with Deborah.

Noah told himself to stay put. He knew Deborah was more than capable of commanding the company and that she didn't need him sticking his nose in, but his flesh got the better of him.

As he came up on them, he overheard Lucious whisper. "What are you waiting for? This is ridiculous!"

Deborah's response was controlled. "I understand how this must seem to you. You are a soldier, and you want to do what soldiers do best – fight. But as your commander, I must seek God's plan and implement it. We cannot win this fight, let alone this war, without him. You know this, so why are you questioning my decision to wait?"

"Because it's stupid. Just like the decision to allow Caleb to remain with us, gathering intelligence to use against us."

Noah saw Deborah take a deep breath. Her expression implied she was thinking, "Please, not this again." Lucious had been adamant about voicing

169

what many of the others felt but did not have the courage to say.

Lucious continued to argue with their commander. "The longer we wait, the more lives we lose and the stronger the enemy becomes. Why are you stalling? What are you afraid of? We can take them. We have never lost a fight!"

Deborah paused for a moment, gaining her composure before she responded to Lucious' attack on her leadership. "Precisely. We have never lost because we have never made a move without listening to his direction first. He leads us!"

Noah felt a wave of guilt wash over him as he admitted to himself that he had wondered the same thing as Lucious. Noah turned to survey their surroundings when Joshua shot him a quizzical look. Noah held up his finger to gesture he would be back in a minute.

Noah knew that Deborah only moved when God instructed her to do so, and if he was telling her to hold their position, then that is exactly what she was going to do. Stepping out from underneath God's umbrella of protection, taking the road that seemingly made sense, over his direction, would only place her soldiers and those they were fighting to protect in jeopardy. She had fought against Satan too long to fall for one of his traps.

Deborah's voice was patient but weary. "Lucious, you know how this works. You know the tactics our enemy uses against us. Please, I urge you to stop and pray about it. You are a formidable soldier, but without God you will be defeated."

Lucious scoffed at her words.

Deborah continued to reason with him. "God has a purpose. Everything he does is to bring about his plan. There are forces at work beyond our comprehension, things we cannot see with our own eyes. Trust in his timing. He is never too early or too late; he is always right on time."

A gentle smile crossed her face as she gave Lucious' hand a firm squeeze. Lucious turned and noticed Noah in the shadows. He shrugged off her attempts to comfort him and marched off toward the other members of the group, making much more noise than Noah would have liked. Deborah turned her attention to Noah.

Noah fumbled for words. "Oh, uh... well... I just wanted to make sure you were all right," he blushed.

Deborah turned to climb up the tree. She gave him a nod that appeared to be an invitation to join her. Noah turned and looked around behind him, wondering if her gesture was intended for someone else. Joshua had been observing everything that was taking place. He smiled at Noah, nodding for him to follow her.

"Not this again," he thought to himself. Climbing trees was not his specialty, and looking like a lumbering oaf in front of everyone wasn't at the top of his list, but... why not?

Once he had maneuvered himself onto a limb next to her, she turned and looked at him. "What is your take on my conversation with Lucious, which you obviously overheard?"

Noah looked at her sheepishly. He probably should have backed off and given them some privacy. Too late now.

"Um, well, I respect your decision, but I would be lying if I said I didn't understand Lucious' position as well. It's not that easy to just shut off your human brain and learn to look at things from a spiritual aspect. I'm not saying he is right. I'm just saying I get where he's coming from."

Noah was taken by surprise when she smiled at him, nearly allowing herself to laugh out loud. "I find your honesty charming... well, most of the time," she quietly chuckled under her breath. "It's one of the reasons I have grown to kinda, well, maybe … like you."

Noah's eyes widened. He thought she found him completely offensive. "Really?" he asked.

There was a playful twinkle in her eye. "Well, at the least I have learned to tolerate you."

For a brief moment, reality seemed to slip away and Noah found himself yearning to kiss her. "Where the heck did that come from?" he asked himself.

Deborah's face took on a serious countenance. "What do you think about Lucious' abilities as a soldier?"

Noah felt as though this was a trick question. From his experience, women loved to ambush men with trick questions. He gave Deborah a skeptical look.

"I think Lucious has the most natural talent out of all of us when it comes to combat. His agility, speed, and power surpass the rest of us, but..."

Noah hesitated, not sure if he wanted to continue. Deborah had taught him that there was great folly in judging others, and besides, he didn't wish to speak ill of his friend. Lucious was a great guy. Then he remembered her comment just a minute ago about appreciating his honesty.

"I am hesitant to answer because I do not wish to judge, but I will admit that I am a little concerned for him."

Deborah nodded. "How so?"

Noah took a deep breath. "Because he has a tendency to rely on his natural abilities. He was plucked out of the flock at a very young age because he stood out from the rest of us. Coaches and trainers took his raw talent and turned him into a fine-tuned machine. He was a beast on the football field, and society worshiped him because of it. We are probably just as much to blame for his ego as Satan is. We helped turn him into what he is now. Let me correct myself. What he was before he met you. God used you to soften him up a bit. He was pretty cocky when he was America's top fantasy football player."

The timing of their conversation seemed strange. It was timely considering what had just transpired between Deborah and Lucious, but it just felt odd considering their circumstances. Noah couldn't resist the temptation to ask.

"So do you know why God wants us to stay put? Do you have a clue what's going on?"

Deborah looked him straight in the eye. "Not a darn clue. I'm trying my hardest to just accept it. It is personally killing me to sit up here while all those innocent people are down there battling for their lives. I don't know, maybe he is waiting on our prayer warriors, or maybe the enemy is occupying the angels and heavenly forces that God is trying to send down to us, so he needs us to wait. If we go charging in there before they are capable of joining us, we're dead meat."

Noah's eyes widened as he nodded. What she said made perfect sense. He had noticed that it took them longer than usual to defeat the group of monsters they had just encountered. Her words had also reminded him of his nieces back at the farm. He hated having to be separated from them.

"Can I ask you why you left Mary behind? Martha I understand. She must stay with her prayer warriors, and they would be vulnerable traveling out here in the open with us. But why Mary?"

Deborah shook her head. "I wish I knew, I really do. Before Danielle left, she forewarned me about this battle. She informed me of exactly who was to join me out here, and who was to stay behind on the farm. To be honest, I understood her decision to leave Mary behind, but I am just as bewildered as the rest of you as to why she insisted that Caleb remain under Rebekah's command."

Caleb's presence had continued to put Noah on edge, especially after the latest incident involving the suspicious newcomer. Matthew had caught him sneaking back into camp a few nights ago all by himself. Caleb claimed that he thought he had seen a fellow soldier venturing out past the protected borders of the farm and went to investigate. Of course, he had refused to tell them who it was he had seen sneaking out of camp in the middle of the night. He claimed that it was too dark to tell exactly who it was.

Noah tried to calm his fragile nerves. He reminded himself that Deborah had left Rebekah in command of the farm, and even though he still wasn't keen on the idea of Joshua being in a relationship with her, he had to admit that she was one mighty warrior.

Out of nowhere, Deborah grabbed his arm, nearly causing him to slip off his branch. Deborah spoke quickly. "Sorry, I didn't mean to frighten you, but God has just given us the go-ahead. We must hurry!"

Deborah beat Noah to the ground. No surprise there, but what was surprising and a tad distressing was the fact that all around them stood a multitude of God's elite angels. Noah did not fail to notice that their weapons were drawn.

MARY

Mary took a long, deep breath before slowly exhaling. She knew she was a child of the one true God, but she was still human and her mixed feelings were tearing her apart. She stood tall with her sword held firmly in both hands. She was alert and ready, but her flesh was screaming. Rebekah stood beside her, never taking her eyes away from the dark vastness that enveloped the land beyond the gate.

Matthew's angel stood guard over them. The angel's grim expression left Mary with an eerie feeling. The angel's presence wasn't much comfort; in fact, it actually made Mary more apprehensive than she already was. She wondered if the angel saw or sensed something in the distance that their human eyes failed to see.

Mary bit the inside of her lip in an attempt to fight back the tears that threatened to escape as she watched her uncle disappear into the darkness without her. When she joined the Army of Angels, she had envisioned herself fighting alongside him and Martha. She couldn't help but wonder if her uncle was following her parents' footsteps into heaven, leaving her and Marty behind.

Speaking of Martha, Mary was thankful that she hadn't been separated from her sister. She couldn't imagine leaving Martha alone on the farm. Granted, she really wasn't alone. Rebekah and several other warriors remained behind. Mary knew Deborah wasn't a fool. She knew it was inevitable that Satan's foul creatures would attack the island.

Events were mounting. It wouldn't be long before this spiritual war climaxed, forcing God to open the gates of heaven so that fire and brimstone would rain down upon the earth. She made herself draw in another slow, deep breath in a vain attempt to calm her nerves.

She felt Rebekah place a reassuring arm around her. She whispered in

Mary's ear. "Don't worry, little sparrow, your uncle is in good hands."

Mary knew that Deborah would do everything in her power to bring her uncle and every other soldier under her command home alive, but she also knew what the others did not. She knew what was still to come. Danielle had not spared her from the truth. Mary knew as soon as she saw Matthew's arm that the rules of the game had already changed.

Rebekah spoke to her. "I have been instructed to assign you first watch."

Rebekah walked beside Mary, waiting until they had passed through the gate and were back on the farm before she leaned in close to Mary, whispering in her ear where she should take up her post. Mary nodded her understanding and headed off in that direction.

She hurried across the yard, staying in the shadows as much as possible. Rascal and Jack clung to her side. Her heart beat faster as she realized her chances of running into the enemy were probably greater in the shadows than out in the open, but it was too late now. She paused for a minute beneath the tree and peered across the pond, hoping to make eye contact with her sister, but Martha's eyes were closed as she prayed.

Mary fought the wave of envy brewing inside her as she watched Luke standing over Martha. Mary noticed that Tristan had been watching her, and it made her blush. She remembered how his lips tasted like pecan pie the first time he had kissed her. It had been so magical.

After they had been sworn in as official members of the Army of Angels, Tristan had invited her to take a walk with him. They had wandered into her mother's garden, talking about their favorite childhood memories, when out of nowhere he had pulled her close to him. She felt his strong muscles brush up against her before his lips met hers. His kiss had been gentle, yet hungry. For the first time in her life, Mary felt emotions stir in her that she had never felt before. She would give anything to be by his side right now.

Mary's spirits had been squashed when she found she would not be joining Martha, Luke, and Tristan on the island. Deborah had insisted that Danielle's orders were to keep Mary away from the center of the fighting. If what the prophetess had told her was true, then it didn't seem to matter where she was – unless Danielle's orders were given in an attempt to keep the others safe.

Mary climbed the ladder and crawled into the treehouse. As she took the binoculars out of their case and began focusing them, her thoughts drifted back to cherished childhood memories. She longed for those carefree days.

Looking through the binoculars, she carefully surveyed the premises, doing a double take near the front gate. "Oh, duh, that would be Matthew's angel," she said to herself.

For a quick second, the faint glow in the distance had caused her heart to skip a beat. Mary scoured the rest of the property before returning full circle to the island, which was supposed to be her focal point.

Time passed slowly, and Mary was fighting to stay awake. Everything had been quiet and rather boring for quite some time when Martha and the rest of the prayer warriors started shouting up to the heavens with a fierce intensity. This was not a good sign. Mary decided she should probably send a few words up to God, too.

It was not long before the mood shifted, as a wonderful presence crept from the center of the island and out over the rest of the farm. There was no denying that the Holy Spirit had descended from heaven and was graciously calming every soul it touched. To her delight, Mary watched as prayer warriors rose and sang praises unto the Lord. Many of them, including Martha, danced with joy. Their faces shone like a full moon, filling Mary's heart with hope and peace.

Her breath caught in her throat as stunning beings illuminated the night with their heavenly radiance and positioned themselves around the island. Reverence spread across the entire farm. Mary found herself joining in as she lifted up her praises to God. She was pretty sure she heard other voices singing out in the distance. Rascal and Jack were sitting at the foot of the tree rooing, as if they were joining in.

Mary scanned the horizon for any sign of trouble while soaking up the uplifting presence of the Holy Spirit. When she rounded back to the island, she couldn't believe her eyes. She lowered the binoculars, rubbed her eyes, and then steeled herself as she raised the binoculars once again.

"Holy crud!"

On top of the gazebo were two breathtakingly beautiful yet frightful creatures. They beamed with the light of heaven as they sang.

"Holy, holy, holy;
Holy is the Lord;
the whole earth is filled with his glory!"

As Mary listened to these heavenly beings, she remembered her uncle reading about them in the book of Isaiah. She could no longer fool herself into believing that this brutal collision between heaven and hell would pass, especially now that God was sending down the big guns.

That was a good thing. Yet, for her ... it wasn't.

JOSHUA

Deborah led the way through the dense foliage, attempting to stay in the shadows. Her weapon was drawn, ready to engage the enemy, with Joshua and other soldiers following her example. The mood was intense as the Army of Angels sped across the terrain with stealth and precision, which was easier said than done. One of the new recruits learned this the hard way when he accidentally stepped on a brittle twig. The sound echoed in the darkness as if a grenade had gone off.

Everyone froze. Joshua held his breath, listening for any sign of Satan's soldiers. Somehow the angels had turned off their brilliant glow so the company could navigate through the terrain without being seen and ambushed.

Joshua's nerves were rattled when he heard the faint call of an owl in the distance. The Army of Angels used the sound of a hooting owl to signal their commander's order to retreat. He couldn't help but wonder if this call was being made by God's creation, or if it was a deceptive call from their enemy.

Deborah signaled for the soldiers to move forward, but Joshua could not shake the eerie sensation that pulsed through him. Every few seconds, he found himself turning around to make sure they weren't being followed.

As they approached the streets of Knoxville, Joshua turned around for what felt like the hundredth time. Only now he was certain that he saw the shadow of a dark figure run past. He was about to alert the others but decided it would probably be prudent to hold off in case it was just his imagination playing tricks on him. Instead, he walked backwards, unable to divert his eyes from the potential threat behind them.

Oblivious to the fact that Deborah had motioned for the company to halt and duck down, Joshua nearly toppled over Noah. At that moment, he was positive he saw another shadow. The enemy was out there, and from what Joshua could gather, they were attempting to surround them.

Joshua gripped his weapon tighter while simultaneously alerting the others. He cried out like a falcon, the army's distress signal. Instantly, his fellow soldiers positioned themselves in a fighting stance. Joshua was blinded as the angels once again glowed with ethereal power. The effect stunned the enemy, allowing the Army of Angels to get a jump on them.

Before Joshua had a chance to blink, he heard his comrades reciting scripture verses, which resulted in a reinforcement of heavenly warriors appearing in their midst. Joshua was alarmed by the silence to his left. Noah was fighting ferociously on his right, and the array of voices that were lifting up the Word of God danced around him, except for one location. Lucious remained silent. He stood before a demon unaccompanied by his guardian angel.

Joshua tried not to be distracted by what was happening to Lucious, but he couldn't hold back the ominous feeling. At that moment, Lucious stumbled backward as the demonic beast ripped a deep laceration in his thigh, cutting him to the bone. Lucious screamed in pain, and Joshua wanted desperately to come to his aid, but the foul creature he was fighting was unrelenting. It took everything Joshua had to keep the demon from overtaking him, even with the power of scripture assisting him. If Joshua turned to help Lucious, they would both be in the same position, and it wouldn't do their comrades any good to have two men down. So Joshua used the best weapon he had: He began to pray for Lucious' soul.

From his peripheral vision, Joshua saw the sadistic, demonic soldier from hell raise its crude weapon high above its head, preparing to bring the blade down on Lucious' skull.

Although Deborah was engaged in her own battle on the opposite side of the field, she was intuitively aware of Lucious' dire situation. True to form, Deborah also fought for Lucious' soul through the power of prayer.

Joshua heard her conversing with God in an unfamiliar tongue in what he assumed to be divine intercession for her friend and fellow soldier. Joshua felt a sense of relief rush over him when he heard the silent warrior's husky voice over the clashing of steel mixed with the aggressive reciting of scripture, and the vile demonic words that spewed from Satan's beasts.

"God, please, I beg of you, please forgive my arrogance. I am nothing without you! All that I am and all that I possess is because of you! Show mercy on your servant and forgive my sinful pride!"

In less than a heartbeat, the satanic axe barely missed Lucious' head and two angels manifested over him, annihilating the devil's minion. Another monster took its place, but this time Lucious had his angel and his personal strength in God fighting with him. Joshua heard Lucious proclaiming his faith with renewed and rejuvenated strength.

"I love you fervently and devotedly, O Lord, my strength. The Lord is my Rock, my Fortress, and my Deliverer; my God, my keen and firm strength in whom I will trust and take refuge, my Shield, and the Horn of my salvation, my High Tower. I will call upon the Lord, who is to be praised; so shall I be saved from my enemies. The cords or bands of death surrounded me, and the torrents of ruin terrified me; the snares of death confronted and came upon me. In my distress I called upon the Lord and cried to my God; He heard my voice out of his temple, and my cry came before him, into his ears. Thank you, Lord, for caring about your wayward servant!"

The company managed to push and fight its way into the center of town. They sent thanks up to heaven that so far the only soldier who had any significant wounds was Lucious. Miraculously, since his angel had appeared, his wounds had stopped bleeding and his strength had returned.

However, Joshua noticed that something seemed to be troubling their commander even when the believers from Knoxville shouted with joy as God's army joined their ranks. Noah shot Joshua a surprised look as their eyes fell upon the many angels that accompanied the townspeople.

"The word about how to fight the Army of Darkness must be getting out," Noah said.

Joshua nodded. "Mainyu and Miller will be pissed."

Noah chuckled. "I sure hope so!" As he looked around him he added, "You know, I had overheard Deborah instructing Matthew to spread the word about how to fight the dark soldiers, wherever and whenever he could while he was out on his scouting missions, but I never thought it would go very far."

The combined forces of the Army of Angels and the townspeople of Knoxville started to make a dent in the Army of Darkness' defenses. Their tactics became more efficient and their success more prominent. Just as they were making some real headway, the night faded away and dawn spread across the horizon. To their relief, Satan's soldiers fell back, scattering in several directions.

Shouts of joy rose to heaven as the believers exalted God in their victory, celebrating the fact that none had perished. Deborah wove through the battlefield of fallen demons, making her way toward some much needed solitude.

Joshua caught Noah watching her. He nudged Noah on the shoulder. "Hey, why don't you go and find out what's up with our commander, and I will check on Lucious."

Noah smiled and nodded.

DEBORAH

Noah had the good intention of allowing Deborah to have this time to herself, but when Joshua suggested that he check on her, he couldn't help himself.

He followed her down a dirt path that led outside of town and watched her climb into a gorgeous, sprawling oak tree. He thanked God that she had finally picked something low to the ground and easy to climb. Deborah smiled as Noah planted himself on a thick branch.

"Better?"

He gave her a puzzled look. "Huh?"

She laughed. "I knew you were following me, so I purposefully picked this tree. I thought you might appreciate it."

They both burst out laughing as they forgot the gravity of their lives for just a moment.

"Why, yes, I much prefer this selection. Thank you for thinking of me."

It wasn't until then that he realized how grateful he was that she had not been harmed.

Noah studied her. "Are you going to tell me why you're not celebrating our victory?" he asked.

She smiled. "That obvious, was I?"

Noah shrugged. "Well..."

Deborah nodded, then took a deep breath. "Something's not right."

"How's that?"

"Do you remember Danielle's parting words to us?" She didn't wait for Noah to answer. "She said that the deepest cells of Sheol were being unlocked, that the vilest of Satan's followers were being set loose upon earth, and that they would no longer be confined by the darkness of night."

Noah nodded. "Yes, I do remember that. It's kinda hard to forget something so terrifying."

She looked deep into his eyes. "Well, where are they? What are they up to? Was this just a ploy of Satan to lure us away from the farm? The people here had already received the message of how to defeat the Army of Darkness. They knew that the Word of God was their only salvation. Yes, we were mighty when our forces joined together, but they weren't in any more danger of dying last night than they would have been if we had stayed on the farm. Something is off."

The two comrades sat in silence as Noah thought about what she said. His voice broke through the still air. "But we are led by God, not Satan, so why would God lead us all the way out here if it's not part of his plan? You said that Danielle had foretold you about this battle, specifically instructing you on who to take with you and who to leave behind."

That last part made him a little anxious. His nieces were at the farm. If Deborah was correct, and all this had been a trick to get them to leave the rest of their group unattended... Noah caught himself. He wasn't going to worry about what he couldn't control. God was in control. "Be still and know that I am God," he said quietly to himself.

"Well said!" A twinkle danced in Deborah's eyes, but then her serious demeanor returned. "I just have this horrible feeling in my gut that I can't shake. Something dreadful is in our midst. I don't know what it is, and it might even be part of God's plan, but I don't think our flesh is going to like it one bit. I could tell that Danielle was holding something back from me. She has never done that before. There's more to this journey than you or I know, and for the first time I am in the dark, totally clueless about the next step."

Noah let out a slight chuckle. "Yeah, well, welcome to my world. Kind of sucks, doesn't it?"

Deborah nodded, and they laughed. Then Noah changed the subject.

"So, what the heck? Joshua and I were right next to Lucious when that craziness was going down, and the worst part was that the beast I was fighting was so powerful, I couldn't help him at all. I seriously thought I was going to watch him die right there in front of me. I felt so helpless."

"You couldn't have helped him. It was his trial. He had to figure it out for himself, but I agree with you. It was definitely not fun to witness. It still scared the crud out of me. If his angels had come a millisecond later, his human existence would have ended!"

Just then they spotted Joshua coming toward them. "Hey guys, I don't mean to interrupt, but I wanted to let you know that everyone is congregating in the high school gym. A bunch of the local women are fixing breakfast for everyone, and they're setting up sleeping arrangements as well."

"That sounds fabulous," Deborah said. "I'm starving, and I'm so tired that I feel like the walking dead."

Joshua cleared his throat. "Deborah, I'm confused," he said. "From how Danielle was speaking the last time we saw her, I thought that the next time we encountered the enemy it was going to be unbearable and far worse than it was. Not that I'm not grateful it was easier than what she made it out to be… But I was just wondering if you thought the same thing. Not to mention that they still retreated at daybreak."

Deborah's mood took a somber turn. "Yeah, I have found that information a bit troubling myself. Unfortunately, I'm not sure what to make of it."

MARY

Mary fought desperately to relax in the presence of the Holy Spirit that had settled over the farm, but a small part of her couldn't help asking why God needed to send the Seraphim. Martha and her warriors were relentless. Song after song rang out to the Lord.

If she had to stand watch and face mankind's darkest hour, this was definitely the best post to have. Mary enjoyed working next to such an amazing group of worshipers. They comforted her spirit as she praised the Lord along with them, until her heart stopped at the verse that asked, "Who will take his place?"

From the first time Mary had heard this song, she could not listen to it without a flood of tears springing forth. The thought of what Jesus must have endured during his journey to the cross tore her apart. To know that her sins caused him to have to face such an unfathomable suffering riddled her with guilt. And yet she was immeasurably thankful at the same time. Mary silently contemplated the song's lyrics.

"Thank you, Lord, for your unbelievable sacrifice so I could receive salvation. I am so unworthy, yet you found me worthy. My heart and soul desperately want to shout, 'Yes, I will gladly take your place!' I am the one who is sinful, who deserves to face the cross, but my flesh is full of fear. My human nature wants to preserve my life, to abstain from such unimaginable pain."

Mary's silent prayer was interrupted as Rebekah poked her head through the trap door.

"Hey beautiful, it seems you had an uneventful watch. But you look exhausted. Go and get some sleep. I'll take the rest of tonight's shift."

Mary nodded, but she was apprehensive to leave. She enjoyed being near her sister and the comfort of the songs and prayers she and her warriors provided. Rebekah nudged her on.

"It's okay. Go and get some rest. If anything happens or we hear any news about your uncle and the rest of the company, someone will come and get you, I promise. Besides, we all need to get as much rest as possible, so take advantage of it while you can." Rebekah's smile was warm and endearing.

"Thanks, Rebekah. I'll do my best."

Before heading across the yard to the farmhouse, Mary walked to the edge of the pond. Her two trusty companions, Jack and Rascal, were happily glued to her side. She was hoping the twins thing would work and her sister would open her eyes and notice her. It took a minute, but sure enough, Martha opened her eyes and looked directly at Mary. A warm smile spread across Martha's face as she mouthed the words "I love you" and blew her a big kiss. Mary wanted to cry. She wanted desperately to stay with her sister. Before obeying Rebekah's orders, Mary mouthed, "I love you, too" and returned Martha's kiss.

"You take care of yourself, Marty girl. I'm going to be depending on you more than you know, more than you could ever imagine," she said to herself before she reluctantly turned and headed across the property.

The farmhouse was disturbingly quiet. Mary was the only female left at the farm besides Rebekah. Well, there was Martha and the women in her group, but they remained out on the island, so that meant Mary was alone in the big old house. The men who were heading off to sleep would be down at the barn with their fellow soldiers.

Mary wandered around the house, looking at the family photos as though she had never seen them before. She wondered if her ancestors could have ever imagined that this is what would happen to the world.

Eventually she went upstairs and fell into bed. As hard as she tried to fall asleep, Martha's empty bed next to hers was too unsettling. Frustrated, she turned on the antique light that had belonged to her great-grandmother. She picked up her worn Bible and thumbed through it. Mary caught her breath as she looked at the pages. Staring up at her was the sixth chapter of Isaiah. Her eyes fell on verse eight. "And I heard the voice of the Lord, saying, whom shall I send? And who will go for us? Then said I, here am I; send me."

A deep sigh passed her lips. Mary could not shake Danielle's words from earlier. She looked up and prayed, her voice trembling, "Oh Lord, grant me strength if this is your will for me. My heart says 'yes,' but my flesh wants to run away. Let your will be done! But Lord, you were the Son of God; I am just the daughter of man. I'm only human!"

A still, small voice responded in her mind, reminding her, "You can do all things through me! I will strengthen you! You are more than a child of man; you are first and foremost a child of the one and only true God. You were born for a purpose, a God-given plan to bring honor and glory to God. Nothing is impossible with me! Do you accept?"

NOAH

The school gym was as quiet as a graveyard except for the snoring that drifted from the men's section. Deborah had made the executive decision to have her entire company sleep instead of posting guards to watch for impending danger. Her soldiers needed the rest.

Before they all headed off to dreamland, they used items from the classrooms and some gym equipment to barricade the doors into the school. Not that the effort would stop the enemy from entering, but it would make quite a racket, alerting her army and the townspeople of their presence.

After eating a warm breakfast, some tossed and turned on the hard flooring. Their tired and sore muscles longed for a plush mattress, but exhaustion finally beat out discomfort and the men and women eventually drifted off to a subconscious state.

Noah was lost in a deep, dreamless sleep when he felt someone shaking him and calling his name. He tried to ignore it, hoping it would go away, but the nagging became increasingly annoying, making it impossible to ignore. Finally, he opened his eyes.

As recollection came to him and he remembered where he was, alarm raced through his core and suddenly he was wide awake, painfully so. Deborah was standing over him, her face as white as a ghost. Perspiration beaded on her forehead, and her voice was rushed. She was talking to him, but at first, he only saw her lips moving. Then his ears were pricked by her words.

"It was all a ploy to lead us away from the farm. We have to get back there immediately!"

Noah shook his head, trying to clear the cobwebs. "Wait, what are you talking about?"

"I don't have time to explain. Get the men up. We're leaving in ten minutes. I'll fill you in on our way back to the farm."

Noah looked up at the small window above and saw dusk giving way to night. They had slept the entire day. "Whoa, wait a minute. It's going to be completely dark in ten minutes. You want us to travel at night?"

Deborah sounded out of breath as she answered him, already heading to the other side of the gym to alert the women. "That no longer matters. Danielle's prophecy has already begun to unfurl, and we are running out of time."

With that she disappeared, weaving her way through the maze of sleeping bodies scattered across the wooden floor.

As Noah jumped to his feet, the implication of her words sunk in. Why would Satan want to lure them away from the farm unless he was planning to attack it? But wouldn't Satan want the Army of Angels there if he was planning a surprise attack? Unless he was targeting Martha and the other prayer warriors, knowing that their company relied heavily on their support.

"Oh God, no… not Martha and Mary."

Noah tried not to panic. That would be playing into Satan's hands. He vowed to remain calm and place his trust in God no matter the circumstances.

"Be still and know that I am God!"

Noah quickly woke up Joshua and the rest of his fellow soldiers when he noticed that Lucious was missing. His heart began to pound in his chest when he noticed his friend coming out of the locker room. He noticed that Lucious was walking with a slight limp.

"Hey, you okay?"

Lucious flashed his game-winning smile. "Yeah, dude. I feel like a rock star." Lucious looked around at all the activity. "What's this all about?"

"Deborah has given the order to return to camp. Are you going to be okay to travel?"

Lucious waved his hand, brushing off Noah's concern. "Yeah, man, no problem. Don't worry about me. But it's dark out. I really think we should wait until morning."

Noah felt a sense of apprehension growing in the pit of his stomach. He nodded. "Yeah, I know what you mean, but she feels strongly about this, so…" Noah shrugged.

Lucious nodded. "Yeah, I gotcha."

In less than ten minutes the company had removed the barricades and was headed down the main road toward home. Some of the townspeople of Knoxville had joined their ranks, making it even harder to disguise their presence.

Noah heard one of the female soldiers, whom he believed was named Trinity, question their commander. "Deborah, shouldn't we be taking cover and using the same path we came in on? What about the enemy?"

Noah noticed the soldier's eyes were bugged out as she scanned the darkness for any sign of movement.

"No, it's not a concern right now," Deborah said. "Satan is done playing a game he cannot win. He knows that his foot soldiers are no match for our angels. He has something far more menacing up his detestable sleeve. This battle was a ploy to lure us away from the farm. Our immediate mission is to return there as soon as humanly possible."

Trinity still looked puzzled. "I don't get it. Why would God allow us to be lured away? We were following his lead, right?"

Lucious piped up. "I agree. We need to turn around and head back to the gym. What could Satan want at the farm anyway? The biggest threat to his forces is right here, plodding down some road in the middle of the night. We are the ones he's looking for."

Noah and Joshua exchanged concerned looks. They recognized the doubt that was being implanted in several of their comrades.

Deborah spoke out in a fierce and forceful voice that Noah had never heard before – and hoped he would never hear again.

"In the name of our Lord Jesus Christ, I demand you to be gone! We are all children of God, washed and bought by the blood of Jesus, and you have no power over us. In the name of Jesus Christ and the blood he shed on the cross for all of our sins, I command you to be gone from us, Satan!"

Noah immediately felt a surge of relief and a calming in his spirit after Deborah's prayer. Their commander picked up her pace as she talked.

"God has a plan. We cannot begin to fathom and understand his greatness. Remember who ultimately receives victory when all is said and done. Satan knows that the events are mounting. He is running out of time, and he is becoming desperate. Victory is near; do not lose sight of the prize! We have to remain strong, steadfast, and unshakable! Do you understand me? Do all of you understand me?"

It was quite a sight to see Deborah and her company of soldiers, all in white, marching down a country road with the city lights in the distance behind them and darkness looming before them. Noah imagined God must have had a huge smile on his face as the group bellowed their answer.

"Yes, ma'am!"

DANIELLE

Danielle sat in front of the fire in her quaint cabin, thinking about Mary. She felt a deep connection with the young woman and longed for her company. In a faint way, Mary reminded her of her little sister, Sarah. She smiled as she recalled the way Sarah would always call her "Elli" instead of Danielle. No one else had ever called her that, not even her parents.

God called Sarah home years ago. Cancer had devoured her body until she could no longer fight it. Tears welled up in Danielle's eyes as she recalled her father and brothers carrying the small casket that held Sarah's ten-year-old body.

Danielle was fourteen when she lost her precious Sarah, but not a day had passed that she didn't think of her sweet soul. Even while she was hospitalized and suffering with cancer, Sarah would give away the gifts that came pouring in from family, church members, and friends, to other kids in her ward. She always shared the gospel with all who would listen. There was no denying that Sarah had a gift. She saved quite a few souls during her stay in the hospital.

The one Danielle remembered vividly was Lilly. She was only eight years old, but what a beauty she was. She had spent months in the hospital fighting the same nasty disease Sarah was fighting. She started out in a room down the hall from Sarah, but they brought her in to be Sarah's roommate the night before a major surgery. The next day, Danielle and her family were visiting Sarah, who was unusually exhausted. When they asked her what was wrong, Sarah was nonchalant.

"Oh, it's nothing really. I'm just tired because Lilly couldn't sleep last night. You know how nerve-wracking it can be the night before a big surgery. So I stayed up with her, and we chatted about girl stuff and God."

A little while later, a nurse came into the room. She wore a solemn expression as she gathered up Lilly's belongings.

"What's going on? Are you guys moving Lilly again?" Sarah asked.

The nurse looked at Sarah and seemed to be struggling with herself. Finally, after a long pause, she found her voice. "Uh... um, no. Sarah, I don't know how to say this, but... something went wrong during surgery. Lilly's heart failed her. I'm afraid she didn't make it. I am so very sorry, honey. I know how close the two of you were."

With tears running down her face, Sarah smiled at the nurse. "That's okay. She's home now. When Lilly couldn't sleep last night, the two of us stayed up praying together. Lilly accepted the Lord. So she is just going back to her real home now. Her suffering has ended, and I will only have a short time of grieving before we can have our girl talks again."

That last statement was chilling. It haunted Danielle and her family. Just two short weeks later, Sarah joined Lilly, and the two of them could enjoy all the girl talks they wanted.

Danielle knew as she watched that little casket pass by that her sister had the unique gift of prophecy. Even though Mary did not have the gift, something in her character reminded Danielle of little Sarah. It was a childlike faith that allowed them to look past all the critics and their scientific arguments and believe with the pure, innocent heart of a child. It was something so rare and breathtaking to witness, even in a community of believers.

Danielle found herself wondering if death was going to hurt. She also wondered why humans feared death so much when heaven is so wonderful. Shouldn't we fear a long life here on earth instead? Was it fear of pain? Fear of leaving our loved ones? Was it the fear that heaven didn't really exist? Or was it the fear that they were not going to make it into heaven? She let out a slight laugh as she contemplated how complex humans were.

Danielle knew that her trial was near. As she inched closer to the fire to fight the sudden chill in the air, she remembered God telling her that she would face the most monumental trial of her life when the climate took an unexpected turn.

"God, give me strength to endure! I cannot do this without you. Thank you, for your Word promises that no matter how dire my situation may appear, you will never leave me nor forsake me. I stand on that promise. Keep me on the path of righteousness. Amen!"

NOAH

As Deborah and her soldiers approached the barren town of Gatlinburg, Noah's heart raced like a thoroughbred's. The closer they got to the farm, the more desperate and apprehensive he felt. What would they encounter when they walked through the gates?

Deborah brought the company to an abrupt halt. She wore a look of confusion. Noah knew exactly what this meant. She would look for a place of solitude to check in with their commander-in-chief. Noah knew just the place, and it was a two-minute walk from where they stood. He nudged Deborah's shoulder.

"Come on, I know what you need."

They had walked a ways when Deborah smiled, her big blue eyes shining up at him.

"I see what you're doing. You're trying to lead me off into the dark to take advantage of me. This is hardly the time or place for such behavior, soldier." Her playful smile lit up the darkness, and not just the physical darkness that surrounded them.

Noah feigned a sense of shock. "Commander, I promise you that I shall never make such an ungentlemanly trespass. You have my word on the matter."

"Are you implying that you do not find me desirable?" she teased.

Noah knew she was just joking in an attempt to break the unspoken tension and the sense of impending doom, but the truth was he found her highly desirable.

Noah continued to chide with her. "What I am saying, Commander, is that you are my superior, therefore I shall exercise full restraint."

"Wow, we are major geeks," she said laughingly.

Noah nodded in agreement, and his expression saddened.

"What is it? What's wrong?" she asked. Deborah placed her delicate hand on his aching shoulder. He loved when she did that, and not only because it made all the pain from his old football injury vanish. Noah hesitated, uncertain if he wanted to share his thoughts.

He shook his head. "It's nothing. I guess I am just homesick for the good old days."

He forced himself to laugh. The truth was he longed to be with Deborah. He longed to have a real relationship with her. He wanted to be able to cuddle on the couch with her and watch movies, or fix a romantic dinner together while sipping a glass of red wine. He wanted to be able to kiss her beautiful lips, and go on long afternoon hikes. He wanted to sit next to her on the porch swing on a lazy summer day, drinking a glass of homemade lemonade. He knew it would probably sound sappy and silly, but these were the memories he cherished most from his childhood.

Deborah was watching him closely.

"Hmm, it just feels like there is something more roaming around that handsome head of yours."

Noah smiled. It was as though she could read his mind. It was both annoying and endearing. No wonder her presence drove him crazy.

Noah shrugged. "I guess I'm sad."

Deborah cocked her head to the side. "About?"

"All that I am going to miss out on. I know heaven is supposed to be beyond amazing, or at least that is what my sister Anna claims, but before I depart for my grand life in the heavens, I had kind of hoped to enjoy some of life's simple pleasures here first. I watched my folks and Anna experience a part of life that until now I never knew I wanted. I watched them build a life with someone they loved. I guess deep down I always wanted that for myself, but was too afraid to pursue it after Emma's death. I watched Joshua suffer after she was ripped away from him, and I never wanted to know what that felt like. But my fear of losing someone I loved cost me from being able to build a life with someone. I never longed for anything grand or extravagant, just simple living with simple pleasures and someone to cherish and spend my life with."

When Deborah responded, her voice was husky with emotion. "That sounds absolutely heavenly."

Noah nodded and then realized they were taking far too long. "I better show you what I brought you out here to see."

He walked around the bend, and then held out his arms. "Voila! God is waiting. I don't want to leave you out here alone, so I'll be just around the corner."

Deborah's eyes focused through the darkness, revealing a large boulder at the edge of a serene, babbling creek. "It's perfect, Noah. Thank you!"

Noah smiled before he wandered off in search of a large rock or log. His body ached from both the physical exertion and the tension that never seemed to leave him alone.

While attempting to find some comfort for his throbbing muscles, he kept an eye out for any sign of the enemy. Noah was beginning to wish he had brought some of the other soldiers with them. Even though he was just around the corner, he still felt too far away from Deborah. The demons were astonishingly swift considering their bulk, and they could pounce on Deborah in seconds.

Suddenly, Deborah came running toward him. "We are to follow the fire! I have no idea what the Holy Spirit is referring to, but those are our instructions." She grimaced in frustration. "I really wish Danielle had given me more information. This isn't like her, and God is being quite vague himself."

Out of nowhere, Noah felt the Holy Spirit speak to him. He ran in front of Deborah and forced her to stop, placing his hands firmly on her shoulders.

"Stop. Take a deep breath."

She gave him a quizzical look as she tried to rein in her impatience. Noah continued to follow the Holy Spirit's orders.

"I wait for the Lord, I wait expectantly, and in his Word do I hope. I am looking and waiting for the Lord more than watchmen for the morning, I say, more than watchmen for the morning. O Israel, hope in the Lord! For with the Lord there is mercy and loving kindness, and with him is plenteous redemption. And he will redeem Israel from all their iniquities. Jehovah Emanuel."

Noah heard her faint voice repeating his words. "God is with us! You are right, Noah. I need to let go and allow God to lead us. I have this feeling that our involvement is coming to an end. This war is escalating to a higher level, a level that we are not called to fight – or at least not in the traditional form that we are used to."

Deborah and Noah hurried back to their comrades and shared what God had conveyed to their commander. Deborah had received confirmation that the time was coming for them to relinquish the fight to another.

They walked down the road, content but anxious for the comforts of the farm. But it appeared God had other plans. The farm would have to wait. A faint scent wafted in from a distance, awakening their senses. Noah and Deborah turned to each other.

"Fire!"

DANIELLE

Danielle had drifted off to sleep in front of the fire. She was awakened by a repulsive stench that caused her to gag. A voice hissed from the corner.

"So pleased you find our company so agreeable."

A chorus of raspy laughter filled the room. Emerging from all four corners were the foulest demonic creatures she had ever seen. The leader remained in the shadows as the other four encircled her. When he spoke, his voice hissed in a way that reminded Danielle of chalk scraping across a chalkboard. It made her body shudder.

"Do you find me offensive? Well, that does hurt my feelings. You see, where I come from, I am revered. Have you ever heard of the Lake of Fire? Such a beautiful place. In fact, I find it quite annoying here. I eagerly wish to return, so why don't you be a good little dear and tell us where she is?"

Danielle steeled herself for the torture she knew she would have to endure. Satan was losing the war. He knew his demons, even these odious beings of death, could not defeat the legions of angels in God's army, so he had to change the game. God would play along, though. He had confidence in his weapon; she would not disappoint him. Danielle wished that God would choose another method, but God never chose the easy route, because his people grew through suffering.

"Believe me, darling, it's in your best interest to accommodate our wishes," the demon hissed. "If you remain stubborn and refuse our request, well, I'm afraid it will not bode well for you." Sarcasm oozed from the rancid creature. "What do you say, pretty? Is it going to be the easy road or the hard road?"

A deep, low laugh rasped out of its putrid lungs. Danielle looked the vile beast in what she hoped was its eyes. It was the same monster she had seen

194

up in the tall pines observing their camp since their first night on the farm.

"Go to hell!"

"Oh dear, you don't know how badly I want to. I am tiring of this horrid place you pathetic creatures call Earth." The beast spit on the wooden floor. The acid from its saliva bubbled and ate through the wood, creating a small hole in the floor. Danielle braced herself.

"Great! Really, God?" she said to herself. "I know I don't have to tell you this, but just for the record, I will do this, but I really, really don't want to!"

The hissing voice returned. "I'm losing my patience." He scowled at the four surrounding Danielle, who remained silent. "Enough of this. Make her talk!"

One of the beasts lifted Danielle by her hair and pulled her across the floor. He flung the door open and dragged her out to a fallen log.

The prophetess shuddered at the sight of razor-sharp, six-inch claws that served as fingernails, and the fangs that barely fit in their mouths. She refused to fight, knowing that she was no match for the demons. Besides, she would not give these repulsive beings the satisfaction.

An ice-cold wind whipped her slender frame as two of the beasts ransacked her cabin for clues. Frustrated when their search turned up empty, they torched the cabin. At least the fire's immense heat provided some relief from the cold. Danielle knew that was the only relief she would get tonight. Two of Satan's monsters tied her face up on the log. Then one of them stuck his putrid face in hers.

"Where is she?"

Danielle closed her eyes stubbornly. The demon who had dragged her out of the cabin ran one of his claws down the length of her leg. She screamed in agony as it dug several inches into her flesh. She willed herself to stay calm, but the adrenaline from the pain caused her heart to race out of control.

The leader sauntered over to her. When he reached the log, he bent over Danielle, his repugnant face an inch away from hers.

"This isn't going to get any easier. If you value your pathetic little life, I suggest you tell us what we came here for. If your God is so wonderful, where are the magnificent angels we've heard so much about? Does your papa think you're unworthy of being saved? Doesn't he love you anymore? Or is he just a fairytale created to keep all you ridiculous humans in line? Face it, dearie, you're on your own. Are you going to be so idiotic as to continue to serve a so-called god who has abandoned you in your hour of need? Because believe me, honey, if you don't start talking, your useless existence will be extinguished!"

As he finished speaking, spit sprayed out of his mouth and fell on the log next to her face. Danielle couldn't see it, but she heard the acid eating away at the bark. Between the beast's rancid breath and the excruciating pain from her wound, Danielle had to fight the urge to throw up. Tied down on her back, the vomit would cause her to choke and die, not that she believed she had much longer to live. Even if she did give them the information they were so desperately seeking, Danielle knew they would just kill her anyway. No, this was the way God had planned it, so this was the way it had to be.

"The Lord is my light and salvation," she cried, her voice losing its quake as she continued. "Whom shall I fear or dread? The Lord is the refuge and stronghold of my life. Of whom shall I be afraid?"

Danielle let out a blood-curdling scream as the beast tore into her flesh again with his talons.

"When the wicked, even my enemies and my foes, came upon me to eat up my flesh, they stumbled... and fell."

A hiss of laughter filled the air. "Oh, really? I don't see us stumbling, my dear, but you are most certainly going to meet your fate tonight!"

Anger spewed from the beast as the realization that his tactics were failing him gnawed at his prideful nerves.

"Though a host encamp against me, my heart shall not fear, though war arise against me, in this will I be confident."

Before Danielle could proclaim another breath of scripture, the leader gave the order.

"Finish her!"

With that, all four beasts spit their venomous saliva into her raw flesh. The unbearable pain caused Danielle to pass out before she could hear the acidic poison bubbling and sizzling inside her wounds. She was unaware of the fact that the poison was seeping into her system, shutting down her vitals, slowly bringing the peace of death.

Finally, her suffering was over.

JOSHUA

Not wanting to lead her soldiers on another wild goose chase, Deborah ordered her company to head back to camp immediately. She pulled Noah, Joshua, and Lucious aside. Looking down at the blood that was seeping through his white pants, Deborah addressed Lucious first.

"I don't understand why your leg isn't healing. I want you to promise me that as soon as you get back to the farm, you will have Rebekah take a look at it."

Lucious nodded. "Sure thing, boss." He looked at her sideways. "But what are you up to? Aren't you going back with the rest of us?"

Deborah shook her head. "I have to check on something first. We'll catch up with you shortly."

Lucious looked at Noah and Joshua. "Do you need me to join you? You could use someone with experience. Who knows what could happen with these two newbies as your backup," he chided.

"Oh, really? Like your gimpy butt could do any better?" Joshua teased.

Lucious shrugged. "Probably."

Lucious saluted the three of them as he limped off to catch up with the rest of the warriors. Joshua and Noah waited for Deborah to let them in on her plan.

Deborah nodded at them. "You two are with me."

The three of them abandoned the road that led back to the farm. Instead, they followed the trail of smoke that grew heavier the deeper they traveled into the forest.

Joshua's heart pounded. There could be only one thing this far out in the wilderness that the enemy wanted: Danielle. He couldn't forget the foreboding message she had delivered the last time she had seen any of them.

The thick trees hid the moon, intensifying the darkness. But what really caught Joshua's attention was the drastic change in temperature. The air had a bite to it, burning their lungs and causing their breath to hover in the air like pillows of smoke. Joshua knew that whatever was causing this strange phenomenon was definitely unnatural.

Their progress was slower than they would have liked because they had to take such cautious, deliberate steps. The frost crunched under their feet and made the boulders they had to scramble over precariously slippery. The last thing they needed was to get injured minutes before having to fight the beasts of hell. And from the ominous feel of things, Joshua's spirit told him this time they were not going to encounter the typical demons they had become accustomed to fighting. Not only had the game changed, but so had its players.

As they cleared the last set of boulders, Deborah, Noah, and Joshua froze in place. The clearing to Danielle's cabin was approximately thirty feet away. What had once been Danielle's home was now a roaring fire.

As their shock began to diminish, the three warriors made out what appeared to be a body tied to a fallen log near the edge of the clearing. There was a foul odor of burning flesh swirled together with the familiar stench of hell. The resulting smell was nauseating. Joshua had to fight to keep from vomiting. They were all too aware of the significance of the vile stench. It could mean only one thing.

They quietly withdrew their weapons as their eyes searched through the darkness for any sign of the enemy. They would be camouflaged somewhere in the shadows, waiting patiently for the perfect moment to strike.

Deborah signaled for Noah and Joshua to take cover before she climbed the nearest pine tree in an attempt to assess the situation. Tension was building. Joshua knew he should be scouring the scene for the vile beasts, but he could not pull his eyes away from his commander. He had a sinking feeling that would not allow him a moment of solace no matter how hard he prayed.

Joshua couldn't help but notice the absence of their angels. Even though he wasn't shouting scripture from the top of his lungs as he had during battle, he was reciting it faithfully inside his head, but still there was no sign of their heavenly comrades. Something wasn't right.

Deborah positioned herself on one of the highest branches and searched the ground for the demons. Tears welled in her eyes when she saw Danielle's remains, blurring her vision for a moment. She had to close her eyes and look away. The picture of her friend tied down, ripped to shreds with her skin burned and peeling away, was more than she could bear.

When Deborah opened her eyes again, that's when she saw it – a dark shadow crouched in a tree twelve feet away. Her nerves were quickly unraveling as she recognized the beast from her recurring nightmares. She scanned the surrounding trees and sucked in her breath. Four other identical demons were also hiding in the trees, ready to drop onto Noah and Joshua below. They would be taken completely off guard, expecting their foe to come at them from the ground. The dark soldiers they had faced previously, even the new hideous ones that possessed a monstrous form, did not have wings.

Joshua and Noah heard Deborah let out a single hoot that mimicked the barn owls from the farm. They knew this was her signal to retreat. The two men looked at each other, neither one of them willing to leave their commander. Joshua felt a sense of relief as she worked her way back down the tree, but something was odd about the way she was descending. She moved in a peculiar way, as though she were being watched. What had she spotted?

Deborah rotated her attention from one demon to the next when something caught her eye. Two of the demons were holding a net between them. Who or what were they trying to catch?

Without warning, a loud crack echoed in the dark. Joshua's eyes were glued on Deborah, but it all happened so quickly that at first he wasn't sure what he was witnessing was real. The branch on which she was standing gave way, and she plummeted toward the forest floor thirty feet below. Noah and Joshua sprinted toward her when they heard the shriek of demons over their head. Five disgusting creatures flew straight at their commander. Suddenly, two veered off and headed right for the two of them.

"Guard and keep yourselves in the love of God!" Joshua shouted. "Expect and patiently wait for the mercy of our Lord Jesus Christ which will bring you unto life eternal."

Joshua could not digest what he saw next. Deborah had just managed to grab a branch and pull herself atop it when the ground shook violently, causing her to lose her balance. Again, she was spiraling toward the hard, unforgiving ground.

One of the demons swirled around her before he raised a menacing set of claws. It struck with swift precision. Its talons tore through her clothing, ripping open her flesh. She screamed from the unbearable pain as blood gushed from her side.

The demons began to make obnoxious clicking sounds deep in their throats. The last thing Joshua saw before the two beasts landed right in front of them was the most bizarre thing ever. It looked as though the creatures were attempting to spit on Deborah.

The winged beast slashed at Joshua, aiming for his throat. Joshua blocked the blow with his sword, but the monster's claws broke the steel weapon in two. Before he had a chance to react, a host of thirteen heavenly

199

creatures appeared. A bright light flashed as the most intimidating and beautiful angel whisked Deborah away.

Noah recognized him. He shouted over to Joshua, "Did you see him? He was one of the angels who accompanied Anna on her visit. I wouldn't want to be on his bad side!"

The remaining twelve angels jumped in, fearlessly combating the five invaders from hell and forcing them to retreat into the darkness, but not before Joshua heard one of the demons boast.

"You may have won this battle, but we will return, and we will not stop until we have the one we were sent for."

An evil hiss spread across the unseen distance as they fled.

MATTHEW

Matthew slowly ascended the stairs in the farmhouse. It had been a while since he had checked in on Mary. As he turned the corner of the second story hallway, he froze for a moment, stunned. Caleb stood just outside Mary's bedroom door. His hand was outstretched in her direction as he spoke with a forceful tone in an unfamiliar language. Matthew's concern turned to anger.

"What do you think you are doing?" Matthew said.

Caleb slowly turned and looked at Matthew, who was eyeballing him suspiciously. For a brief moment, Matthew thought he saw a golden glow in Caleb's eyes. He shook his head. The lack of sleep must be getting to him.

Caleb simply turned and began to walk away. As he passed by Matthew, he spoke in a low tone. "My apologies."

Matthew's tongue got the better of him.

"Why are you still here?" Matthew nodded in the direction of Mary's room. "You have to know we won't let you hurt her."

Caleb offered a single nod. He started to walk away, then paused and looked back at Matthew. "You cannot stop what has already been put in motion. It's too late."

Matthew saw an expression of sadness cross Caleb's face. He was about to ask what Caleb meant by that, but he had already disappeared around the corner.

After checking on Mary, relieved to see that she was fast asleep and unharmed, Matthew rushed out to the treehouse to relay his encounter with Caleb to Rebekah. Her face lit up with a warm smile as his head popped through the trap door.

"Hey you, am I glad to see a friendly face. Keeping watch can get a little lonely." She paused as she noticed Matthew's grim expression. "Oh no, what's happened?"

"I still haven't received word from any of our people," he said. Their return was taking longer than they had anticipated, causing a slight sense of concern to be planted in the hearts of those who had stayed behind. Matthew continued. "I came to inform you of an odd situation I just had with Caleb."

After sharing the incident with his leader, Rebekah ordered him to keep a close eye on Caleb. She informed Matthew of the location of Caleb's assigned post and asked him to watch Caleb from a safe distance. Matthew headed back down through the trap door when he stopped to ask, "But what about Mary? Shouldn't someone be guarding her?"

Rebekah shook her head. "As long as she is in the house, she is protected. Danielle, Deborah, and I prayed a hedge of protection throughout the house, not to mention the hedge of protection that we all prayed around the property."

Matthew accepted her answer and left to fulfill his assignment. He thought about what Rebekah had said and it did make sense. All of the injuries the army had sustained had happened outside the farm's protective barrier. Well, actually he was the only one who had suffered an injury, but the fact remained that it didn't happen on the farm. Luke had been wounded, but that had happened before the arrival of the Army of Angels.

As Matthew jogged across the farm toward Caleb's post, he was elated at the sight of several of their soldiers returning. He searched for Deborah, but was unable to locate her amongst the throng of individuals. There were several new faces mixed in with familiar ones. He spotted Lucious and ran up to him.

Matthew was filled with alarm as he saw his friend's bloody leg and peppered him with questions. "Are you okay? What happened? Where is Deborah?"

Lucious chuckled. "Where is Rebekah? Deborah ordered me to check in with her immediately."

Matthew waved his hand. "Follow me."

Matthew assisted Lucious up the stairs and through the trap door. Rebekah and Matthew listened closely to what Lucious had to say as Rebekah prayed over his wound.

The three soldiers exchanged troubled expressions when Lucious informed them that Deborah had taken Joshua and Noah with her to investigate the fire out in the forest. An unspoken concern for Danielle filled their hearts.

Lucious excused himself. He was anxious to exchange his blood-soaked pants for some new ones. Rebekah asked Matthew to stay behind for a moment to lift up a prayer for the three warriors who still remained in enemy territory. Then he left to spy on Caleb.

Rebekah also asked him to send a replacement for her post so she could welcome the newcomers from Knoxville. She did not relish having so much responsibility placed upon her shoulders. She longed for Danielle and Deborah's return.

MARY

Mary had no idea how long she had been enjoying the wonderful escape of being unconscious, lost in a world of peaceful slumber, before the real world pulled her back. Her bed shook as a thunderous crack pierced the sky and a bolt of light sped past her window.

Mary sat up, trying to catch her breath from being jolted awake from a dead sleep. She sent up a quick prayer. "Lord, please let this be good news!"

Mary had barely managed to get her robe wrapped around her when she heard feet racing up the stairs. She grabbed her weapon and ducked behind the largest piece of furniture in her room. It took her a moment before she mustered the courage to peek around the armoire, relieved to see her fellow comrades.

Anxious to join the others, she closed the door and quickly changed into her clothes. She sheathed her sword and followed the pandemonium into her parents' bedroom.

Mary's gaze fell upon the blood-soaked bedding and the deep, jagged gash in the side of one of their female soldiers. A man she did not recognize hovered over the victim, concealing the warrior's identity. Many in the room knelt reverently before God, lifting up prayers on her behalf.

Mary felt a sense of guilt at her relief that it obviously was not her uncle. She opened her mouth to ask who the wounded soldier was, noting that the frame was too petite to be Martha or Danielle, when the stranger turned to retrieve something from his medical bag, revealing the victim's face. It was Deborah.

Mary stumbled back against the wall, her head spinning. How could this have happened to Deborah, of all people? She was their commander and the most skillful soldier among them.

Mary rested against the wall, taking slow, deep breaths as she tried to collect herself. That was when she spotted Rebekah on the other side of Deborah, holding her friend's hand while gently soothing her forehead. Then it dawned on her: Where was Uncle Noah? No matter how much he tried to deny his affection for Deborah, even to himself, Mary had seen the way he looked at their commander. So why wasn't he by Deborah's side?

Mary wove her way through the group of stunned individuals until she reached Rebekah.

"What happened to her, and why isn't my uncle and Joshua here? Has something happened to them? Are they still alive?" Her voice and lips trembled uncontrollably as she fought to hold back tears.

Rebekah gave her an affectionate, sorrowful expression that caused bile to churn in Mary's stomach.

"I'm so sorry, Mary, but we don't know where they are, or if they're okay." Tears rolled down the elder warrior's face. The man she had grown to love and her best friend's fate were hanging in the balance. Rebekah paused as if she were contemplating whether she should continue.

"Please, please tell me. I have to know!" Mary begged.

Rebekah nodded her understanding. After all, Mary was a sworn member of the Army of Angels. She was no longer an innocent bystander, but a true soldier for Christ.

"Your uncle and Joshua are the only warriors who did not return to camp," she said finally.

"Oh... I see. Thank you for being honest with me."

Rebekah nodded as tears continued to flow down her face. She knew there was nothing she could say that would alleviate Mary's concern. There was certainly nothing anyone could say to relieve hers.

As Mary drew back, she looked into Deborah's face. It was peaceful, and Mary thanked God that at least he was kind enough to allow her to remain unconscious, ignorant of the dire trauma her body was suffering.

Mary made her way down the staircase, through the kitchen door, and out into the English garden her mother loved so much. She knelt in front of the bench her mother had sat on for hours at a time while reading her Bible and talking with her Heavenly Father – the same bench where Mary first spoke to Deborah about becoming a member of the Army of Angels.

The two amazing women reminded Mary so much of each other, and now it looked as though she was about to lose Deborah, too. She had no idea whether her uncle was still alive or dead, but one thing she did know was that he would have no desire to go on living if Deborah was taken away from him. How much sorrow and loss could one man endure? Her mother had always promised her and her sister that God would never give them more than they could handle, but Mary was seriously beginning to think that her infallible God had her confused with someone else, because she was at her limit.

"God, we are now entering into a realm beyond my capabilities. I need you to gird me up and pump my veins with your strength, because I am empty. If you want me to take on the role you have laid out before me, you need to help me transcend my human capabilities, for without you I am finished."

Mary felt the Holy Spirit prompting her to read the letter her mother had left for her and Martha the night she left to join God in heaven. Mary had avoided reading her mother's last words to her for years. She didn't think she could handle the flood of emotions that she was positive would accompany her hearing her mother's voice through the words Anna left on paper.

The past few weeks Mary had felt compelled to keep the letter with her, carrying it secretly next to her heart. Out of obedience, Mary pulled out the folded letter. Her eyes filled with tears at the sight of her mother's handwriting. It drove home how much she truly missed and longed for her mother's presence. For a few minutes, Mary just stared at the familiar writing before venturing to read her mother's final words.

"My dear precious angels,

My heart aches for the two of you. Heaven will not be truly perfect until we are all together again. I know the road ahead will not be an easy one, but I do know that God has great plans for both of you. Do not shrink back in fear from your calling. I beg the two of you to march forward with a bold heart, confident that God is in control! You are left behind to exist during the darkest times known to mankind. I am afraid that life as you once knew it will soon be forever lost to you, but please hold tight to the promises of God. Remember that our life here on Earth is fleeting, but if you remain steadfast and confident in his love for you, and follow his plan for your lives, you will not be found wanting, lacking, or disappointed, but rather you will find yourselves traveling down streets of gold where the enemy no longer can torture you, for he has no power or authority in God's realm. We all must lose our life here to gain eternal bliss with him in heaven. Remember, this, too, shall pass, but behold the wonders and glory of God in heaven when he calls you home! Your father and I will never leave you or forsake you. We will be walking with both of you for every step that you take during your remaining years here – as will your Heavenly Father. Call upon his name to rise you up above your circumstances so that he can plant your steps firmly on the path of righteousness. I will be at the gates of heaven waiting to welcome you home!

All of our love, always and forever,

Mom."

Mary's shoulders shook uncontrollably as she whispered, "I love you more."

NOAH

Noah was completely transfixed. The fact that some of the beasts who fought for the Army of Darkness possessed the ability to fly, well, it took the battle to a whole new level, literally. Noah could not shake the image of swords forged of heavenly steel clashing with the razor-sharp claws of hell, as black and white forms spiraled and swirled in a vicious dance amongst the treetops.

Noah was miffed. Why hadn't the angels wiped out these creatures? How did God expect the Army of Angels to defend themselves against this elite demonic foe? Look at what happened to Deborah, and she was their commander. Scripture didn't save her! Noah felt anger toward God welling up within him. This was not good.

"Get away from me, Satan!" he yelled. "You have no power over me. I have been washed by the blood of Jesus. As a child of the one true God, I am set free!"

Noah turned to find Joshua and the twelve angels watching him. Noah was thankful that the awful things from the depths of hell had disappeared, but something inside him told him that this would not be the last time they would encounter them. A morbid part of Noah wanted to investigate the log in the clearing. He wanted to know exactly what these vile things were capable of, but Noah knew that if he allowed his curiosity to get the better of him, he would never be able to erase the appalling truth from his memory.

Joshua walked over to Noah. "I pray to God that the body on that log isn't Danielle. Do you think it could possibly be an animal?" Joshua asked hopefully.

Noah shot him a look. "We can try and convince ourselves that that's the case."

Noah looked at the fire, wondering if the monsters were still out there keeping a watch over the clearing, hoping that others will come to bury the body. Alarm washed over Noah as he remembered their parting words.

Joshua caught Noah's expression. "What, what is it?"

Noah lowered his voice. "It just dawned on me that killing Danielle wasn't the sole purpose of their mission. They're looking for someone else."

The truth of what Noah said registered with Joshua. "But who and why?"

"If I were a betting man, I would put my money on Deborah. After all, she is our commander. Everyone knows that the best way to kill a snake is to chop of its head, and since she is our leader, well..."

Then another thought popped into his overtaxed brain. Could it be Martha? She was responsible for leading the prayer warriors who provided their soldiers with supernatural fuel to defeat Satan's forces.

Joshua looked around. "Hey, do you notice something?"

Noah shook his head. "No, what?"

Joshua replied, "The frigid, cold air. It's gone."

The two of them paused for a moment to admire the beauty of the lush green wilderness beyond the clearing. The sun was peeking over the eastern mountains, sending shards of warm rays through the tall pines toward the valley. Noah took a slow, deep breath of clean air before reciting the words Deborah had insisted he memorize.

"Be still and know that I am God."

Joshua approached the angels. He hesitantly asked one of them, "Do you know if Deborah is alive?"

The angel shook his head. "I'm afraid I don't know."

Noah piped up, "What happened? What took you guys so long to join us?"

Another angel spoke. "We were called from several locations. Gabriel and I were engaged in a deadly altercation just outside the farm protecting one of our own. Satan is trying to divide our forces in an attempt to weaken us."

Joshua looked over at the log. "Why didn't someone come to save her?" Tears welled up in his eyes as he looked upon what was most likely Danielle's lifeless body.

The angel's voice was husky with emotion. "Some must perish in order to save the many."

Noah's head was spinning. What exactly was that supposed to mean? His eyes flew open wide. "Do you know who the demons are after?"

The angel with the husky voice nodded his head, but before Noah could ask him who it was, the angels were being beckoned away.

Noah and Joshua felt alone and vulnerable. They resumed their arduous trek back to the farm, climbing over and through the rugged terrain. They traveled as quickly as possible, not knowing how much time they had since the beasts they had encountered did not fear the daylight. They picked up their pace, knowing that they had to warn the others of Satan's plot before it was too late.

MATTHEW

Matthew weaved his way through the shadows in an attempt to observe Caleb without being detected. As he crouched behind some dense brush, peering through the bare patches, Matthew instinctively withdrew his dagger from his boot as footsteps approached from somewhere behind him. He quietly shifted his position, staying out of view of the person headed toward Caleb.

Matthew's mind was racing with possible scenarios of who it might be, but he was almost certain the oncoming footsteps belonged to Caleb's contact with the Army of Darkness.

Matthew was stunned when he realized it was Lucious. He knew Lucious did not agree with Danielle's decision to allow Caleb to join their ranks. Matthew's body became tense as the thought passed through his mind. What if Lucious is planning to harm Caleb? Why else would he come all the way out here to visit with a man he openly despised?

As Matthew inched closer, he saw Lucious pull out his dagger. To his amazement, Caleb did not panic, nor did he draw his weapon. Instead, his voice remained calm and steady.

"Hello, Lucious. What brings you all the way out here tonight?"

Lucious' voice burned with anger. "Don't pretend you don't know who I am and what I've done. Did you really think that I would let you live after you discovered my little secret?"

Caleb laughed. "Did you really think we didn't know?"

Matthew heard the confusion in Lucious' voice. "We?"

Matthew fought to stifle a gasp as he saw several dark soldiers surrounding Lucious. He was about to shout out a warning to alert his friend when right before his eyes Caleb morphed into a majestic being.

One of the soldiers hissed. "Well, well, well, lookie here, boys. It looks like we have a mighty warrior from heaven all by his lonesome with nobody around to help him. Such a pity."

Both Lucious' and Matthew's jaws dropped to the floor. In his wildest dreams Matthew never would have guessed that Caleb had been sent from God. Shame rushed over him as he felt the sting of his sin. Judgment belonged to the Lord. Caleb had been treated unfairly by the members of God's army because they had passed unfair judgment on one of God's elite warriors.

Matthew had always judged Jesus' persecutors. He had never understood how they could have misjudged Jesus and sentenced him to death, but what he had found most astonishing was Jesus' response: "Forgive them Father, for they know not what they do." He had never understood how Jesus could be so passionate toward those who had just tortured and murdered him in cold blood. He had never been more appreciative of Jesus' compassion toward those who had sinned against him as he was this very moment.

"God, please forgive me, for I truly did not know what I was doing. This is precisely why you and you alone should be the one to sit and judge the hearts and actions of men."

Matthew noticed that Lucious' leg was dripping with blood. He heard Caleb's voice addressing Lucious. "You know the truth. The truth will set you free. Turn from your sin and be healed. You cannot serve two masters. You must make a decision."

Lucious scoffed. "It's too late for me. God could never forgive me of my crimes against him, but I can keep the others from finding out the truth of who I am and what I've done. Satan will reward me if I deliver her to him."

Caleb shook his head. "You don't have to do this. Walk away from his lies! Jesus' blood will cover your sin! You saw the healing power of the Lord. He saved you on the battlefield in Knoxville. My brother was one of the two who intervened and saved you from the blow that would have taken your life."

Lucious looked down at his bleeding wound. "What do you call this?"

"The Bible warns us of what will happen if we attempt to serve two masters. God saved you, but you allowed Satan to plant fear into your heart, convincing you that God would cast you aside for what you have done, but that is a lie! Your wound was healed by the power of God, but you listened to the enemy. You turned your back on the one who made you, the one who loves you. He cannot bless you if you serve Satan."

Caleb's next words were ominous. "Besides, the die has been cast. She has willingly accepted God's plan for her."

Lucious was skeptical. "If that is true, then why are you here? If you aren't here to save her, then what are you here for?" Lucious looked pleased with himself.

Caleb laughed. "Such little understanding. I'm not here to save her; I am here to strengthen her, to pray over her soul. God never abandons those who seek him. Her fate is sealed. The fate of everyone else rides on her shoulders."

"Please. There is no way she can withstand what is laid out before her. She will fold, and when she does you will have wished you had chosen differently. It's not too late to join us."

Matthew's head was spinning. In the moment it took him to blink, a ferocious brawl broke out in front of him. Several mighty angels were suddenly fighting alongside Caleb. Matthew wanted to join the fight, but something inside him told him to stay put.

After what seemed like an eternity, God's forces finally defeated their opponents. Lucious' lifeless body lay face down on the ground. Matthew felt the sting of his salty tears pooling in his eyes. He had been praying with all his might that Lucious would return to God's fold, but his prayers were not enough to sway him.

Matthew startled at Caleb's voice as the angel looked mournfully over Lucious' body.

"This is the sucky part of free will."

"You knew I was here?" Matthew said.

Caleb chuckled. "You seriously thought I didn't know? To an angel, humans are about as stealthy as an elephant tramping around in a forest."

Matthew didn't know what to say. "Oh..."

Caleb smiled. "Come on. We need to hurry. Your sister is on her way back." With that, a loud crack shuddered through the sky. "See."

Matthew became focused. "I have to tell her about Lucious, and... you."

Caleb let out a hearty laugh before returning to his human form. Matthew stared at him. "Why did you do that? Don't you prefer being an angel?"

Caleb nodded. "Actually, yes, I do, but who is going to believe you unless I show them?"

Matthew thought about it. "Yeah, good point."

Caleb let out a deep sigh. "Humans! O, ye of little faith."

Matthew followed Caleb's lead as the angel hurried to the farmhouse. He was surprised to see that another angel stood guard on the porch steps. Matthew tried not to stare, but his presence demanded respect.

Caleb rolled his eyes at Matthew's reaction, and his voice was oozing with sarcasm. "Close your mouth. He's not God," Caleb scoffed before he formally introduced them. "Matthew, I would like you to meet my older brother, Michael. Michael, this is Deborah's younger brother, Matthew."

Matthew stood transfixed. It took him a minute to regain his wits. He leaned over and whispered to Caleb. "Is he the Michael?"

Caleb let out an exasperated sigh. "Yes, he is the Michael. Michael the Arch Angel. Why is it the rest of us just become a pile of manure whenever you or Gabriel are around?"

Michael laughed at Caleb's frustration. He looked at Matthew. "I hope you don't give your sister a hard time just because she holds a prestigious title. What's up with the little brother complex?"

Caleb brushed off Michael's comment. He nodded upstairs. "How is she doing?"

Michael's face turned somber. "She's definitely had better days. I suggest you hurry."

Matthew started to become concerned. "Who? Who has had better days?"

Caleb ignored Matthew's questions as he sped up the stairs. He paused at the threshold. It bothered him to see her like this. Matthew had been right behind Caleb and nearly knocked the angel over when his eyes fell on his sister, fighting for her life just a few feet away. He shot Caleb a look.

"What happened to her? Is she going to be okay?"

Caleb strode up beside Deborah, dismissing the unpleasant looks he was receiving from several members of the group. Reuben, the stocky, red-haired soldier, stepped between Caleb and Deborah. "What, you came to finish the job your friends started?" he said as he whipped out his dagger, holding it to Caleb's throat.

Matthew pleaded with him. "Please, put your weapon away. Caleb is not who or what you think he is. We have judged him unfairly." Matthew choked on his next words. "Lucious was the traitor."

Several of the members began to form a circle around Matthew and Caleb. Matthew was trying to think of how to explain everything so that his friends could understand when Caleb changed into his true form. It was a good thing the room had tall ceilings. Everyone shrunk back and gasped.

Matthew gestured with his hand. "Yeah, I was trying to get to that part." Matthew looked down at his sister. Her skin was pale. He looked up at Caleb. "Isn't there anything you can do to save her?"

Caleb shook his head. "No, that decision isn't up to me. All I can do is lay my hands on her and appeal to God on her behalf."

Matthew looked over at the doctor who had fought beside Deborah in Knoxville and who had traveled with her back to the farm. Matthew's voice cracked as he attempted to fight back his emotions. "What are her chances? Can you operate or something?"

The doctor lowered his eyes. "I'm sorry, but she has been gravely injured. I have done everything I can possibly do, considering the circumstances." The doctor cleared his throat before continuing. "Next to a miracle, I'm afraid there isn't anything else I can do for her."

Caleb sighed. "Ye of little faith." He looked around the room. "I want everybody to hold hands and pray together. Have you not heard of the power you as believers possess when two or more of you come together? For Pete's sake."

Caleb's bedside manner left something to be desired, but his heart was true and his faith was unshakable. "I want you to call upon Jehovah Raffa."

Several of the members of the congregation looked at him with a quizzical expression. Caleb sighed again. "What do they teach you people in Sunday School?" Caleb shook his head before he explained that Jehovah Raffa means "God heals."

A hushed "Oh" spread throughout the room.

Caleb laid his strong hands over Deborah and began to pray in tongues. Matthew didn't have a clue as to what his new friend was saying, but he didn't care. If anyone could bring about the miracle Deborah so desperately needed, it was Caleb.

MARTHA

Martha and her warriors could not help but notice the mayhem that was taking place across the pond. She turned her gaze toward heaven.

"God, I don't know what is going on. I don't know the specific needs of my fellow soldiers, but you do! Lord, I thank you for your unfailing love. I thank you that no matter what our circumstances may be, you are there for us. You are our rock, our stronghold during the storm, our eternal salvation!"

Martha's prayers were interrupted as the ground shook beneath her feet. A violent crack throbbed in her ears seconds before a heavenly light illuminated the hazy dawn. The uproar across the pond turned to pandemonium.

"Okay, God, I'm not going to lie. It's becoming extremely difficult to stay focused on my task. I'm fighting to make sense out of all this craziness. Please give my mind peace or at least direction so that I'm able to perform the job you have given me. I need a little help here, please."

Martha opened her eyes to find Matthew running across the yard in their direction.

"Thank you!

Martha was shocked when Matthew stepped out of the boat and onto the island. She had expected him to deliver the news and return quickly to the others, but instead, he strode straight toward her.

"I need to speak with you in private."

Martha searched his body language for clues. He appeared calm, but he had a wild look in his eyes. She willed herself to remain calm, but her body rebelled against her orders. Her heart beat sporadically, and her hands were wet with perspiration.

"Get control of yourself. God is on the throne!" she whispered to herself.

Matthew's eyes connected with hers, and she knew instantly how difficult it was for him to say what he was about to say.

"I have come to ask that you and your warriors lift four of our own up in prayer."

Martha felt the ground sway beneath her.

"We are almost certain that Danielle is no longer with us." he said. "Pray that her soul finds comfort with the Lord."

Matthew's sharp reflexes allowed him to catch Martha. He helped her keep her balance as he led her to a nearby stump. Once she was sitting down, he waited for her to regain her bearings before he continued.

"Pray for your Uncle Noah and Joshua's safety."

Martha's eyes widened with panic.

"According to the angel who rescued her, they were with my sister deep in the forest when they were ambushed by the enemy," Matthew explained. "At this point, no one knows what happened to them."

Martha didn't know how much more of this she could take. But so far Matthew had only reported about three soldiers. There was still one left. Matthew gave her a minute to take it all in before she nodded for him to continue.

"And although it is probably futile, I would like to make a request."

Martha nodded. "Of course. What is it?"

"Would you please pray for Lucious' soul?"

Martha was confused. "I don't understand. I thought his leg had been prayed over and was healed?"

"Well..." Matthew updated Martha on the mind-blowing events that he had witnessed between Caleb and Lucious.

Martha smiled. "I always liked him," she said, referring to Caleb.

Matthew laughed. "Yeah, the rest of us never really quite got that."

Martha gently held his arm. "I want you to know and share with the others that we will be doing all that we can to defeat Satan and slam the gates of hell so hard that they will remain shut tight forever, with all of its vile inhabitants locked securely inside."

Matthew couldn't help but notice the transformation in Martha. Instead of destroying her faith, this news appeared to stir up a fire in her soul.

"Oh, and make sure you tell everyone else that until God says otherwise, my uncle and Joshua are alive. Thinking anything else is accepting the lies the enemy is trying to blacken our souls into believing. And we should be thanking God that Danielle is enjoying her eternal home with her Creator. She is finally in heaven where we all belong. We can be sorry for our loss, because she will be greatly missed, but we must first celebrate her victory and her amazing reward. As far as everything else is concerned... we will not lose hope, for the power of heaven is made full by the abundance of our hope and trust in our Father!"

She embraced Matthew, nearly squeezing the air out of him. Matthew offered her a warm smile before he headed off toward the dinghy that would carry him back across the pond.

Martha reached down and pulled out her mother's note she had been carrying next to her heart when a message from heaven sent her running after Matthew.

"Wait! Wait!" She reached the boat just as Matthew settled down on the seat. He looked up, concerned. "Please make sure you seek Mary out right away and give this to her."

Matthew nodded. "Sure. Is everything okay?"

Martha offered Matthew a sly grin. "God is on the throne, my friend. How could anything not be okay?"

NOAH

Noah and Joshua were making decent time. Of course, the sunlight and lack of slippery frost helped. Noah's mind kept torturing him with thoughts of the worst-case scenarios. Had the demons already reached the farm? Would Martha have enough protection if they came after her? Was Deborah still alive? If Deborah didn't make it, who would be there to protect Mary from Caleb?

The thoughts just went on and on, until he heard a still, small voice inside his head remind him. "Be still and know that I am God."

Joshua broke the unbearable silence. It was as if he could read Noah's mind. "Don't worry, God has it all under control."

Noah nodded, but the truth was he didn't know what he would do if something happened to any of his girls, and that included Deborah.

"When did you know that Emma… and now Rebekah? When did you know that you loved them?"

Joshua hid his smile, not wanting to embarrass Noah. It had been obvious to him for quite some time that his friend was falling for their commander. Joshua's voice became husky when he talked about Emma. There was a part of him that would always love her.

"I loved Emma from the first day I saw her, but the first time I realized that I was in love with her was the day she rolled up her sleeves and helped me work on my Mustang. She knew her way around an engine better than most guys." Joshua shrugged. "I don't know, I guess I found it kinda sexy, ya know?"

Noah laughed. "I guess if I wasn't her brother I would have found it sexy, but to me, I found it annoying and humiliating that my sister was a better mechanic than I was."

The two became quiet for a minute before Noah asked, "What about

Rebekah? When did you know with her?"

Joshua shot Noah a sideways glance. "Are you sure you want to discuss this? I know it's a difficult subject for you."

Noah shrugged. "I'm kind of getting used to seeing the two of you together. I guess all of this crazy mayhem has made the past seem like it took place in another lifetime or something. Our past almost doesn't seem real anymore."

Joshua nodded. "Yeah, I get that."

Noah looked at his friend. "Well? Are you going to tell me or not?"

Joshua chuckled. "Why the sudden interest?" he asked with a sly smile.

Noah wasn't sure if he was ready to admit to anyone else that he had fallen in love with Deborah. It was difficult enough to admit it to himself. It made him feel vulnerable, and that was a feeling he was still struggling with.

"I'm just trying to keep my mind off of everything. I thought a little conversation would do the trick, but if you don't want to talk about it, I understand."

"Uh-huh, okay, well... I guess the first time I knew I was in love with Rebekah was when she called you a lovable blowhard." Joshua let out a hearty laugh.

Noah looked offended. "What? When did she call me that? And you fell in love with her over that?"

Joshua was laughing so hard, all he could manage was a slight nod.

"Well, at least she did call me lovable, but blowhard? Really? That hurts, man..."

Noah and Joshua both stopped dead in their tracks a few feet outside the gate. There, standing on the front steps of the farmhouse was the glorious angel that had scooped up Deborah and carried her away.

Joshua spoke without taking his eyes off the heavenly being. "The fact that the angel is still here is a good sign, right?"

Reality had smacked them both in the head. Their playful banter had been a nice respite, but it had been too short.

Rebekah was the first one to see them come through the gate. She ran over and threw her arms around Joshua, praising God that he was okay. To her surprise, Noah refrained from making his typical snide comment.

Rebekah's heart was heavy as she wondered how much they knew about what had unfolded. She did not want to be the one to tell Noah about Deborah, but at the same time, she didn't want him to have to hear it from someone else. However, she wouldn't have a chance.

Noah looked at Rebekah. "We need to sound the alarm!" Noah looked at Joshua. "Gather everyone together in the barn!" Then he turned his attention back to Rebekah. "Where is Deborah? Is she alive?"

Rebekah lowered her eyes. "Yes, she is still holding on, but Noah, I... I just want you to be prepared. She's in pretty rough shape."

Noah nodded. "Yeah, we were there. We saw the whole thing! Those bast- … er, those monsters are still alive. They attacked Deborah and we think they killed Danielle." He looked over at Michael. "The angels didn't finish them off, and we overheard them threatening to return. They're after someone in particular. They said they wouldn't stop until they got the one they were sent for. I thought for sure you were going to tell me that they had taken Deborah. We need to post soldiers to stand over her twenty-four, seven. We also need soldiers to guard over Martha and her warriors."

Panic filled his eyes, "Martha. I forgot to ask, is she okay? They didn't come for her, did they?"

"Whoa, take a deep breath," Rebekah said calmly. "We haven't seen a sign of the beasts anywhere. I'll sound the alarm and inform the rest of the army about them, but first I want you to go and see Deborah. Joshua and I can address the soldiers."

Noah nodded. He had decided to enter through the kitchen door, wanting to avoid the angel standing guard in the front. The truth was the heavenly host intimidated him a little. As he approached the farmhouse, a faint, familiar odor assaulted his nostrils and he felt a slight chill in the air. His heart skipped a beat. Were they coming for Deborah? He ran full speed into the house and up the stairs. When he reached her bedside, relief rushed over him as he saw her lying there, but then reality struck, bringing Noah to his knees.

Her pale body was motionless except for the shallow, small movement of her chest as it barely rose and fell. He took her delicate hand in his, willing her to wake up. What could Satan possibly want with her now, except to finish the job he had started? Was that why his beasts had not been seen? Were they waiting to see if she expired on her own?

Noah wanted to excuse everyone from the room so he could have a brief moment alone with her, but he knew that would leave them vulnerable, creating the perfect opportunity for Satan's forces to finish the job.

That was when it dawned on Noah that Caleb was in the room, standing next to Matthew. Noah jumped to his feet as he questioned Matthew.

"What the hell is he doing in here?"

Before Matthew could answer, Noah lunged after Caleb. He had the angel pinned against the wall. "This is all your fault! I should kill you right here and now."

Matthew tried to pull Noah off of Caleb. "No, Noah, you have it all wrong! We all did! Lucious was the traitor, not Caleb."

Noah released his grip. "What?"

Matthew sighed. He addressed Caleb. "You know, this wouldn't keep happening if you had a more pleasant demeanor."

Caleb shrugged. "God didn't assign this mission to me because I have a cheery disposition. He appointed me because he knew I wouldn't let him down. I think a steadfast spirit trumps perkiness."

Matthew rolled his eyes. "Whatever." Then he looked at Noah, who was staring at the two of them in disbelief.

"Would somebody please tell me what is going on around here?"

Matthew's expression became sullen. "Lucious was Mainyu's spy. He was the soldier Caleb had followed out into the forest. We saw what the enemy wanted us to see. Caleb is actually an angel."

Noah let out a sarcastic chuckle. "Yeah, right."

Caleb smirked at Noah as he transformed into his heavenly form. Noah took a step back. "Holy mother of..."

Noah found himself repeating a verse Anna always used to say. "But don't forget to be friendly to outsiders, for in so doing, some people, without knowing it, have entertained angels." He stood there rubbing his chin, stunned by the turn of events.

"Wow! I guess we totally misjudged you!" A sly smile crept across Noah's face. "But in our defense, Matthew has a valid point. You really do need to work on your attitude."

Caleb rolled his eyes. "Of course, that was the problem, because everybody should have a pleasant disposition while they're being judged for something they didn't do."

Noah shook his head. "True, but you are an angel."

"And your point is?"

"My point is that you are a member of God's heavenly host. You are above all of our pathetic human weaknesses."

"Seriously?" Caleb looked at Matthew. "What on Earth are they teaching you people? Do you guys not know that Satan is a fallen angel? Do you really think that Satan and his followers would have been cast out of heaven if they lacked human weaknesses?"

Noah shook his head, "No. I guess you have a point, but why do they act as though they are so much better than the rest of us?"

Caleb scoffed. "Because they are messed up. Heck, they even believe that they are better than their creator." Caleb looked at Noah as if he were studying him. "You haven't been letting their self-righteous, superior attitude get in your head have you?"

Noah shrugged. "Well, it kind of does feel as though we are on the bottom of the food chain in the supernatural world."

Caleb scowled at Noah, who jumped as the angel placed his hand on Noah and shouted. "In the name of Jesus Christ, by the power and the authority of his blood shed on the cross, I demand you to be gone!"

Caleb smiled at Noah. "Better?"

Noah nodded. He looked over at Matthew. "Is he always this aggressive?"

Matthew chuckled. "Yep. In fact, he's the angel version of you."

Both Caleb and Noah gave Matthew a dirty look. Deborah's younger brother uttered under his breath, "Or not..."

Caleb gestured toward Deborah. "Matthew, myself, and Doc will give you a moment alone."

Noah nodded. "Thanks."

Noah pulled up a chair and sat next to Deborah. He wanted so badly to tell her what he had overheard in the wilderness, but a small part of him appreciated the fact that she was unconscious, because he knew he would be tempted to tell her. He also knew that if she did know, Deborah would be jumping out of bed, jeopardizing her life to fight for the lives of others. Maybe this really was a blessing from God. It didn't feel like a blessing, but Noah was beginning to learn that with God, you never knew what to expect.

Noah leaned over and whispered in her ear. "Don't you dare think about quitting on me! Do you hear me? You have a company to lead, and your people are counting on you. I have to go, but I will return shortly, and I fully expect to see those big, beautiful blue eyes of yours when I do."

He whispered something inaudible in her ear and then kissed her gently on the forehead.

Noah stood up and joined Caleb and Matthew just outside the bedroom door. He was telling them what he had overheard in the forest and filling them in on the bleak reality of their chances against their new foe, when he spotted Joshua waiting for him on the landing. Noah excused himself, and nodded for Joshua to follow him out.

Joshua waited until they were out of earshot before he spoke. "We checked on Martha and her warriors, and they are sound."

Noah exhaled a deep sigh of relief, but then he noticed the grim expression on Joshua's face. "What? What has happened?"

Joshua lowered his voice. "When we sounded the alarm, everyone reported to the barn. All except one."

Noah's pulse quickened. Confusion filled his mind. If Martha was okay, and Deborah was upstairs, then who was missing? Who would be that important to their enemy?

As Joshua led Noah out toward the garden, he continued to explain what little he knew.

"Mary. Mary didn't respond to the alarm."

Noah looked at him, baffled. "Mary? Why Mary?"

They stopped just short of the bench on which Anna so dearly loved to sit. Rebekah was there waiting for them.

"I don't understand. What's going on?" Noah asked. "Why's Rebekah here?"

"Joshua asked me to come here, because apparently I am the last person to have seen Mary." Rebekah paused as she took a deep breath in a futile attempt to calm her nerves. She adored Mary and the idea of her sweet young friend in the hands of their enemy shook her to her core.

"Matthew had just returned from delivering news to Martha on the island. Martha had requested that he give something to Mary for her. He was anxious to spend some time with his sister, so I volunteered to do it. It took me quite a while to locate her, because she was out here alone. I warned her that it wasn't prudent to wander around all by herself. She thanked me for my concern and assured me that she would be up to see Deborah in a moment."

Noah was still trying to put all of the pieces together. He knew he was missing something, but what?

"What did Martha ask Matthew to deliver to Mary?"

Tears poured down Rebekah's face as she slowly shook her head. "It was a small piece of paper folded in half. I didn't read it, so I don't know what it said."

MARY

Mary could not shake the dreadful apprehension that continued to grow inside her no matter how hard she prayed. Rebekah's ominous parting words didn't help. She contemplated rushing back inside the house, but decided to stay in the garden for a moment so she could read Martha's note in private. She was beginning to regret her decision to have Rebekah take Rascal and Jack in the house with her, but her two loyal companions had been acting out of sorts, making it difficult for her to concentrate.

As soon as Mary laid her eyes on the writing that was scribbled across the small, torn piece of paper, she recognized her mother's penmanship. She laughed quietly under her breath.

"Wow, you sure have a lot to say to me lately."

Mary barely had time to read the note before a bitter cold filled the air.

"That's strange," she thought to herself. "And what's up with the horrible stench?"

In an instant, Mary found herself gagging from the horrible odor. She pushed the note deep into her pocket, and just as she was turning to escape the smell, a shadow fell over her. She reached for her sword, but a raspy voice hissed just inches behind her.

"I wouldn't do that if I were you."

A heavy weight knocked Mary to the ground. She tried to stand but found she was being pulled into the air. She struggled violently to escape, but was unsuccessful. To her horror, she realized that she was caught in a net that was swiftly rising into the sky. Above her, two black, menacing creatures held the net in what appeared to be talons, like a predatory bird holds its prey.

Frantic, she looked around for help. Fear raced through her body as she realized there wasn't a single soul nearby, except for three additional black creatures that were flying cover, ready to fend off any foe that might get in their way.

Mary fought to stay coherent. She scoured the horizon for any landmarks that would clue her in to where her captors were taking her. Her stomach was doing back-flips. She had always had a fear of heights. Her delicate fingers clung to the netting so hard it was causing the material to cut into her flesh. Eventually, as they climbed higher and higher, the lack of oxygen was too much for her body to sustain its normal functions. She collapsed into a small heap at the bottom of the net, thousands of feet above the ground. The creature who flew cover below let out a screech to alert its two comrades above.

"Our orders are to bring her to him alive! We need to lower our altitude before we lose her."

NOAH

Noah shook his head, angry and dismayed.

"I don't get it. Have we done something to cause God to turn his back on us? What did we do? We were completely protected in God's favor, and now we are almost certain that Danielle is dead, the only person who might be able to confirm that is lying unconscious, hanging on to life by her fingernails, and now ... and now Mary is missing. Oh, and I almost forgot, one of our trusted friends and comrades turned out to be a traitor. It's like we fell out of favor with God overnight!"

Noah looked at Joshua and Rebekah. "I just don't know what to make of all of this or what to do next."

Joshua related to the exasperation in his friend's voice. It seemed as though everything was spiraling out of control and they couldn't hit the stop button.

Noah turned to Rebekah. "We need you to go back to the barn and inform the others of everything. Tell them every detail. It's crucial that we put our heads together. Pray that someone saw something that will help us put the pieces together."

He turned to Joshua. "You and I are going to go pay Marty a visit."

MARTHA

Once again, Martha's prayers were interrupted as Luke informed her that her uncle and Joshua were on the island requesting to speak with her. She was elated to hear the news of her uncle's safety. Martha ran up to Noah and wrapped her long, slender arms around him.

"God is good! We were all worried about you. What happened? I feel so isolated way out here."

Martha's joy was overshadowed by the somber expressions her uncle and Joshua were wearing. She exhaled a deep sigh. "By the look on your faces, I don't have too much cause to celebrate. Is it Deborah?"

Noah shook his head. "No, Deborah is in the exact same condition. She hasn't regained consciousness, but I am sending up prayers of thanksgiving that she is still breathing."

Martha looked confused. "I don't understand. Why the dour faces? God has returned the two of you back to us safe and sound, and Deborah still has a chance ..."

Noah wasted no time filling in the blanks. "Mary has disappeared. She has simply vanished."

Martha's jaw dropped as she reacted in stunned silence.

"Rebekah was the last person to see her," Noah continued. "She said that she had delivered a note to Mary at your request. We're hoping that whatever was on that note might help lead us to her."

Martha's voice trembled as she answered. "The note was from Mom. She slipped it into my hand during her visit ... with the angels. Just as Matthew was climbing into the dinghy to go back across, I felt the Holy Spirit urging me to share it with Mary."

Joshua's voice was soft and comforting. "Don't worry. We'll find your sister, but first, can you remember what the note said?"

Martha nodded. "Yes, but I don't believe it will help. This whole thing … it's starting to make sense to me. I think."

"What do you mean?" Noah asked.

Martha straightened herself and looked her uncle dead in the eye. "I mean I believe Mary is beyond our physical reach. All we can do is pray like we have never prayed before. The two of you need to gather all of our warriors, including Deborah, and move everyone here onto the island. If my spirit is hearing God correctly, there is going to be a climactic collision, and we cannot be divided. Our forces aren't strong enough to hold off the demons if we are spread out. The beginning of the end has come!"

Both men looked at each other with a wild look in their eyes. Noah looked back to Martha. "Marty, how much time do we have before they are here?"

Martha shook her head. "I'm not sure. But something tells me you must hurry!"

Noah and Joshua ran full speed toward the boat. Before they got in, Noah turned back toward Martha. "Wait, you never told us what the note said."

She walked over to her uncle and Joshua and lowered her voice so as not to alarm the others. "It said, 'One shall be sacrificed for the salvation of all.' I believe with all my heart that Mary is that 'one' and if I'm correct, she is going to need every one of us in her prayer corner. From this point forward, you will learn to fight my way. There will be no need for swords or any other physical weapon. We will fight with the fiercest weapon that we possess: the Word of God. The angels will come by the legions. The sky over us will be full of terror. The final battle between heaven and hell will take place before our very eyes."

Noah furrowed his eyebrows in confusion. "But what exactly are they fighting for?"

Martha bent down and whispered in his ear. "For our souls. The fate of our future is being placed entirely upon Mary's shoulders! God has instructed us to intercede on her behalf. We're to pray without ceasing, for her torment will exceed anything mortal man has ever known."

Noah felt paralyzed by shock and horror, but Martha urged him into action. "It is imperative that we are all under the shield of this heavenly hedge of protection. The Army of Darkness is heading straight toward us as we speak. They are assigned with the task of annihilating us so that Mary will be left alone to fend for herself against the ruler of sin. God hasn't forgotten us, nor will he abandon or forsake us. He has ordered the entire heavenly host to engage in this war. They fight to the death for our very souls. Now go! Anyone who isn't on the island before the enemy arrives won't stand a chance. Hurry!"

Martha walked around to the front of the boat and shoved it into the water.

MARY

Mary looked about her frantically, trying to find some clue that would enlighten her as to where she was. It took her eyes a while to adjust to the darkness. She recognized one clue that caused her spirits to plunge: a vile, noxious odor.

"Well, hello there, sleepy head. We were beginning to wonder if you were ever going to wake up. Travel really can mess with your inner clock, or so I've heard."

Mary whipped around, squinting in the darkness in search of the owner of the low, seductive voice. It sounded as though it belonged to a human. Her heart jumped for joy at the prospect that someone had rescued her. Did this individual somehow overtake Satan's elite forces? But what about the formidable stench that filled her lungs? Could it be possible that she was simply smelling their dead remains somewhere close by?

A svelte young man came into view, and circled around in front of Mary. She was struck by how incredibly handsome he was. His complexion was flawless, and his rich brown hair brought out the remarkable brightness of his blue eyes. When he spoke, his voice carried a tender, compassionate tone that put Mary at ease. She felt the rigid tension begin to ebb from her body.

"Where am I?" She looked up at the stranger, waiting for his response.

"Aw, don't worry. You're safe with me here in my kingdom." He smiled at her before he let out a soft laugh.

Mary cleared her throat. "Um, did you say your 'kingdom'?"

His smile broadened. "Yes, you shall be my honored guest. We must equip you with proper accommodations."

Mary was baffled. Who was this guy?

"I'm sorry, but I'm a little confused. What country are we in? Are you some kind of ... royalty?"

A sly grin spread across his face. "Why yes, you didn't know? I have been called many things, but I personally prefer the expression 'Prince of Darkness.'"

A sadistic laugh rose from deep within his bowels. "Welcome to Sheol, Mary."

The darkness around her began to spin. Her heart felt as though it had stopped beating altogether. She reached down and pinched herself on the leg, hoping she would wake up and this would just be a horrendous nightmare. But the pinch hurt far too much, and to her dismay she didn't find herself waking up in the farmhouse.

"Oh, please, do not fret. I mean you no harm. There's just one teensy little request I have of you, and then you may either stay here with me or join your friends."

Mary stared at him, refusing to bite.

"Now, don't be like that, Mary. I promise you that no harm will come to you. You just need to repeat these words, 'Nullus Deus,' and I will set you free."

Mary closed her eyes and took a long, deep breath. It turned out to be a very bad decision. Her lungs burned from the toxic fumes that oozed from the foul creatures hiding in the shadows. Mary knew this was her moment of truth. Fear jolted through her body. She had no illusions about what would happen if she refused to cooperate. Danielle had forewarned her about all that was expected of her.

Mary wiped the perspiration from her forehead with a trembling hand. As she pulled her hand down, an involuntary gasp escaped her lips as she saw that blood was smeared across her hand. She knew the Latin words Satan was demanding her to proclaim. She also knew the ramifications of her obeying his command. All the souls in heaven, along with all the souls remaining on Earth, were counting upon her being able to withstand the torture this monster had in store for her.

It was mind-blowing how Satan was the most beautiful being Mary had ever seen. She had imagined him to be despicable and repulsive, like his followers. But he was the master of deception, she reminded herself, so she really shouldn't have been surprised.

Mary rose slowly to her feet and looked into Satan's deep blue eyes. "David said, 'Only the fool hath said in his heart, there is no God!' And I, Satan, am no fool!"

PERSEPHONE MILLER

Persephone reached across her desk and answered her phone. Angra was calling from his personal line. "Hello, my handsome prince."

"Meet me in the gardens."

She rolled her eyes as she hung up the phone. "Now what?" she said to herself. "I swear this man is the biggest drama queen I have ever met."

As she was walking to meet Mainyu, her boss' messenger came running up to her. He handed her a sealed letter, which she quickly tore open. She eagerly devoured the information, armed and ready to meet the world leader.

Angra scowled when she arrived. "What took you so bloody long?" He couldn't help but notice the look of victory on her face. "And wipe that stupid expression off your face. Your man has failed. Not only has his cover been blown, but he has been sent back to us, dead," Mainyu snarled.

Persephone feigned a pout. "Oh darn, what a pity."

He glared at her with a steely expression. "How dare you mock me! Have you already been dipping into the whiskey? Your agent failed. His mission has been compromised. Do you not understand the ramifications of what has happened?"

Persephone let out a seductive chuckle. "Actually, that is a wonderful idea. I think I will pour me a little mid-day libation to celebrate." She paused for effect, enjoying the impatience that was brewing within him. "You see, Angra, Lucious served his purpose. He may have been killed, but not before he completed his mission."

Mainyu looked at her, puzzled. "What is it you think you know?"

Persephone gave him a sly smile. "I just happen to know that their commander is knocking on death's door." She clicked her tongue together several times. "Such awful news. Just think of all those rebels out there

232

fighting without their devout leader. Oh, and another bit of information you might be interested in hearing is the fact that their prophetess has been eliminated. I'm sure she is having a smashing time in heaven."

Persephone was thoroughly enjoying the moment. "And, you might be interested in knowing that our master has her in his possession as we speak." Persephone gave Angra a sultry look. "It's just a matter of time before she buckles. From what I've heard, she has a very unhealthy fear of ... death."

A sadistic sense of joy was welling up in Mainyu, but then his cautious demeanor took over. "How can I be sure that what you are telling me is true?" He looked at her skeptically.

Persephone smirked. "We have worked together for how long and you still can't find it in yourself to trust me? Will it ever register with you that we are on the same team?" She glared at him as she handed him the letter. "I broke the seal myself."

Mainyu eyeballed the seal of Satan. He nodded. "Very well." He walked over and whispered in her ear. "You were saying something about celebrating?"

NOAH

Noah and Joshua jumped out of the dinghy as soon as it landed on the other side. Joshua tore off toward the barn as Noah raced toward the farmhouse.

Noah ran straight past Michael and didn't stop until he was at Deborah's side, pausing for only a moment to take in her serene beauty. He regretted never telling her how he felt about her. He looked up at Caleb and Matthew.

Caleb gave Noah a knowing look as he gestured to Matthew. "Hurry, follow Noah." Caleb then addressed Noah. "Don't worry, I will stand guard until all of our comrades are safely on the island, and my brother, Michael, will watch over you as you carry your commander to safety."

Noah nodded. "You know, I just want to say thanks, and that I am sorry. It was wrong of me to judge you, and it only makes things worse that I misjudged you."

"Eh, it's okay. After all, you are only human," Caleb said with a laugh.

Rebekah came running into the room. She looked up at Noah with intensity brewing in her eyes. "What about Deborah?"

With all the excitement, Noah had forgotten all about the doctor who still tended to Deborah. "Doc will carry her IV. You can carry his other supplies. I'll carry Deborah myself."

Rebekah nodded and began placing the doctor's supplies into his bag. She ran ahead of them while Noah and the doctor maneuvered their way through the doorway and down the stairs, ensuring Deborah's IV was intact. Noah carried her in his arms as gently as he could, trying not to jar her too much. Her head rested against his chest. When she let out a soft groan, Noah stopped, afraid he may have hurt her, but Doc urged him on.

"Don't stop," he said. "As soon as we get onto the island, we can set her

234

up in a comfortable place. Just think of how she will benefit from the presence of all those prayer warriors."

By the time they arrived with Deborah at the water's edge, all of the others had crossed the pond, holding on to hope that the three of them would make it across to safety in time. Martha had the boat sent back, so it was waiting for them as they reached the water's edge. First the two men laid Deborah down in the boat. Doc got in with the IV, but before Noah had a chance to join them, the ground shook violently. Noah pushed the boat as hard as he could into the water, stranding himself at the shore.

Martha gave him a panicked look. "Uncle Noah! What are you doing?" she yelled, as Tristan and Luke pulled the boat across the water as fast as they could.

Tristan and Luke dragged the boat and its two occupants up onto the island just as a thunderous crack vibrated across the sky. A number of Satan's demons appeared overhead and Martha immediately burst out in prayer. True to Caleb's word, Michael and Caleb were instantly at Noah's side, ferociously fighting off the attacking creatures in an attempt to protect Noah.

Noah looked up just as two razor-sharp talons stretched down to scoop him up. He heard Caleb's voice shouting to him over the clashing steel. "Dive into the water!"

Noah dove deep and turned to watch from the depths below. He saw a brilliant light hovering over him, then he saw Michael's sword aglow with fire piercing deep into the chest of the swooping beast. The monster shrieked in pain as Michael withdrew his weapon from the dark creature. Satan's soldier was ablaze as the holy fire devoured its soul, leaving nothing but a handful of toxic ashes scattered across the water's surface above.

No longer able to hold his breath, Noah quickly swam toward the edge of the island. As soon as his head emerged, Luke and Tristan were there to pull him to safety. Noah lay motionless for a moment as he tried to take it all in.

The scene was indescribable. The sky was literally raining fire. Brilliant angels illuminated the island below as they warred with Satan's forces. The Seraphim were boldly shouting praises to heaven and the sound of their voices gave Noah a strange sense of peace and comfort – strange because the world was being turned upside down and chaos appeared to have taken the throne.

Noah scanned the island and was amazed. Martha's forethought was remarkable. She had a pallet set up under the gazebo for Deborah. A group of prayer warriors recited scripture in one corner, while another group prayed in tongues and a third group offered up praise and worship to God. He also saw a circle of immense light coming from a ring of angels placed strategically around the entire island. Above them, four angels hovered over the island, each taking a post, East, West, North, and South. The Seraphim were positioned directly in the center on top of the gazebo.

The sky rang with the sound of heaven-forged steel colliding against the claws and blazing swords of hell, as thunder and lightning pierced the sky. A violent hailstorm pummeled the Earth, but miraculously, it bounced harmlessly off the invisible shield of protection that covered this sacred piece of land and its inhabitants.

Noah remembered a scripture his grandmother used to quote. He smiled as he found himself reciting the familiar passage. It was as if she had prepared him for this precise moment.

"And the heathen nations raged, but your wrath came, the time when the dead will be judged and your servants the prophets and saints rewarded, and those who revere your name, both low and high and small and great, and the time for destroying the corrupters of the earth. Then the sanctuary of God in heaven was thrown open, and the ark of his covenant was seen standing inside in his sanctuary; and there were flashes of lightning, loud rumblings, peals of thunder, and earthquake, and a terrific hailstorm."

MARY

Before the Prince of Darkness had a chance to respond to her defiant words, Mary heard what sounded like the world coming to an end in the far-off distance. Satan turned to one of the creatures behind her.

"You fool! You neglected to close the portal upon your return. I suggest you correct your mistake before I decide you are more of a liability than an asset."

She heard the demon whimper in fear as it scurried off to appease its master.

Satan turned his attention back to Mary. "Here is where I beg to differ with you. If there truly is a God, and he is all powerful, then why are you here? Why didn't he save you?"

He shot the cowering monsters a scolding look. "Where are his mighty angels? Hmm? It appears, young lady, that your awesome and mighty God has abandoned you. He has left you to fend for yourself in the hands of your enemy. Maybe he knows who the true principality is and has accepted defeat. Now say the words!"

Mary spoke with an eerie sense of calm. "Greater is he who is in me than he who is in the world!" She saw the rage brewing underneath his cool demeanor, but Satan quickly composed himself as he let out a slow, sadistic laugh that shook the ground, causing small crevices to form under their feet.

"Oh, we shall see about that, little one. I have existed long before your kind. Are you so naïve that you seriously believe you can win this fight? You are no match for me! Simply say the two little words I ask of you, and I shall give you the world. I will allow you and your friends to live, and I shall make you my bride. Think about it. You would be queen over all the earth. Every knee shall bend and every head shall bow to you for all eternity."

Mary thought of the horrible suffering her mother had endured during her last days on Earth. She remembered Deborah's lifeless body as she lay there fighting to survive the wicked wound Satan's demon had inflicted upon her at his request. His dark soldiers had been stealing souls and wreaking havoc on Earth, causing misery and sorrow wherever they went. She swallowed hard and exhaled slowly before responding.

"You cannot offer what is not yours to give. Our souls belong to God alone! Do with me what you will, but victory belongs to my Lord in heaven. Jesus will squash the head of the serpent. So it is written in the book of truth. Nothing you do or say can change that!"

Her words provoked his anger. Satan could no longer disguise his true self as the darkest, foulest, evil transformed him into the most sinister and bone-chilling monster she had ever seen. He circled her slowly, stopping to stand directly in front of her. His saliva sprayed her as he spoke.

"I shall not ask again," he said, his voice no longer soft and soothing, but deep and menacing. "Say the words or suffer the consequences. The choice is yours."

His maniacal growl sent chills down her spine. Mary was scared to death. She knew what torture the Master of the Lake of Fire had up his sleeve. She closed her eyes and sent up a silent prayer.

"God, strength now, I need your strength!"

The Holy Spirit reminded her of a scripture her sister was fond of proclaiming. Mary shouted it as loud as she could, hoping that God and his heavenly host could hear her.

"Be self-controlled and alert. Your enemy the devil prowls around like a roaring lion looking for someone to devour. Resist him, stand firm in the faith, because you know that your brothers throughout the world are undergoing the same kind of sufferings."

She had barely finished speaking when an unbearable pain shot through her head. She felt her body being hurled through the air by Satan's dizzying blow. The last thought she had was the realization that her body was about to hit the ground hard.

MARTHA

Martha had found a peace in God that was not true to her natural character. Something deep inside reassured her that everything was going to be okay. Her only source of worry came from the uncanny connection she had with Mary, that crazy twins thing everyone always talked about. She felt the magnitude of the excruciating terror that ravaged Mary's mind.

Martha hated not knowing where her sister was or what she was going through, but at least she knew how to pray for her. Whatever their enemy had in store for Mary, Martha was hell-bent on defeating him. Martha continually went from group to group, informing them of what Mary needed prayer for, but her need never changed: strength to overcome the tremendous fear and unimaginable suffering.

Martha was speaking with Noah, who was glued to Deborah's side, when she stopped suddenly. She was squinting her eyes as if she were experiencing extreme pain.

Noah grabbed her arm. "Marty, what is it? Are you okay? Marty ..."

It took a moment before she could respond. "Yes, yes I'm okay, but I don't know about Mary. I sensed this searing pain, and then everything went dark. I can't read her right now. I'm afraid something has happened to her."

Martha and Noah clasped each other's hands and fought off their angst with prayer, as they read from the Bible.

"Cast your burden on the Lord, releasing the weight of it, and he will sustain you; he will never allow the consistently righteous to be moved. But you, O God, will bring down the wicked into the pit of destruction; men of blood and treachery shall not live out half their days. But I will trust in, lean on, and confidently rely on you."

They paused before continuing. "He has redeemed my life in peace from the battle that was against me so that none came near me, for they were many who strove with me. Behold, God is my helper and ally; the Lord is my upholder and is with them who uphold my life. He will pay back evil to my enemies; in your faithfulness, Lord, put an end to them. With a freewill offering I will sacrifice to you; I will give thanks and praise your name, O Lord, for it is good. For he has delivered me out of every trouble, and my eye has looked in triumph on my enemies. I will thank you and confide in you forever, because you have delivered me and kept me safe. I will wait on, hope in, and expect in your name, for it is good, in the presence of your saints, your kind and pious ones."

Martha caught her breath, squeezing Noah's strong, firm hands. "I feel her. I can feel her again!"

MARY

Mary recovered consciousness, but a large part of her wished she had remained in that oblivious state, unaware of what she was about to endure. She took in her surroundings and then closed her eyes and lifted up her petition in silence.

"Lord, help me and equip me with your power, wisdom, and strength to withstand the terrors and unbelievable suffering during the midst of my darkest hours on Earth. Lift me above my human abilities. In Jesus' precious and holy name I pray, Amen."

Satan was quite pleased with himself as he took in the cleverness of his plan. Mary stood in the very courtyard where Jesus had been persecuted and sentenced to death. It was as though they had stepped through a portal that transported them back in time.

Strangers surrounded her, speaking a language she could not understand. But she didn't have to comprehend their tongue to decipher their meaning. They looked upon her with contempt and hatred, just as they had looked upon her Savior thousands of years ago.

Mary's voice trembled, but her words did not fail her. "Now the Lord spoke to Paul in the night by a vision, 'Do not be afraid, but speak, and do not keep silent, for I am with you' ..."

She inhaled slowly before continuing, "For I, the Lord your God, hold your right hand. I am the Lord, who says to you, fear not; I will help you! Behold, God, my salvation! I will trust and not be afraid, for the Lord God is my strength and song; yes, he has become my salvation. The Lord is on my side; I will not fear! What can man do to me? The Lord is on my side and takes my part. He is among those who help me; therefore shall I see my desire established upon those who hate me."

Satan let out a demonic laugh as a rancid stench choked the air. "Oh, but how innocent and naïve you are, child. You actually think scripture will work on me?" He approached her until he was just mere inches from her ear. "I am not a lowly, pathetic, and powerless mortal. My powers supersede those of Sheol's foulest monsters. There are none in this realm equal to me!"

He nodded to two of the beasts. "Enough of this. If she loves her precious Jesus so much, let her feel his pain!"

The dark creatures hissed with pleasure. One grabbed her so violently it ripped her shoulder out of its socket. Mary bit her lip as she fought back her screams. She did not want to give Satan and his demented followers any satisfaction. Blood trickled down her chin as she bit deep into her flesh.

The wicked creature dragged her to a pole, where the other beast was waiting for her, smiling sadistically. Once she was strapped to the pole, the two vile beings flogged her delicate flesh with the same barbaric weapons the Roman soldiers had used to torture Jesus.

The pain was too great for her to withstand. Her blood-curdling screams filled the courtyard. Tears and blood plummeted to the ground as Mary closed her eyes and tried to endure the inconceivable nightmare.

"Lord, my spirit is willing but my flesh is weak," she prayed.

By the time the flogging stopped, Mary's young flesh had been ripped and mutilated, and blood pooled on the ground around her. Mary's legs were so weak she could barely stand. She kept her eyes clenched shut, but she knew something evil had approached her due to the detestable odor of its breath. Satan was whispering in her ear once again.

"Are you having fun yet?" His obnoxious laughter filled the courtyard. "You know you have the power to put an end to all this needless suffering. Simply say the words, and you shall be set free."

Mary's body trembled uncontrollably from the searing pain that ravaged her entire being. Vomit spewed from her mouth, splashing all over Satan. Her resolve was weakening.

"God? Hello? I need you! I need you this very instant!" she shouted to heaven inside her head, not wanting to reveal her true state of mind to those around her.

The Holy Spirit moved in Mary, urging her to open her eyes. She shook her head slightly. She knew she would not be able to stand the sight of her wounds and her own blood.

"God, you know I faint at the sight of blood."

But she heard it again, louder this time.

"Fine."

Mary opened her eyes slowly, expecting to see Satan's gruesome and disfigured face. Instead, standing before the crowd, she saw Danielle. Tears of gratitude ran down her face, stinging her flesh as they landed on the open wounds on her shoulders.

"Thank you, Lord, thank you!"

Danielle did not utter a single word, but her eyes spoke volumes. She stood before Mary, shining brilliantly with a glow that resembled that of the angels. The prophetess did not possess wings, but her presence more than disturbed Satan and his followers. They hissed and snarled at her, but they were unable to touch her. In fact, they took care to keep a safe distance from her.

Satan scoffed. "Do you really think she can save you? She couldn't even save herself."

As Mary focused on Danielle's presence, she found the courage to lift up scripture unto her Heavenly Father.

"You whom I, the Lord, have taken from the ends of the earth and have called you from the corners of it, and said to you, you are my servant, I have chosen you and not cast you off. Fear not, for I am with you; do not look around you in terror and be dismayed, for I am your God. I will strengthen and harden you to difficulties, yes, I will help you; yes, I will hold you up and retain you with my victorious right hand of rightness and justice. Behold, all they who are enraged and inflamed against you shall be as nothing and shall perish. You shall seek those who contend with you but shall not find them; they who war against you shall be as nothing, as nothing at all. For I the Lord your God hold your right hand; I am the Lord, who says to you, fear not; I will help you!"

Satan hissed. "You pathetic fool! If your God is for you, I sure wouldn't want to be his enemy. He has turned his back on you and left you to suffer! Just like he did your friend over there. So where is he, hmm? Why isn't he saving you? Maybe you aren't his precious little darling after all? Face it, he has forsaken you, he has abandoned you, and you will suffer and die at the hands of your enemy. I will destroy you! You will not live to see another day. Two little words will save your life and spare you all of this: Nullus Deus."

Mary stared at the ground, avoiding the hideous presence of the Prince of Darkness. Then she slowly lifted her head and held it high. A smile crept across her face as she stared Satan down, taking in every inch of his repulsiveness. When she finally spoke, there was pure joy in her voice.

"Oh, ye of little faith! God has already saved me. You may torture me and brutally rip my very last breath from this human body, but," her voice rang with confidence, "you will never be able to undo the power of salvation that Jesus willingly and lovingly chose to endure on the cross for my soul. You may take my human life, but Jesus owns my soul! I am not of this world! You have spent centuries upon centuries desperately and pathetically trying to reverse a loss that cost you the war. The verdict is in. You lost!"

Vexation poured out of Satan. "You're filled with courage and honor now, but I will break you, and then your soul will belong to me! Jesus may have won the battle of the cross, but you, my dear, are no Jesus. You are an unworthy sinner, and you're about to meet the ramifications of your sins!"

Mary chuckled. "Liar! The Word declares that I have been made worthy by the blood of Jesus that he shed on the cross for my sins. You deceitful snake! My sins have been washed clean by his blood, and you know this. How dare you speak such lies to me! You have no power over me!"

His fury boiled over. "Finish her!"

The dark creatures of hell picked up Mary and flung her at the cross. Danielle came up beside her and lifted the heavy burden with her. As the two women hefted the cross, one of the demons crammed a crown of thorns down upon Mary's head. Blood caught in her eyelashes, making it difficult for her to see. She stumbled and fell on the uneven path.

The weight of the cross was too much for Danielle to carry alone, and part of the cross came smashing down on Mary's leg, causing her to let out an agonizing scream. Danielle managed to lift the cross enough for Mary to drag her wounded leg out from beneath it. As Danielle knelt down to lift the cross, she spoke softly in her friend's ear.

"This, too, shall pass. Your load here in this place is heavy, but in heaven you shall be set free from the wickedness and torment. You have nearly completed your journey."

Danielle offered Mary a sweet, knowing smile that comforted her spirit, but as Mary tried to stand, she fell once again. The weight of her cross was too much for her wounded body to carry.

"Lord, what do I do?"

Mary could hear the followers of Satan taunting her with evil, slanderous insults. They laughed at her suffering and threw jagged rocks at her and Danielle. But the crowd hushed when two glowing, heavenly figures emerged in the distance. Mary's parents walked right past the onlookers without acknowledging their existence. Joel assisted Danielle in carrying his daughter's cross as Anna lifted her daughter under her shoulders and helped her walk the final stretch to the Place of the Skull.

Danielle stood with her parents as another familiar face appeared in the crowd. Mary's soul was uplifted as her eyes fell upon little Lizzy, who stood in front of Danielle, smiling up at Mary with big, encouraging eyes. Mary felt comforted by their presence as she heard their voices lifting her up in prayer.

As Satan's soldiers hammered the nails through Mary's flesh, pinning her to the cross, Mary witnessed the veil between the three worlds – hell, Earth, and heaven – start to lift.

The demons nailed a sign to her cross, which read, "Daughter of the one and only true God." They concluded their final acts of persecution by hoisting Mary's cross straight into the air, forcing the weight of her body to asphyxiate her. Tears poured down her face, plunging several feet to the ground.

Mary did not cry due to the tremendous pain that pulsated through her body. Her tears were caused by the warmth in her heart as she watched her parents, Lizzy, and Danielle praying fervently for her just a few feet away, and as Martha, her Uncle Noah, Tristan, and the rest of her comrades prayed for her soul on the island. The faith that these wonderful people possessed enabled her to withstand the impossible. Love and heartfelt thankfulness overwhelmed her spirit.

Mary was struggling to breathe when one of the soldiers from the Army of Darkness drove his sword deep into her side. As her blood spilled and life passed from her, Mary spoke her final words.

"Then shall your light break forth like the morning. Thank you, Abba..."

MARTHA

Heaven and hell clashed in a brawl to the death. The magnitude of the impact was literally ground-breaking. Earth was being torn to pieces. Great crevices formed, dividing the Parks property. Land that had stood for thousands of years was being ripped apart. The only piece of land that stood firm and unshakable was their tiny island.

Martha surveyed the chaos that surrounded them, amazed that she wasn't terrified to her core. She was, however, extremely unnerved by the intense level of anxiety and agonizing pain she sensed from Mary. She comforted herself by repeating her uncle's mantra, "Be still and know that I am God."

"God, I know you love my sister even more than I do, but it is so difficult for me to feel her suffering and not be able to put an end to it! I know that your ways are not our ways and that you have a divine reason for the anguish and torture she is undergoing, but Lord, as her sister, I pray that you raise her above her situation. Bring her strength, courage, endurance, and most of all an abundant faith in you! May your will be done! I love you and I thank you for loving all of us in spite of our sins. Thank you for seeing the good in us and for never giving up on us..."

A violent clash rang throughout the atmosphere, interrupting Martha's prayers and the prayers of everyone else on the island. She looked up as every living soul caught their breath.

God had lifted the veil between heaven, hell, and Earth. All at once, every person on the island was able to see Mary – beaten, bruised, and bloody, hanging on the cross.

There wasn't a dry eye among them as many warriors fell to their knees. Martha stumbled backward, and Luke caught her in his arms. She could barely breathe. Tristan was screaming, "No!" as he ran toward the boat.

246

Noah bolted after him, managing to catch him just in time. Rascal and Jack whimpered and howled, making it difficult for the others to hear Rebekah's cry.

"Look, there's Danielle!" she shouted.

All eyes fell on the four saints – Danielle, Anna, Joel, and Lizzy – who were kneeling before Mary, diligently praising God. As the Army of Angels stood in shock and bewilderment, a quiet voice broke the silence. Deborah's bright blue eyes flew open, and her voice rang out.

"Thank you, Father… It is finished!"

Martha and Noah shared the same confounded emotions. They were relieved and joyful that Deborah had returned to them, but also disturbed and troubled at the sight of Mary's lifeless body.

Martha struggled to make sense of everything that had just transpired when a splendid and majestic sight caused her to fall to her knees. Jesus had descended from his throne with a formidable force of angels, including Michael and Caleb. She had been so shaken by the horrible sight of her sister that she hadn't noticed that the war between heaven and hell had ended. Joshua pointed.

"Look, there's Satan. He's standing to the right of Mary's cross."

Fear exuded from his very being. He spun around in a futile attempt to flee, only to find his soldiers had been slain and replaced by an impenetrable wall of angels who fearlessly blocked his flight. In a split-second, Satan transformed himself into a slithering snake in a desperate attempt to flee the wrath of God.

Jesus stomped on the serpent's head, defeating his foe once and for all. He looked up toward heaven and raised his beautiful voice.

"It is finished!"

Shouts of joy rang out throughout all three kingdoms. Adrenaline energized the entire island as all of God's soldiers gazed upon their Savior. Jesus walked over to the cross and instructed his angels to lower it. As Mary's body lay limp on the cross, Jesus gently removed every nail from her body. Then he removed the crown of thorns from her head and took Mary up into his loving arms. He prayed over her, tears of sorrow and joy flowing down his face and onto hers. Their Savior prayed in an unknown tongue, but everyone knew in their hearts what he was doing.

Martha wept uncontrollably, impatient for the opportunity to see her sister and her parents again. She found herself wondering what God had in store.

During the battle, Earth and all of Satan's followers had been completely destroyed. Nothing remained, with the exception of the island. The tiny land mass that once stood on her family's property was surrounded by nothing but empty space. They were literally "not of this world" anymore.

MARY

Mary slowly opened her eyes, dazed and confused. From what she could gather, her life had been restored. She celebrated the fact that all the pain that had wracked her body was gone. She looked down and took a dreadful inventory of herself. She was still broken and bruised, and still possessed a grotesque gash in her side.

She was fighting the urge to gag as she looked up at Jesus in confusion. To her amazement, he laughed at her. For some reason, the thought of Jesus being a God who laughed had never crossed her mind.

"I just thought I would be completely healed," she said sheepishly.

Jesus shook his head. "I have left the rest for you."

She smiled up at him. "Really?"

Mary could hear the joy in his voice. "Mm hmm."

Mary was a little nervous to be performing her own miracle in front of him. It was kind of like singing a famous song in front of the artist who made the song famous. She closed her eyes, raised her voice and boldly proclaimed, "In the name of Jesus Christ my Lord and Savior, I command my body to be healed!"

"Well, how was that?" she asked.

Jesus chuckled. "Take a look for yourself."

She was overjoyed to find her body had been restored to perfection. Overcome with relief and swelling with euphoria, she flung herself into his arms and embraced him with the biggest bear hug she could muster.

Mary was astonished and thrilled to find that Jesus was so loving and personable. He treated her just like her Uncle Noah had always treated her, like a loving older brother. As they stood wrapped in her exuberant embrace, he looked down at her.

"Are you ready?"

"Huh? Ready for what?"

Jesus smiled. "Ready to go home! Your Heavenly Father is eager to see you, along with a few other people you might know."

Mary offered up a vigorous nod. "Heck yeah. Let's do this!"

For the first time in a very long while, Mary felt the freedom of being nothing more than a young teenage girl. What a tremendous comfort it was to have the weight of the world lifted from her shoulders.

NOAH

Noah's heart was pounding out of his chest. Heaven was everything he had ever imagined and then some. All of the newcomers were in total awe of its beauty, which surpassed anything God had created on Earth.

The best part, aside from being in God's presence – nothing could top that – was seeing his entire family together again. He had been concerned about what would happen when Emma saw Joshua again, but to his surprise and relief, the flame she had once carried for him had passed. In fact, she, Rebekah, and Deborah had become the three amigos.

No one could stop questioning why they had ever fought so hard to stay on Earth. Noah gathered that it was probably because humankind's ultimate fear was the unknown. Yes, the Bible had spoken of the wonders of heaven, but without any firsthand knowledge, that small shred of doubt created a depth of fear that no one had fully overcome. Now all of their trials and tribulations had been laid to rest. They were where they belonged.

Noah had asked God why he had allowed Deborah to be injured when they needed her the most. God had simply smiled and said, "One, to teach you to rely on me and not others, and two, to see if you had finally learned to trust me and believe that I love you and am watching out for you, no matter how unjust and unfair life may be."

Joshua laid a firm hand on Noah's shoulder. "Take a deep breath. Your prayers have been answered, and in heaven, no less."

The two childhood friends let out a hearty laugh.

"You're right," Noah said. "I don't know why I'm so nervous. You'd think that I was about to meet God for the first time – again."

Joshua nodded. "Seriously, that was some intense stuff!"

Noah's mind wandered back to that day. He remembered how anxious he was, waiting to be called into God's throne room. It was kind of like waiting to be called into the school principal's office. He didn't know what to expect. Was God going to be a bright, magnificent light, or a human figure? What would God say to him?

Noah's thoughts were brought back to the present as the music began to play. "Okay, God, I can do this. What could possibly go wrong? We're in heaven!"

The forest was strewn with decorations. The rows of chairs were neatly aligned and filled with all of his dearest friends and loved ones. His parents, along with Emma, Anna, and Joel, all sat in the front row with the biggest, cheesiest smiles plastered across their faces. He showered them with an anxious and excited expression. Candles flickered, and the fresh, clean scent of pine filled his nostrils.

Noah smiled patiently as Mary rounded the corner and came into view, followed by Martha, Danielle, and Rebekah. The four women were absolutely radiant. He caught a glimpse of Joshua out of the corner of his eye. Joshua could not stop staring at Rebekah. Noah cleared his throat to get Joshua's attention before he started drooling. Joshua shrugged.

"Yeah, right, thanks," he whispered under his breath.

The two men struggled to suppress their laughter.

There was a pause that made Noah wonder if something was wrong. He felt a slight sense of panic, but then his fears were alleviated as Deborah rounded the corner. The entire congregation inhaled deeply as they rose to their feet. It was ironic, seeing as Noah felt as though he was going to fall down. But then Jesus stepped up to the podium, and Noah's legs regained their strength. With Jesus by his side, he could do anything!

Tears filled Noah's eyes as he looked upon Deborah with wonder. She was the most resplendent sight he had ever seen, glowing with heavenly beauty.

For a quick moment, Noah took his eyes off his wife-to-be and looked across at the four women lined up on the other side. He mouthed a silent "Thank you." Noah knew that without the sacrifice and steadfast persistence of these four women, this moment wouldn't be possible.

His gaze lingered on Mary. He would never be able to fathom the magnitude of her pain and suffering that day. A young child of God, frail in all of her humanity, had conquered the evil darkness of hell. Noah choked up as Mary mouthed back, "I love you more."

Noah turned his attention back to Deborah, who was just an arm's reach away. The rest of the ceremony was a blur, with the exception of their first kiss as husband and wife. Noah had been apprehensive about kissing her in front of an audience, but when the time came, nothing had ever felt more natural. Afterward, Deborah looked up at him with that playful grin of hers.

"Who knew that all a girl needed to do was almost die to get your attention?"

As she gave Noah a flirtatious wink, he was surprised to hear Jesus and Joshua laughing together.

Mary had warned him of this. Who knew Jesus had a sense of humor? Funny how that seemed to strike everyone as odd.

ABOUT THE AUTHOR

C. L. Peck is the author of the award-winning novel "A Midnight Song" and the soon-to-be released children's books "EMMA Volumes 1 & 2."

Mrs. Peck is celebrating the release of her first adult Christian novel, "The Last Call." According to the author, it is the first of several novels. She currently is finishing a secular novel and has started work on two additional Christian novels.

Mrs. Peck hopes "The Last Call" will have as profound an impact on her audience as it did her during the writing process. She humbly acknowledges that God is the true author: "The ideas all came from the Big Guy upstairs." She also stated, "God would give me just enough information to write a chapter. After that, I was stumped. I would ask, 'Okay, now what?' and within no time He responded. And so it went, chapter after chapter."

Mrs. Peck is the proud mother of her two adult children, Casey and Alissa. She lives on the Central Coast of California with her husband, Tony, who puts his years of experience in the field of journalism to good use as her editor. Her elderly parents reside with the couple, along with a plethora of pets. The latest addition to the family is a collection of fluffy chicks who currently reside in their kitchen – in a brooder, of course. You can read about her novice backyard chicken adventures in her blog, "A Chick's Life."

www.ingramcontent.com/pod-product-compliance
Lightning Source LLC
Chambersburg PA
CBHW070551130626
46556CB00001B/110